THE SINS OF THE FATHERS

By

Richard Leslie Brock

The characters and events portrayed in this book are fictitious. Any similarity to real persons, living or dead, is coincidental and not intended by the author.

ISBN: 9798838723574

Cover design by: Art Painter
Library of Congress Control Number: 2018675309
Printed in the United States of America

ABOUT THE AUTHOR

This is the author's third novel after **Laguna Diary** and **The House of Ilya**.

For the **Sins of the Fathers**, Brock relies on his academic background from UCI and UCLA in Classical History, Folklore and Mythology, along with 1,000's of miles on the Pacific Crest Trail, Muir Trail, and two winters in Alaska for his wilderness experience in the telling of this novel.

A CABIN ON THE MOUNTAIN

Steele awoke with a headache burrowing through his forehead all the way back to where he once had a cowlick of raven black hair. It was three in the morning. But it wasn't the buffeting wind outside that woke him and caused him to raise his head. It always blew like that this time of year. But sometimes, in his predawn stupor, he would ask himself: *why always wake at three?* Still confused, he lay his head back down and fixed his eyes on the dark underside of the cedar-planked roof. *Why not one or two,* he mused amid the blackness of the room?f Then he laid his hands over his face and eyes and rubbed until he remembered.

Dismissing his self-talk as the idle ruminations of an old man, he lifted his right leg off the cot using both hands and pivoted until it hovered above the floor. Then he let it drop while still clasping his knee and harnessed the dead weight of his falling leg to help lift his upper body into a sitting position. It was awkward since his left leg was still stretched out on the sheets. Now sitting with one foot on the floor and one still on the cot, he reached for his outstretched leg. Using both hands again, he raised it off the covers and then let his foot fall until it hit the floor beside his right. Once both legs and feet were grounded together on the wooden planks, he sat bolt upright on his cot until the blood in his brain stabilized, the pain in his forehead subsided, and the room stopped spinning.

Then, with a downward push of his arms against the stiff rail of the cot and a feeble lift from what was left of his leg muscles, he raised his body to a standing position and assessed his balance to ensure he could stay upright. Feeling almost stable, he turned and walked on wobbly legs to the front door. Once there, he opened it to feel an arid wind blowing left to right across the dry lake toward the Great Salt Basin. *South to north,* he noted as he looked west toward Utah. He stepped carefully to avoid stubbing his barefoot toes on some unseen thing along the way. Such obstacles ranged from an open cabinet door, rusty nail-heads, or a slithering critter that had come through the gaping space under the one-hundred-year-old door.

Years before, a small shrub had rooted ten feet away and two steps down from the porch. He could see the dry woody texture of its branches by the light of the stars. Steele avoided splinters lurking on the weathered deck and stair-steps and then walked on thickly calloused feet across coarse granite sand and jagged pebbles with his thin white hair and beard flying in the wind. *Just like Old King Lear,* he mused on his appearance. As he sauntered out, he reached for his manhood which was hanging past his low-hanging testicles. The three together formed a triad of loose and dangling appendages that were buffeted by the dry wind.

Ever since he started with the new blood-pressure medication, his phallus had begun to hang lower, freer, bigger, and thicker. Despite the engorgement, it was supple, swung with each step, and felt heavy. His pendulous features tugged at his groin and felt good at his age. As he neared the shrub, he grasped his organ with a steady right hand and aimed it at the mesquite. *It will like this*, he thought. *Any piss loosed upon this dried-out spot has to be a good thing for plants desperate for moisture,* he rationalized.

But still, he worried that there might be something sinister in his urine that could kill it. Then he dismissed the thought and simply enjoyed the rare steadiness of his right hand, the draining of his bladder, and the thick stream of sour urine that pierced the dry air and bubbled when it hit the ground. As he continued to rain on the plant, the late summer wind buffeted his back and blew his testicles back and forth. *Just like that pair of bells on that Spanish Mission in Santa Fe*, he mused. Standing naked in the blowing wind, he felt the animal in him again—a male animal. He had not felt it for years as he descended into old age and drunkenness. It felt so manly, he almost roared. He did not, but even if he had, there was no one this high on the unnamed mountain that would have heard him.

He took no pleasure in the handling of his privates, and it had nothing to do with sex. It was about gender; it was about being man and not being woman. His mind meandered to the feminine side of humankind and how women might feel their gender from the weight of their breasts, or from their inertia as they swung when turning their body toward a waiting lover. *May be like that,* he thought struggling to bridge the gap between man and woman. Feeling his manhood confirmed a part of who he was, so he wondered what confirmed womanhood for women. Then he shifted his thoughts to men and women together. He concluded that in the mutual joy of sensing their pendent features, man and woman celebrate them and affirm who they are as gendered creatures sharing the earth. The thought had the ring of a well-argued thesis. But he had been wrong often enough about the nature of women before. Womanly reprimands had taught him to keep such thoughts secret. Soon he was scolding himself. His musing ended with a reprimand to cease with his self-indulgence.

As he shook himself dry, he looked up at the stars. The high altitude gave him a view of the night sky in a way that the flatlands below could not. The air was thinner here and parched. It lacked the lowland moisture that fogged the crispness of the stars. And this far away from cities and towns, the air was free from the invasive glow of distant streetlamps. Here he was again, finding himself on his familiar perch set eight-thousand feet above the plain below and pissing naked on a lonesome bush under a canopy of brilliant stars burning bright from trillions of miles away.

His soul sated from the scene, he turned back toward the unlit cabin and navigated toward the refrigerator. Hiding his eyes with one hand from the bright light that would escape from its opening, he reached around the partially cracked door with his eyes closed and felt for the jug of milk among the assortment of bottles and jars. Then, with his eyes still covered, he pulled out the jug, opened it, took two large gulps, returned it to the refrigerator, and closed the door so that he could open his eyes once again in the peaceful darkness. *Not sure why,* he thought, *but two gulps are good for two or even three more hours of delicious sleep. Maybe it's that tryptophan?* Soon he was back in bed. Dreamland resumed after he pulled his covers up to his white-bearded chin. Sometimes he dreamed of tasks that needed to be done, lists to be made, or items to be fixed. Other times, there was that girl from Leadville. These dreams were welcome—not like the ones that once terrorized him every night for most of his adult life. It was much better than that.

An hour later he woke up with a start remembering that *Leon Posey don't have anything to swing and nothing left to heft.* Leaving the thought behind like a wet rag leaking wastewater down a dark drain, he slept soundly for two more hours.

Steele's daughter Molly was now forty-one. Her daughter Allie was almost eighteen. She mostly had the look of Molly who was born with fiery sparklers reflecting from her wide-open eyes on the Fourth of July. But the pinched brow between Allie's eyes betrayed a hint of the scowl Leon Posey wore for most of his life until he became a broken man incapable of scaring anyone with a mean look on his face. Both women looked good in faded blue jeans with starched white shirts, braided ponytails, and boots. They resembled twins except Molly's hair was a curly golden blonde and Allie's was straight and jet-black. The girls were coming up to check on the old man and try to talk him down from the mountain before winter pounced or he died before it came. They were soon to arrive at the cabin in Steele's beat-up half-ton Chevy that he called Mc Tavish in memory of his old friend and his sheepherding partner Ganiz. It was going on sixty years old.

Steele had been up since sunrise checking on the waterwheel. All three of the lightbulbs in the cabin had begun to flicker the evening before so he knew something needed fixing at the generator. He had built the waterwheel contraption himself. He constructed it using nothing but a saw, hand tools, some lumber from down below, long bolts, and a span of three-inch galvanized pipe for the axle which spun on a greased wooden cradle much like the spoked wheels on an old buckboard. The axle had a pulley and a belt connected to a salvaged car generator and a store-bought inverter. Both were anchored to a flat rock with a layer of concrete and bolts. The rickety contrivance created a steady stream of electricity and sent it to the cabin via a wire snaked through a hundred feet of steel pipe laid above ground. It wasn't to code, it was crude, and the galvanized pipe he used for the axle on the wheel had to be changed out every year due to rust and wear. But it worked.

A few hundred years or maybe a thousand years earlier, a landslide tore down from higher reaches of the mountain. It spread rocks and mud across the channel of the old stream that once fed a now dry lake and diverted it to a plateau below the cabin where it meandered until it flung itself off a cliff. Traces of the old streambed leading to the dry lake could still be seen. Sometimes Steele wished that the stream still fed the lake and ran nearer to the cabin that he had leased from the government twenty-five years before. The shack had been built illegally on federal land sometime around 1880 or 1890 but no one was sure. The government claimed it now. Legend rumored that it was built by three rustlers who were brothers from a failed cattle ranch in the Disappointment Country. Steele's Federal lease was good until 2030 when he would be eighty-seven. Steele often mused that the destiny of the cabin was linked to his own. If nothing else, its crumbling remains, and its dark past were a metaphor for his serpentine life. And Steele was drawn to it even though he had a real house down below on a sheep ranch.

But despite that sprawling ranch, even there he preferred to live in what the girls called the bungalow in the pasture. It was built on a small rise just up from the main house. But the bungalow was really nothing more than a two-room cabin converted from an outbuilding. From its vantage in the pasture, Steele saw it as holding vigil over the ranch. He was unsure where the feeling came from. But the cabin that had become a bungalow gave him a comfort as it guarded the house from the unknowns that had circled Steele's head for most of his life.

Returning his thoughts to the streambed and the dry lake, he thought it would have been nice to have a lake to fish in. *But the lake dried up a century ago*, Steele admonished. He had little patience for *what-if* conversations from anyone including himself. Maybe it would have been nice, but nature had firmly decided the stream's course eons ago, so it was a useless thought. *What if* had no power to change what was. In place of what might have been, nature had left a fast-running creek strong enough to generate a thousand watts of electricity twenty-four hours a day in spring, summer, and fall until the stream finally froze in winter. That translated to enough power to support three weak lightbulbs, a CB radio to keep in touch with Molly, and to help Allie with her homework. It also powered the refrigerator even if not a TV.

When people asked him how he lived up there without a television, he told them there was no TV signal up there anyway. "Besides, I'd rather read a book," he would answer, knowing it was a haughty response to a fair question. Then, just to get their dander up by sounding learned, he added —"or maybe write one." Truth was, he read a lot. A dog-eared copy of one of his favorites lay upon his crude desk. It was the third book of Horace's *Odes*. A bookmark lay open to a passage written in Latin. Next to it was Steele's handwritten translation: *"For the sins of your fathers you, must suffer."*

When winter came, the creek froze, and the generator stopped making electricity. In that season, he would use kerosene lamps for reading and drag the refrigerator out onto the porch where it stayed cold without power. He kept the bears out of it with a padlock and chain. For heat, he burned logs cut from downed trees, and he slept a lot. It was a simple life for a man whose life had not been simple. He had been living here off and on for years, ever since he delivered justice to Leon Posey for what he did to Molly and Morgan. He only stayed at the sheep ranch during the short lambing season and for visits with Molly and Allie a few times a month. But now, a change was coming. A bookend was closing in on his story.

When he reached the paddlewheel, he quickly saw what was causing the problem with the generator and his flickering lights. A tree had lost a branch in the wind and it fell into the stream and floated up against the wheel. There, it began rubbing and making it slow down and run unevenly. As he removed the branch, he heard a honk along with the roar of a straining engine and a barking dog. The dog sounded like his new dog Fergus that had been staying with the girls back on the ranch. That commotion was followed by the whinny of Maverick in the corral. Steele looked back and saw a slow-moving trail of rust colored dust following a faded blue truck up the fire road to the only structure on the mountain except for the unmanned ranger tower. Steele had climbed that tower one evening and saw the twelve streetlights on main street streaming fifty miles toward him across the salt flats from Monticello, Utah. He considered the tower to the silent partner of the rustlers cabin.

"Molly—Allie, been expecting ya. Come on in."

Fergus bolted from the bed of the truck and jumped all over Steele almost knocking him down in his excitement to see him. Then Steele raised his finger and glared at Fergus who immediately stopped jumping and laid down at his feet. But his tail was wagging so hard he was surrounded by dust.

"Long ride?"

"No. Gritty though," said Molly as she spat sand.

"Yeah, I saw the red cloud following you up the road."

"Like a fly on you know."

"Yeah, I know. Hungry?"

"No," interjected Allie — "Thirsty."

"Coke, beer, Orange Crush, Dad's Root Beer?"

"Wine's good," said the girls with a hopeful tone.

"I expected that. Red or white?"

"I'll take a pinot noir. Room temperature," answered Molly.

"Chilled white for me," announced his granddaughter.

"Sorry, don't got no chilled white. Things sure have changed a lot since they put in Telluride. Used to be all beer and whiskey around here. Now — well now it's wine. And not just wine — special kinds of wine — special brands of wine — special glasses for different wines— different temperatures for wine. Wonder what my Basque friends think about it — them drinking home-made red out of a sun warmed bota bag and all?"

"But Pops, you like wine," defended Allie who looked to Molly for support.

"Table wine. I like table wine. Like when I took your grandmother, Marija back to her old country on that road trip through Slovenia stopping at farmhouses with her before she died. She had just found out she was pregnant with you Molly," he added as he tossed her a wink. Molly drank in his story about the mother she never got to meet. "Great trip. The farmers, they'd pull out a table and two chairs, serve us sliced meat with fresh tomatoes, lettuce, olives, onions, and cheese, and whatever wine they had that day. When I asked what kind of wine the white was, they said it was *belo*. When I asked about the red, they said *rdeča*. Didn't matter which farm. The answer was always the same. So yeah, I like wine — red wine, and white wine—wine you drink but don't make the center of conversation. Did I tell you about dessert? Potiča — best bread I ever ate — even better than Basque bread."

"We're not the enemy Pop," answered Molly, mildly disgruntled at Steele's lecture. "We don't even ski like the wine snobs you were talking about at Telluride. We hike, so don't get cranky." Molly was good at being in control. Then she turned to Allie and instructed her to take a little walk over to the creek. Allie complied but pouted off with a miffed look in her eyes aimed directly at her mother.

As Allie sauntered toward the waterwheel kicking up loose rocks with her pointed-toe cowboy boots along the way, Steele blurted out an assertion with a tone of pique: "I know why you're here."

"Yeah, so?"

"So, I don't want to leave this place and go back to the ranch for winter."

"Oh, Pop. Why so stubborn."

"Because I'm dying."

Molly had already learned the diagnosis of brain cancer from the doctor after she bent his arm despite his concerns about privacy. "This is Colorado Doctor Clark, not New York. My father is sick, and I know it." Soon after browbeating him mercilessly, the doctor gave her all the information he had on Steel. So, it wasn't news to Molly. She and Allie were only there because they knew. It was the whole point.

"We're all dying Pop. You've been telling me that my whole life. You said it about my mom who I never got to meet. You said it about Morgan after Leon killed him at the bar. You said it about Dort, the only man you lost during that war. You even said it about our old dog Malcolm when he died. What's so different now?"

"The difference is that it's me that's dying, and I want to be the boss of my own death."

"Come on Pop, nobody's the boss of their own death," she whined. "You're just afraid of looking weak and frail. Or maybe having someone see you when you look weak and frail? Which is it?"

"Both, I guess?" finally answering without a barb attached.

"You think you won't look weak and frail shivering in the cold all by yourself while you die up here? You think we'll be protected at home while we sit by a warm fire knowing you are up here enduring some horrible death all alone. You think we won't be wondering what we'll find up here in spring assuming the bears don't get to you first. C'mon Pop, come on home. It's time. It's your time. And we'll be there for you just like you were there for me, Morgan, Allie, and Dort."

Steele's body slumped as he chewed on her words. Attached as he was to the peace he had finally obtained in this broken-down cabin where he could hear himself think and feel, he knew she was right. *We all die, just like Molly said.* Staying here was only about living on until he died sometime in the far off. But it wasn't far off anymore. He needed to start living his end, and it was not something he could argue about, put off, or deny.

"Which room will I have?"

"Any room you want Pop."

"I want the cabin."

"You mean the bungalow?"

"Yeah, that old shack in the sheep pasture —the cabin."

"Ok, you got it. Why the cabin?"

"You want the short answer or the long answer?"

"Long."

"Can't now. But someday I'll tell you if I figure it out myself."

"All right then. Now, can we talk about why I 'm here in the first place other than to take you home?"

"Talk?"

"About Allie and Leon."

Steel stiffened when he heard Leon's name and tried to process how Allie and Leon could be mentioned in the same sentence. Then he wondered what business Molly might have with the rapist father of her only child. *Maybe he died,* he hoped. Anything less than that was bad news.

Molly watched as Steele's face paled. "Pop?"

"Yeah, I'm here."

"Let's start with the easy part. Allie wants to meet the man that fathered her."

"You mean the man that raped you on a pool table in front of his gang of thugs?"

"Yeah, that asshole."

"Well at least we're off to a good start—but asshole is a bit weak."

"It's the first word that came to mind," deflected Molly. "But you know, I was half expecting this to happen. I mean, she's never met the man that had a part in seeding her. Yeah, yeah, I know. When she first brought it up, I was piqued just like you are I expect. Then, I remembered how desperate I was to meet the mother I never knew. I'd fantasized about her for most of my life and devoured every fact you told me about her—like her father and mother being killed in Slovenia, her grandparents and her leaving their country to come to America—Leadville and all. I always wondered what Marija's half of me makes me who I am. I also wonder if her half skipped me and landed on Allie? I think maybe it did. Funny what's passed along and what skips a generation.

Anyway, it comes down to this. Allie's found Posey. He's is alive but dying. She should take the chance to see him if she feels the need just like I've always needed to meet my mother but never will. Allie knows she was born of rape so it's not like a family reunion. I think she just wants to look him in the face — maybe to put to rest her fears that she's like him."

"She's not."

"I know Pop, and you helped make her that way. You and I— we did a good job. She's a good kid. But she needs to know that for herself—feel it in her bones."

"Fair enough. So, when does this meeting with Lucifer in the flesh happen?"

"Don't know yet. Allie's still working on it."

"Best be soon. I'm dying you know."

"Yeah, Pop. I know—meningioma."

The three of them teamed up to prepare the cabin for the coming winter and for their return to the ranch. Steele pried the belt off the pulley that drove the generator to stop the flow of electricity. Then he returned to the cabin to empty the refrigerator and chain the door shut. Of course, the chain on the door would not be enough to stop someone from breaking through a window. But there was nothing inside of value except Steele's CB radio, his .270 Remington, and his 1911 model .45 pistol, and he would take those with him in the truck.

As they prepared the cabin for their departure, Steele basked in the subtle glow of being called *Pop* by Allie just like Molly called him Pop. In a way, they were both daughters. *Being Pop was the best job I ever had,* he thought as his mind turned to his own father. "Son of a bitch," he muttered. But he stopped his vilification in midstream. He didn't need any more sadness to deal with on this day.

Allie busied herself with Maverick, the spirited black and white Pinto mare Steele had culled from the wild herd down in the Disappointment Country. She was only 15 hands tall and weighed a mere thousand pounds, but she was sweet and sassy just like Allie. The wild herd had multiplied from a string of ten stolen horses that a Canadian horse thief had driven down from Calgary in the early 1900s to sell to Colorado ranchers. But he had to abandon them when the law got on his trail.

Steel knew it was illegal to take Maverick from the herd, and, truth be told, it was a modern-day act of rustling. The herd was protected by federal law. But ranchers had been arguing loudly that the herd had grown too large and wanted it culled. They were competing with their cattle for feed. Local papers were saying that rangers were talking of thinning them out. *Why don't they just say it,* thought Steele? *Thinning means taking them from the wild.* They wouldn't miss one horse in their roundup of the mustangs the ranchers were calling a nuisance.

Rather, in his view, he would be saving the rangers the trouble of running one of them down by adopting it instead. *Thank you very much, Mr. Steele,* he mused they might say. *Thank you for helping us do our job. Well done Mr. Steele.* The end would the same —one less horse in the herd for the rangers to have to take from the wild and lock up in a federal pen. Truth was that Steele liked the idea of being a little bit of a rustler. It made him feel like the right man for the old cabin and connected him to olden times before the mountains were taken over by the wine-drinking ski crowd and their investors.

Allie sang a lullaby to Maverick and stroked her flank to keep her calm as she gently cinched the saddle straps and slid the bitless halter over Maverick's head. Steele had trained the horse to take direction from the soft pull on the reins and pressure from his knees and taught Allie how to use the technique. Allie and Maverick seemed to have a few things in common. First, neither one liked a bit in their mouth. Second, they were both petite and pretty with Allie's long black ponytail mirroring Maverick's horsetail in a girly kind of way. Third, they both looked sleek from behind and seemed built for speed. *Just like Marija,* he thought. Fourth, Maverick liked every story Allie ever told her. And Allie had many stories to tell Maverick on the long rides between the ranch and the cabin.

Not that Maverick understood the words, she just liked the sound of Allie's voice. Steele liked it too as he remembered his father was a good storyteller as well. *Must have passed through me to Allie*, he mused. But storytelling was one of the only good things he could remember about his father.

Molly folded the few clothes that Steele kept with him and put them in an old cardboard box for the ride home. Steele chained the door shut on the cabin.

"Everybody ready," she yelled out the driver's side window?

"Ready," said Steele from the cabin porch.

Allie trotted Maverick over to the truck. After putting both hands on the pommel of the saddle, she leaned over with a protesting squeak from the leather so that she could meet Molly's eyes as she sat in the truck. Allie asserted a ready look without saying a word. Steele walked over beside Maverick and dropped his army issue .45 into the saddlebag making sure Allie saw him do it.

"I won't need that Pop."

"I hope you won't. But this is still wild country."
"Safer than a billiards bar in Nucla."

"Got me there, honey! Got me there," he acknowledged as he threw a knowing glance toward Molly. "See you this afternoon."

Allie liked that Steele appreciated her nose for danger. And she liked that he trusted her with his pistol. Still, she did not like guns. But out of respect for Steele's gesture, she bit her tongue. Allie made a clicking sound and Maverick quickly went into a gentle walk. The morning sun refracted off the truck window causing Steele to squint and hold his hand above his eyes to shade the glare. He wanted to watch his granddaughter ride slowly down the mountain. In the distance, he could hear her singing a song to Maverick. The ride would take her several hours, but she knew a lot of stories and songs. Steele followed them with his eyes until the dirt road rounded a bend and they went out of view.

"You gonna lollygag all day?" asked Molly as she started the engine.

Closing the passenger door and sitting down, Steele replied: "Naw, I'm ready. You want me to drive?"

"Nope. I like driving."

Just like Marija, thought Steele. "Well then, let's go. Time's a wastin.' Don't have all day. Let's giddyap n' go already," he exclaimed while slapping the dashboard in mock anger.

Molly chafed at Steele's playful effort to be in control and have the last word with his order to depart. But rather than go tit-for-tat with him, she shook her head, gunned the engine, and popped the clutch. That caused the rear wheels to spin in the red Colorado dirt. Steele's head snapped back and tapped the back window while the dust she scuffed up obscured the parting view Steele was hoping to have of the cabin. *May be the last time I see it,* he whined to himself. Steele looked over his shoulder just before the truck reached the bend in the road. Enough of the dust had settled, and he could see how decrepit the old structure really was. *Must be how people see me,* he thought as he dropped his guard momentarily and mused on his life.

BACK AT THE RANCH

The old truck passed Allie and Maverick on the way down the mountain and spread a cloud of rusty dust for them to suffer through. Fergus barked at them from the bed of the truck as they passed by. In dog reckoning, he worried that Molly and Steele were unaware that they were leaving part of the family behind. So, he barked at the cabin to let them know of their mistake.

Steele waited until the dust cleared enough, then he looked to see Allie behind them in the distance. He was sure he could see her mouth moving and that she was still singing to Maverick. He hoped she would be back at the ranch by late afternoon or at least before dark even though she was taking the old Ute Indian trail instead going by the side of the highway to get home. Steele liked Ute trail better too. It was not infrequent that cars edged too close to horses and riders on the narrow road.

Riding the Ute trail was also more interesting than following the narrow strip of oily-smelling asphalt with its view of discarded grocery bags and beer cans. The Ute trail led to the same place anyway. It was good that Allie had similar thoughts. Sometimes he opined it was funny that the settlers who invaded the land thought Indians were know-nothing savages. But they mostly made roads that followed Indian paths.

Allie glanced to her left and saw the Lone Cone in the distance near Norwood with the setting sun behind the peak. She remembered Steele telling her there was a government cabin there too. It was like Steele's cabin on his unnamed mountain.

Since no one had ever bothered to name his craggy little peak, Steele took to calling it Steele Mountain. But he was the only one to call it that. The cabin on the Lone Cone was different than the rustler's cabin. Not only did the mountain have a name, but it also had running water, a flushing toilet, an outhouse for winter when the pipes froze, a stove, refrigerator, and electricity brought in by utility poles from Norwood. It was built in 1936, and the Forest Service now rented it out for a hundred dollars a day mainly to people that Steele called the Telluride crowd. Steele was fond of noting that no rustlers ever lived there.

The trip down the mountain from Steele's cabin didn't take long—half an hour on the winding dirt road for the truck. Allie and Maverick would take hours to reach the Ranch. Back in the kitchen of the main house, Steele was quick to get back to the conversation Molly had started at the cabin. "So, what's this about Allie," Steele blurted out as Molly poured red table wine into his glass?

"She tracked Posey down. People her age know a lot of ways to find people on a computer. And you know how obsessed she is about her genealogy. If you were to ask her, she could probably find your dad too–maybe dead—maybe alive. Be that as it may, Leon Posey's in a hospice in Phoenix. A place called the Calvary House."

Steele deflected. "Did you ever wonder about the irony of your rapist having the same first name as my father?"

"Not really. Coincidence happens. Shit happens. Who knows?" Then seeing a lack of conviction on Steele's face, she added. "You're not him Pop. I know who you are, and so does Allie. You're our Pop. Your dad never was a pop — even though you called him Pop. He never deserved the title. Pops are important people. Your father Leon Steele was not important."

"Did Leon Posey deserve me to blow off his pecker and

balls?"

"I don't know. At the time it felt right —me raped — Morgan dead. Now, it feels a bit harsh. But don't forget, he murdered Morgan, and his daddy the Sheriff wasn't going to let the law hang him for killing a queer. And they certainly weren't going to punish him for raping me because they never knew. Nobody knew except Leon, Ellen, his cronies, and me. I didn't tell, and they weren't about to incriminate themselves. So, it was my secret to keep. Hell, you didn't know I was raped until I had to tell you seventeen years ago. Besides, you didn't kill Leon, but Leon did kill Morgan. You just castrated him and told him to leave and never come back. Heck, that wasn't even an eye for an eye. More like an eye for a dingleberry if you ask me."

Steele winced at Molly's words – *"never come back,"* the words Steele said to Leon as he sat bleeding from his crotch. Sounded like what the former Sheriff Pickett told his pop when he handed him the injunction issued by the court. But Steele's order to Leon to *never come back* didn't come from a court of law. It came from the working end of Steele's pistol. Still, Steele didn't like the connection of his words to Leon, and the court's same words to his pop.

"Might have been better if I'd killed him. A man without a home, a pecker, or a pair of balls is only partly a man."

"Well, maybe Leon decided to be a girl. That happens these days," mused Molly to ease the tension.

"Humph," he answered, which told Molly nothing. "Why's he in a hospice?"

"He got the cancer of the Pancreas."

"That kind of cancer moves fast. Real fast. Not like mine."

"Allie knows that, so she needs to get there soon. She just didn't want to do it be behind her pop's back."

Steele was flattered again and filled with some grandfatherly pride. He was also proud that she was so capable with a computer. These were skills that he knew had passed him by as if he was of another age — which he was. He felt a tear well up and gripped the side arms of the chair to hold it back as he pondered and dreaded the thought of Allie finding his lost father with her computer.

"You all right Pop?"

"Yeah. I was passing gas. Sorry."

"You hungry?"

"Not yet. I'd rather wait for Allie. But another glass of wine sounds good. How's old Leon paying for hospice?"

"Doesn't have to. Allie found an ad for it. Says it's free for Medicare and Medicaid folks."

"Free," he pondered?

Watching his mind race, she cut him off. "Hospice is free here too. Allie and me. We're your hospice."

"Oh, I know that," he said presumptively even as he lied. The thought of his daughter and granddaughter having to watch him slip down a slow ugly slide toward death still bothered him. If dying in the cabin on the mountain was off the table, then maybe there was another way. He held the thought.

Steele excused himself and went outside with his glass of wine and walked toward the working end of his ranch. He no longer ran the place year-round to care for his own herd. And he had stopped driving them to the high country in summer for grazing with his partner Ganiz. He and Molly decided to specialize and that freed Steele and Ganiz to semi-retire for most of the year or even fully retire if he let Allie and Molly take care of it all—which they did.

Their specialty was lambing. Since the surrounding sheep country was perched at almost six-thousand-feet, winter snow averaged over a foot and a half. Lambs are mostly born winter through spring. Because of the cold, they need to shelter from the weather and to huddle with their mother ewes for several weeks after they lamb. Even spring was cold at this altitude with snow still lingering on the ground to summer.

Thus, Steele built his business to take in lambing ewes from other ranches during the lambing season, hire some help to manage the surge, and then be done with it after just a few months at most. But it wasn't just about the convenience of having nine or ten months off every year. Lambing was the most enjoyable part of being a sheep rancher. *If you've never seen a flock of lambs hopping and frolicking,* he thought *—well, you haven't seen anything.*

Steele sat on a large white stone that dominated the pasture, sipped his wine, and looked out toward the Ute trail near the highway. There he saw Allie and Maverick a half-mile away. Speed-loving Allie had given Maverick the reins for a final gallop home. Allie's black ponytail flew with the wind and matched the flying tail of Maverick as they cut through the mountain air dodging granite boulders along the way.

Relieved and excited to see them, he turned too quickly and stumbled. Losing his balance was becoming a frequent occurrence, and he wondered if it just came with age or had something to do with the cancer. Either way, it addled him. Barging through the door to the house with some bluster to mask his embarrassment over tripping outside, he announced — "she's almost here." Then he went back out to greet Allie.

"Sore?"

"Not really. Maverick did great," she answered as she stood on her tiptoes to remove the tack. Steele helped with the saddle and opened the gate to the corral so that Maverick could reach her hay and water and greet the roan, his other horse.

"So, I understand you want to talk?"

"Yep. You ready Pops?"

"After dinner and maybe a few more glasses of wine."

"Table wine I presume?"

"Nothing less for me."

"You know Pop, after we get done with this talk, I'd like to learn more about Grandma Marija. Maybe do some Genealogy and find out which village she came from. I'm one-quarter Slovenian after all. Mom home?"

"Yep. She's fixing a chicken dinner if my nose still works."
"It's chicken. I've been smelling it for a mile."

"Think it's Chicken Piccata? I think you love Piccata as much as I do."

"Sorry, Pop. My nose isn't that good. Mom says it's because I smoke. But chicken Picatta is a pleasant thought. You go check on dinner and Mom while I brush Maverick. I'll be in as soon as I wash the horse smell off me at my house."

"Your house?"

"Yeah. I've taken up in the cabin since Ganiz died."

Steele hung his head and had the look of guilt on his face. "I wish I had been here when he passed instead of up on the mountain that day."

"Yes, well it was his time. Guess you'll be taking the cabin now that you'll be staying on the ranch, right?"

"Yeah. Sorry Allie. I'm not going to be comfortable in the house." Steele gave a glance to the cabin. "Sure will miss that old guy sitting on the porch. Any reason you haven't been staying in the big house?"

"Sort of. Me and Mom, well, you know we're a lot alike. Sometimes that's good. Sometimes, not so good. With me in the cabin, we get along better. Besides, she doesn't like my smoking. Says it stinks."

"Understood." With that, Steele left Allie to secure Maverick in the corral she shared with the roan mare and get to her shower. Unlike Maverick, the roan had no given name. It was just called *the roan*. The roan hadn't seen Maverick for two weeks, so they greeted each other by putting their nostrils close together and breathing in their scent. Steele watched them for a moment and then went off to check on Molly in the kitchen.

"So, what's for dinner?"

"Chicken Marsala on linguine."

"What, no Piccata?"

"Do you want to make it," she asked turning away from

the stove to face him while holding a spoon straight up like a weapon?

Thinking better of challenging her, he replied. "Naw." Don't even know why I asked. Who needs Chicken Piccata when we already have already have Chicken Marsala?"

"More wine?"

"Sure."

"Help yourself."

With that, Steele poured full glass of red and tried to keep from spilling it as he tiptoed over to his favorite chair by the window. Fortunately, there was no carpet between here and there as dribbles of red followed him to the chair. As he eased into his seat, Fergus curled up quietly beside him. Soon Allie came in fresh from her shower in the cabin all cleaned up and went in to help Molly.

"Chicken Marsala. I just knew it was Marsala. I've been smelling it for miles."

"Liar," countered Steele.

Molly sensed she had been left out of a prior conversation and let it go. What was the saying, she wondered? *Let sleeping arguments lie*, she thought as she poured herself a flute of champagne and looked up at the ceiling still holding the thought —*Or was it dogs*?

"I'll have some of that," piped Allie as she pointed to Molly's flute.

"It doesn't go with Marsala."

"Ha, champagne goes with everything! Besides, you're drinking it."

Molly thought for less than a second before breaking out in giggles and agreeing with Allie wholeheartedly. Allie, who had already filled a glass with chardonnay, poured it down the sink. She refilled it with champagne even though it was a chardonnay glass. The girls were now in a mood and did a wiggly dance back into the kitchen for a bit of girl talk, one with a flute, one with a chard glass, but both filled with bubbly. Steele watched and felt utterly blessed to have two such lively women in his life.

There was a knock at the door. Steele was closest so he got up to answer. At the door was a beautiful woman who looked surprised to see Steele. "Um, excuse me sir. Is Molly home?"

"Yes, she is," answered Steele, not knowing how to handle a stranger at the door when dinner was just about to be served. "I'll get her."

Molly saw who it was and frowned, strode out of the kitchen, grabbed the hand of the woman, and slammed the door behind her. Then they walked out toward the road with Molly gesticulating wildly as if she were angry. Steele watched.

"Who is that?" he asked Allie.

Allie responded thinking everyone already knew. "It's her lover Emily Pops."

Steele did not recognize Molly's childhood friend not only because she had grown up; she had also taken to cutting her hair short like a boy. *She was the one*, he suddenly recalled. He had caught her and Molly kissing in the barn when they were teens. *They were just practicing for kissing boys,* he remembered they had said. Still, he was speechless. *Molly's Lover?* He sat back in his chair and cocked his head to the side as if that angle would help him understand what he did not know but should have.

THE NEXT DAY AT THE RANCH

The next day Steele got up early with the usual headache after sleeping on the couch in the main house. The cabin in the pasture was not yet ready for him, because Allie still needed to move her things out. It was dark as he stumbled through the kitchen looking for the coffee percolator with the glass bubble on the top. He filled the strainer basket with five full measures of Yuban and put three cups of water in the belly of the pot. *Richness worth a second cup,* ran the TV jingle in his head.

Five measures of Yuban to three cups of water ensured that the coffee would pour like syrup when it was done. It was his version of expresso. He sniffed the dry coffee with pleasure as the aroma drifted up from the wide mouth of the can, and he dropped spoonfulls of it into the silverish aluminum filter basket. Coffee always smelled better than it tasted. *Kind of like that baker's chocolate in Mom's pantry that smelled so good but tasted and so awful when I snuck a bite as a kid,* he recalled. And he did not forget the beating he got when was caught by his mother as he spit the awful stuff into the sink.

"That's one chocolate cake we'll never have," scolded his mother Ginny. She was always putting things into the communal context of family. The message was clear. Glenn Steele had stolen a spare luxury from the clan. Her scolding still stung.

Allie was first to smell the coffee and shuffled in with her old pair of Star Wars slippers and sat down at the table. She had slept the night with her mother on the King bed. Arriving at the table, she yawned, and waited to be served with her eyes still half closed.

"Milk and sugar," he asked?

"Naw. Straight up Pop," you know that.

"Yeah. I was just checking. Things change you know."

As he set Allie's cup down, Molly stepped in wearing only a long tee shirt that barely covered her bottom. Her flip flops announced her approach from down the hallway.

"Morning," muttered Steele offering his greeting to both of them.

"Morning," mumbled both the girls as Molly straddled the chair and took her place at the table. All of them knew that the breakfast dance would soon begin. Allie would be first. She would boil her eggs then fry her bacon crisp then press all the fat out of it. Steele would fry three eggs over easy, fry the bacon rare, and then pour the bacon grease left in the pan over his eggs as if it were syrup. Molly picked three pieces of bacon from Allie's plate which is why Allie fried six strips when she only wanted three. And when Steele wasn't looking, Molly lifted one of his eggs to her plate but left a trail of egg yolk on the table that led directly to the perpetrator.

"You're welcome," said Steele dryly.

No one mentioned the revelation about Molly and Emily that blurted out the day before. *It's Molly's tale to tell,* he thought. But he was addled by it and knew enough about himself that it wasn't going to go away. *Wonder what else*

I've missed since I've been hiding in the cabin up there on the mountain?

Allie was good with computers—not games like most of her high-school friends. She had become obsessed with genealogy. It was driven by wanting to know who she was. As the child of a rapist and murderer, she was desperate to find out whose genes lurked beyond her biological father, Leon Posey. She started her research with the Latter Day Saints and Colorado's State Archives of Vital Statistics. But Soon she was mining on-line genealogy sites. Finally, she subscribed to a website that offered DNA testing where she could compare her genes with a database of other members.

Before her test results came in, she had constructed a well-researched family tree. It was orderly and seemed to stand as settled proof of her pedigree through Glenn Steele and grandmother Marija. Glenn Steele came from a long line of Steeles who came from Scotland. She laughed when her website informed her that the Steele surname was a diminutive for a person who was hard and durable. That fit, she thought when she recalled what he did to Leon Posey. But she also thought it left out his soft side. Marija came from Slovenia with her grandparents after her parents were slaughtered by Tito partisans during that war.

One night as she continued her research, her computer signaled that a new email had just arrived in her in-box. It was the DNA report she had been waiting weeks for. Excited, she opened the attached file confident it would confirm everything her neatly constructed well-researched family tree asserted about her family line. But her brow wrinkled into a scowl as she read the report. *Impossible*, she thought.

The report did not link her to a specific person in the database, but it did attest that she was 1/16th American Indian.

It even located the approximate place where the indigenous genes probably came from —the Mogollon Range in Arizona. *But from who? Leon, Marija, Glenn Steele, Morgan, her mom, Pop Steele? How could that be,* she asked herself? She went back over what she had already posted on her family tree and realized that the tree she had spent the last year constructing was now useless. DNA had eviscerated its foundation.

Steele was as shocked as Allie at the news. But after quickly assessing all the candidates as the source of the indigenous genes, he suspected his father. *He never mentioned his parents at all! Why not? It was as if he came from some sort of spontaneous generation. Could one of Pop's parents been an Indian? Could be,* he mused. *Golly,* he thought, a word he no longer used except when having an ineffable thought. Pushing that notion further, he tried to imagine the prospect. *Me with an Indian grandpa or an Indian grandma?*

Glenn Steele never had much of an opinion one way or the other about Indians. Growing up in the Uncompaghre, they were part of the landscape. They had always been here. And he didn't begrudge their presence. In fact, they made it interesting in his view. Now he learned that he might be a part of that landscape too, but not in the way he could have anticipated.

In this part of the country, the dominant tribe was Ute. Utah was named for them. Utes knew nothing about boundary lines when the land was theirs. Boundary lines were what white men drew on maps without Ute permission. Utes, on the other hand, understood territory from landmarks, not maps. Within those landmarks their territory stretched from Utah into Colorado. It had been that way for centuries with adjustments after conflicts with competing tribes. One of those landmarks was *uncompaghre*—a Ute word for "dirty water." Steele's ranch was built near the river called the Uncompaghre. In a way, his ranch was nothing more than a place name in the land of the Ute that once guided them through their territory.

But if Glenn Steele lacked strong opinions about the Utes, their boundary markers, or any other tribal matters for that matter, Pop Steele did not. He hated Indians on principle but had a special dislike of the Apache. It didn't matter that the Jicarilla Apache were closely related to the Utes who he at least tolerated. Pop Steele's special loathing of Apaches was the reason Glenn Steele did not believe the town rumor about him taking up with an Apache woman. That was still the leading gossip after Pop Steele was kicked out of the house by the law for domestic abuse.

"Oh yeah," people would say, "I heard your father went north to Idaho with a squaw named Apache Jane." If nothing else was clear to Glenn Steele about his father, his animosity toward Apaches and Indians generally was plain. *No, Leon Steele would not have liked being part Indian,* thought Steele when he heard the news about the DNA. He might well have gone to Idaho as some said—who knows—but if he did, Steele bet it was not with an Indian, especially an Apache.

Allie kept at her research. Then, late one evening while sitting at her computer she exclaimed—"I've got it Pop." Steele was sitting in the kitchen enjoying a late-night dessert of torn toast, milk, and sugar and was startled enough to spill a spoon of it on the plastic red and white checked tablecloth.

"You found what?" responded Steele with grumpy annoyance at the interruption.

"I found your Pop in a census! A 1960 Census. He was in Arizona then—in a place called Black Canyon. Says his occupation was '*sheepherder*.'"

1960, mused Steele. *Five years after I bashed his skull to save Jesse — five years after Pop got banished from the family after I called the sheriff—and now a sheepherder no less!*

Steele's right hand hadn't shaken for months. But he could not deny that it was beginning to tremble again now, just like before—right after his father left —then Dort—then Morgan—then Posey—right after each one. The sudden news of his father and the census was just the latest trigger. Now an army of uninvited memories began marauding through his brain riding the welted back of his childhood remembrances.

Pop Steele might as well have appeared live in the doorway to the house with his menacing voice, a bottle of whiskey in one hand, and a knife in the other. Steele knew what his shaking hand augured and decided it was best to shield the girls. He rose from his chair and gave an exaggerated yawn to disguise the tension that was building inside him. Soon after, he stretched his arms out wide to show how tired he was, even though he was not. Then he announced that he needed a little air. On his way out the door, he pulled his down coat off its hook, grabbed a bottle of whiskey off the countertop, and made his way to the cabin though he stumbled in the dark. The weathered steps creaked as he trudged up the uneven planks to the porch. Then he eased himself down into the old rocking chair where Ganiz had spent most of his last days on earth. Soon, he began to drink. After toasting a few to Ganiz, he put down the bottle, slumped down into the creaky chair, and felt his eyes begin to twitch behind his lids as he sank into a drunken dream. That was when he heard a voice calling him from the dark somewhere in the pasture.

"Pop?"

KIT AND KABOODLE

Leon Steele had become a mean drunk long before his son Glenn was twelve years old. He wasn't always that way. Glenn kept four good memories of his Pop before he got bitter.

The first one was that whenever his Pop got hold of an apple, he would pull out his switchblade knife and carefully cut it into quarters. He never used a paring knife from the kitchen. Using the switchblade made it seem personal because it was. Engraved on both sides of the tempered steel blade were three British cavalry soldiers riding at a gallop while swinging their swords at an unseen enemy. Fitted into the bone handle was a logo that said "Sheffield." After pressing a button on the side, the spring-loaded blade swung open with a jerk hard enough to jolt his hand. Then, after slicing the apple into quarters, he would give Glenn one of them. He still remembered the image of his Pop's hairless hand as he held out the quarter to him like a special gift. But his Pop never ate the rest of the apple with him. He always skulked over to a hidden corner and ate the remaining quarters by himself.

The second one was when he taught Steele how to gentle a wild horse. Steele was eight when his father captured a wild mustang while working the Desolation. Steele expected to see the horse saddled against its will and then ridden mercilessly until it gave up trying to buck the hated hominid, the impertinent saddle, and the halter off. He had seen cowboys do it that way in the movies, and he remembered John Wayne dominating a bronco in *Hondo*. But to his surprise, Pop had a kinder way to gentle a wild horse. And it seemed important for Pop to show his young son the right way to do it.

The third one was the slow-motion image of his father reaching out to lift a low hanging branch of an oakbrush. He remembered his hand looked strong. Large veins popped up from under his hairless skin and were filled with blood. Under the branch was a resting bullsnake. Disturbed, it quickly slithered deeper under the bush to escape the humans that had discovered it. Steele was too young to understand it then. But later he realized that his father was teaching him something again. What the subject of this lesson was did not matter. What mattered was that Pop thought he was worthy of being taught.

The last one was when Steele was five. An older boy had been picking on him for weeks with taunts and sometimes with kicks and fists. Finally, young Steele decided to put an end to it. The next time the larger boy came over to bully him, he didn't hesitate. He kicked him in the groin without warning and the larger boy went down holding his crotch crying "No fair, no fair."

That got the attention of the bully's father who came running out of his house, grabbed Steele by the shoulders, and began shaking him like a rag doll. Steele was on the verge of passing out when he heard his father say: "Get your god damned hands off my boy," which was soon followed by the sound of a loud crack as his father's fist crashed into the man's jaw. The man dropped to the ground with a thud unconscious next to his suffering son. "Don't touch my boy again," warned Steele's father as he carried his son back into the house. "Ever," he added in a tone wrapped with deadly menace.

Years later, on a hot humid day on a smelly Kansas oil field near Plainfield, Leon Steele was standing in the shade of a heavily laden truck sneaking a snort of whiskey. Suddenly,

the load of drilling pipe on the trailer shifted, and two tons of steel fell off and crushed his legs. His wife Ginny had married him mainly because he was the best dancer around for miles and told a good story, especially when he drank. Ginny loved to dance and listen to his tales. But after the pipe crushed his legs, Pop Steele's dancing days were over, and his stories turned bitter. Ginny's love of dancing died with his stove-up legs and his drinking became incessant.

From that day forward, he never sliced an apple for Glenn again. But despite the alcohol addiction, he was capable enough to trade three scrawny chickens and some tall tales around a campfire for something worth much more than three hens. Even drunk, he was a natural-born horse-trader.

After his legs were crushed, horse-trading became his work-in-trade. The nature of his work was simple. After roping some wild mustangs in the Disappointment Country and breaking them to saddle and bit, he tied a string of them to his wagon. Like some families in and around Nucla, they were poor and couldn't afford a car or truck. With the mustangs secured by a rope, he added odds and ends behind the seat of the buckboard.

What was in the back of the wagon for trade along with the partially tamed horses tied to it was called his kit and kaboodle. When he was all loaded up, he gave a click of his tongue to the horse pulling the wagon and left at dawn heading for the Disappointment with the mustangs in tow. He would leave without a word to his wife. Ginny would glance out the kitchen window as he rode off while she nursed the youngest of their skinny threadbare brood. She wanted to make sure he was really gone, and secretly wished he would not return to impregnate her again. She was wore out.

When he finally did return a few weeks or months later,

he would have three better horses in tow and better kit and kaboodle along with a load of whiskey which would not last long. Any affability he possessed before returning home, he squandered among the strangers he spent time with at the camps and saloons. He spent it on male camaraderie, whisky, horse- trading, and storytelling. By the time he returned to the crumbling house they rented just outside Nucla near the Disappointment Country, there was little charm left in him to share with his wife and nine children. And when the whiskey ran out at the house, he would drag twelve-year-old Glenn Steele up to the hard buckboard seat with him and head back out to a notorious tavern in the Disappointment. There he got glasses of cheap whiskey to drink at the bar and bought more bottles to bring home.

There was at least one shooting there a month, and old man Pickett, Nucla's town Sheriff did his best to avoid the place unless somebody died. Being wounded was not enough to warrant the dangerous ride to investigate. That danger didn't bother Pop Steele or cause him worry about his son. He needed the boy in case he got too drunk to guide the wagon back home. Steele remembered one trip when he was told to hold the wagon-horse while Pop disembarked and walked on bent legs toward the tavern. Flickering light from the burning fireplace inside escaped the double door entrance and lit the bare ground outside. His pop drank whiskey at the bar and then persuaded the surly owner that he was good for what he owed him on his next trip back.

"Better be," growled the owner who had a Colt .45 revolver slung sloppily over his groin rather than his hip. Reaching below the bar near where a shotgun leaned, he pulled out a long piece of paper with Pop Steele's name at the top. Using a short pencil, he made a new notation near the bottom. His credit limit met, Pop Steele and his son took the two-hour ride back guided by moonlight. Young Steele shivered in the night air without a jacket, and his pop drank himself into oblivion.

Some people drink and feel sleepy. Some people drink and feel happy like his pop once did. When he was courting his mother Ginny in Bazaar Kansas booze just went along with telling tall tales, dancing with Ginny into the night, and keeping her laughing. Others drink and get sloppy. But after Pop lost his legs and Ginny along with them, Pop got mean. And on this trip, Steele was afraid of being alone with him for the long ride home. He felt relieved when Pop flopped over sideways on the seat and passed out—for the moment at least. And Steele was happy to take the reins so that he could hurry the horse. He wanted to get home before Pop woke up.

As he got closer and closer to the house, he held back from thinking he was safe too soon. Then his eyes caught sight of the dim light coming from the kitchen window of their house ahead. He ground his teeth in fear for the five minutes it took to cross the distance until he was there. He locked the brake quietly, jumped off the wagon, and ran inside leaving Pop in a heap in the cold night air under a quarter moon. It was late—three in the morning. He felt bad about leaving him there, and he worried that it was too cold to leave him like that. He even considered covering him with a blanket but thought better of it. That act of kindness could warrant a beating if he woke him. In the end, weariness took over the twelve year-old, and he crawled into bed. As he slept, the wagon-horse and three new horses he traded for at the saloon quietly munched on grass that blew back and forth in the wind in concert with the horses' manes.

The house near Nucla was the best house the Steele family had ever lived in. It was only the second time that they had lived in a house they paid rent for. Pop Steele had dragged his family from spot to spot mainly going west from St. Joseph Missouri to Bazaar Kansas, to Salina, Fort Hays, the Plainville oil fields, Reno Kansas, then Salida Colorado, Gunnison, and finally Nucla. He never said why or how he came to St. Joseph, or why he kept on the move after he left Missouri. He hired out on farms and ranches along the way and he kept Ginny pregnant almost every year of the next ten. He never owned a house of his own and the family either squatted or begged for shelter in a rancher's or farmer's outbuilding along the way. They were homeless.

Steele was last to go to sleep in the household after leaving his father in the buckboard. Not long after that, Pop Steele burst through the front door on one of the new horses yelling at everyone and brandishing his switchblade knife. Despite being the elder of his siblings, Steele was not the biggest of the brothers. Jesse was as big as a man and well-muscled from all the work he did hiring out lifting hay bales on a ranch nearby. Pop Steele was having to duck his head down low almost to the pommel of his saddle because of the low ceiling. But he was slashing the air sideways with his knife while cursing everyone in the house including his wife, Ginny.

"Where are you, you white bitch?"

Jesse and Steele circled their drunken father until they saw an opening and pulled him off the mustang to the floor. The terrified horse wheeled and crashed out the window breaking its foreleg. Its screaming outside from the pain only added to the chaos. Jesse grabbed for the wrist of his father's knife-hand while Steele lay prone over his crippled legs to keep him down. But pop managed to slash Jesse's arm before he could get a good grip on his wrist. The blade sliced an artery and blood spurted over the three of them like a pulsing fountain as they wrestled on the floor and smeared blood over them.

It was then that the old man kicked twelve-year-old

Steele off his crooked legs and got to his feet and crouched while still brandishing the switchblade at his two sons. Pop decided to take on Jesse first. The angry whites of his eyes and teeth showed even in the dim light coming from his mother's bedroom. As he took a menacing step toward Jesse, Glenn Steele ran to the counter by the sink, picked up his mother's rolling pin, and ran back behind his father as he continued to slash at Jesse.

Then Steele raised the roller high over his father's head and sent it crashing down. The blow left a peculiar dent that ran from his pop's forehead to a cowlick at the back of his skull. Blood was flowing into his rolled back eyes before his head hit the floor and bounced. After Pop fell unconscious from the strike to his head, Steele's mother Ginny calmly stepped over him and went to a baby crying in a crib, opened her blouse, and began nursing. Then she uttered three words that would change their lives.

"Get the Sheriff."

Jesse wrapped his knife wound with a dish-towel while Glenn Steele ran to a distant neighbor and used their phone to call the Sheriff. Then he returned to the house, pulled his father's pistol out of its holster, and shot the screaming horse between the eyes. It had a splintered bone sticking out of the skin of its broken foreleg. The smoking pistol was still in his hand hanging at his side when he saw the Sheriff coming up the road with flashing red lights. The sheriff had come quickly. He knew the way. Young Steele was standing near the front door still holding the pistol and was lit up by his headlights as the black and white neared the house. The sheriff got out of the police car, walked past Glenn Steele and the dead horse, ignored the pistol, and then strode into the house through the front door.

When he saw Leon Steele unconscious on the kitchen floor, he decided to take him to the hospital in Montrose in his police car. Steele watched as his father's head bounced down the stairs as the Sheriff dragged him by his feet across the dirt while kicking up dust into the cruiser's headlights. Then he loaded him in the trunk and slammed it shut. The sheriff didn't want blood on his cloth seats.

"Where are you taking him, asked a worried Steele."

"Don't worry son. He won't be back to bother you again."

No, I mean where are you taking him?"

"Hospital in Montrose," answered the Sheriff. "Then to jail if he lives."

If he lives? Fretted Steele. With that, the Sheriff went back in the house to retrieve the switchblade. He folded the blade with a click when it locked and took it as evidence for the judge. Soon after that, he drove off siren blaring and lights flashing to Montrose Memorial Hospital. Steele watched as the Sheriff sped away into the night with his father locked in the trunk. Then he glanced back at the house and saw the younger children crowding the windows watching the scene with wide open eyes. Steele shuddered at what he had done. In his effort to save Jesse, he may have killed his own father. And if Leon Steele survived, he was almost certain to go to jail. What would Glenn say to his brothers and sisters when there was no father to bring home food to eat or money for rent.

Later he would learn that his father's wound looked worse than it was. The doctor said he was lucky to be alive. But he also said that he would carry that dent for the rest of his life. Pop Steele was hospitalized for a week before they discharged him and then he went to jail to be held on a charge of attempted murder. But the prosecutor declined to prosecute him. He said it was a case of domestic abuse. *So, a man who tries to kill his sons goes free, while a man does the same to a stranger goes to jail*, mused Glenn?

Before they let Glenn's father out of the local jail, something called an injunction was issued by the county court in Montrose. It said Pop Steele had to leave the family and never come back. Upon his discharge, he picked up the entirety of his worldly possessions from a police clerk: a wedding ring made of bronze, an empty wallet, and a switchblade knife. Then, he entered the lonely world of a man on foot without a family, a job, money, or a place to live. Young Steele read the words on the legal papers delivered by the sheriff, but he could not comprehend the law. What he could understand was that his father's name was on it, and that he, Glenn Steele, was responsible for the fact that Leon Steele could never come home again.

Ginny didn't live long after that. "She was wore out," Steele would say.

STEELE WAKES UP ON THE PORCH

Steel woke up in Ganiz's rocking chair to the sound of Molly's voice and the gentle touch of her hand on his shoulder.

"Come on back in the house pop. It's cold. You can't sit out here in the open."

Stiff from sitting on the exposed porch for so long, Steele stood up on wobbly legs, looked around because he was unsure where he was after his boyhood dream about kit and kaboodle. He stretched to clear his head. "Why don't I just go inside the cabin?"

"We pulled all the sheets out of there to wash them for you—remember? There's no bedding and no blankets. Come in the house. Your bed's ready, there's a fire going, and it's warm."

"But..."

"No buts this time Pop. Tonight, you're mine," she ordered with a mock frown as she stooped to get under his shoulder, grabbed his arm, and helped him walk down the steps from the porch. Then they crossed some open pasture until they reached the main house and shuffled down the hall to the bedroom. "Sit on the bed Pop," she ordered. He obeyed and sat with his head hanging low and his chin resting passively on his chest while she removed his coat from his limp arms. Allie heard the commotion and appeared in the doorway. Without a word from Molly, she went to his feet to pull off his boots. Soon he was lying in his wool underwear with a soft pillow under his head and a sleepy drool oozing from the corner of his beard stubbled mouth. Molly and Allie left him safe and warm in his room.

Steele was tired, drunk, and falling back into a deep sleep when he heard the voice of his father again. In his dream state, he saw Leon Steele sitting alone on the white rock in the pasture with the glow of a campfire on his face as embers flitted like fireflies high into the midnight sky. A bottle of whiskey was at his side.

"C'mon over." He beckoned with his hand. "I got a tale to tell."

RIDING THE LINE

Riding the line became a full-time job for Glenn Steele when he turned sixteen. By then, he had been head of household for four years—ever since he saved his brother Jesse by smashing that rolling pin on his knife wielding father's head. And ever since getting Leon Steele kicked out of his house when Glenn called the sheriff. Steele was always saving people—people like his brothers and sisters who suddenly became motherless and fatherless but stayed safe and fed because of him.

Riding line was hardest in winter. Cattle ranches along the western slope of the Rockies used men or boys like Steele to ride fence —what they also called "the line." The job was to maintain barbed wire fences and recover cattle that may have escaped their range. Teddy Roosevelt, Steele recalled, was once a line-rider and called it a tough job, especially in winter when snow often collected into near impassible snowdrifts that even a long-legged horse could not plow through.

Summer storms packed their own dangers. They hurled thunderous bolts of lightning down toward tall riders riding tall horses on exposed land cleared of tall trees for pasture. Food was beans and jerky, beans and jerky, and beans and jerky with lots of coffee in between. But truth be told, each week Steele wheedled some extras from the ranch kitchen — some bread, a jug of milk, and a little butter which he kept frozen in winter along with some sugar for his favorite dessert of warm milk and torn buttered toast.

Line-riders often rode in twos and shared a shack for shelter. Not Steele who called his solo shack a cabin. He preferred to be alone, because that was the way he was, but also, because he was completing high school by mail. Having quiet time to study was a benefit. Soon after he got a diploma, he began correspondence courses for college and completed half the credits needed for a bachelor's degree before he was eighteen. Psychology and Roman literature teased his interests, probably because neither was practical. Steele was full enough of practical.

In an arrangement with the ranch that employed him, he took part of his wages in the form of a cow that he sent home to Nucla so that his orphaned siblings would have milk to supplement their diet. The rest of his earnings were sent direct to his brother James who paid the rent, food, and utilities. They called James the accountant. The eldest of the girls was Helen. They were calling her mother by the time she was eight. Neighbors helped out as they could with hand-me-downs, old bread, an occasional hot dinner, and apples from their trees. The town doctor donated his time. Old man Pickett, the town sheriff before Posey's father took over, checked in on them most every day. The landlord was Widow Jensen. She raised eight children on her own after her husband died young. It was not a surprise when she lowered the rent for her impoverished tenants. It was by these acts of kindness and the wages Steele earned by riding the line that kept the family together in their ramshackle abode in Nucla.

One day in mid-January found Steele in the line cabin warming his hands around a glowing red metal stove with a flat top on it for cooking. He took one slice of bread and buttered both sides then flopped it on the stove for a few seconds. Then he flipped it over and did the same with the other side while a mist of fried butter rose to the ceiling, and the smell of burning toast filled the small room. Taking a fork to nudge the toast into a bowl, he let it cool from hot to warm. After a few moments more, he tore it into pieces, sugared it, and poured half a cup of warmed milk over it and said "ah," when the first spoonful hit his lips.

The next day found him riding fence back toward the ranch. Along the way he fixed broken barbed wire and gathered strays. He arrived at the ranch at sundown, picked up supplies, and started to head back toward the cabin as light snow started to fall ahead of a gathering storm.

The foreman met Steele at the supply shack. Like most of the ranch hands, he liked Steele. He was hardworking, didn't cuss, smoke, or drink, and he could always rely on him to do what he said he would do. He also knew that he had a whole family of younger siblings who were depending on him.

"You goin' back in this storm Steele?

"Have to. I'm the line-rider."

"Yeah, but one night won't make a difference. Cattle won't be moving much, and you're current on your fence mending. Why don't you stay over just for the night? The outbuilding over there has a bed and a stove in it."

"Yes sir, but I'm the line-rider."

"So, you are son. So, you are," acquiescing to his sense of mission. Now, listen up. If you have any trouble finding the cutoff that intersects the line toward the cabin, ride the line back. Don't be foolish and get lost looking for the cabin. That line fence over there is your lifeline back here, and if you wander too far away from it in a storm like this, you may not find your way back at all.

"Yes sir. Good advice. I'll see you in a week.

"Or later tonight."

Yes, sir. Next week.

"Take care son." *Stubborn kid,* he thought. *Good kid, but* stubborn.

Other than the cold, the wind, and the dark, following the fence in the general direction of the cabin was no challenge. The hard part was knowing where the cabin was upslope and east from the fence when the snow was blinding, the clouds blocked all the light from the stars and moon, and no feature of the landscape could be seen from the fence line. Most important, the cabin would not be visible from the line. It was too far up the slope from the fence. He would just have to have a sense for where it was without any markers to guide him. *Easy,* he said to himself as he whistled himself past the graveyard.

His horse was named Blue. She spent most of her time in winter under a lean-to behind the cabin. Steele worried that between the snow, wind, and cold that the lean-to might not be enough protection for her in this kind of storm. While the cabin was small and the floor not built to support a horse, she might have to spend the night inside if they ever found the old shack.

Two hours out from the ranch house, drifts began piling up such that Blue was straining to push through the snow that reached to her chest. Despite the cold, she was sweating from exertion. That clinched it. She could not be put away wet under the lean-to. She wouldn't make it. *That's ok. I like you Blue. The cabin is not much, and I'm happy to share and to have the company. Just don't piss in it. I hate the smell of horse piss.*

After two and a half hours, Steele began to worry. On a

summer ride at a regular pace, it would take two hours to go from the line cabin to the ranch. With the drifts slowing Blue down, it was hard to tell how much added time it would take between the ranch and the cabin. But he was hoping he could get close by navigating by time and distance.

Time and distance worked like this. If it took two hours in good weather to get from the ranch to the cabin, how long might it take in bad weather in deep snow? It sounded like an elementary school math problem except it involved life and death. A half hour more, hour more, two hours? To his relief, he was able to eliminate one variable from the puzzle. It was definitely more than the two hours it took on a sunny day to get back to the cabin. So, when he reached the two-hour mark there was no need for concern, but it did signal that it was time to start looking. The cabin would certainly be somewhere further up the line. *But how much further?*

As they rode, he looked for signs. But the fresh carpet of snow was covering up all marks. He knew the cabin was roughly 100 feet up a slope east from the fence as he rode the fence north. Did he dare make a turn east, go 50 or sixty feet and then turn to go parallel with the fence and hope to see the cabin from just fifty feet away. *No*, he thought. It was worse than that. Visibility was less than 20 feet. He would have to ride east away from the fence at least eighty feet, then turn left paralleling the fence. But from that distance, he would no longer be able to see the fence, and the fence was his lifeline. *But what if I wander further away from the line without ever seeing or running into the cabin? I will never know that I've wandered off a parallel path with the fence if I can't to see it.*

It was then that he hit upon a plan. First, he was confident that he was still short of the cabin. He had only been gone from the ranch for two and a half hours, and the drifts had been so deep and time consuming that it was unlikely that they had ridden past the cabin already. That meant the cabin would still somewhere ahead. *Had to be.* Next, if he made a hard right turn east, rode eighty feet, then turned left parallel with the line, he could go, say, one hundred feet. And if he did not find the cabin he could backtrack and do it all over again one hundred feet further up the line more using the fence as a lifeline. *Time consuming, but it should work.*

When three hours of using that search method passed, he got scared. In his most extreme estimate, he should have reached the cabin after three hours but with all the constant backtracking it was hard to calculate. Now the cold was getting to his brain such that he could no longer think straight. Doggedly, he kept on. At four hours he was about to give up, not just because he had not found the cabin, but because Blue was on her last legs. Steele could no longer feel his feet, knees, thighs, or hands. *Should've turned around an hour ago.*

For a moment he allowed himself to mourn his dilemma and apologized to Blue for their defeat. He let his head sink down and listened to wind driven snowflakes flitting off his hat and face. It was a peaceful sound, and he gave into his sleepiness even though he knew better. Many had died taking such a rest in bitter cold because they never woke up. They died frozen in the saddle. But just as he nodded off, Blue gave out a loud snort and then farted loudly into the icy wind. Steele snapped awake and started laughing. Somehow it seemed funny even though she farted a lot. *You do that on purpose to wake me up Blue?*

"Good girl," he shouted. "Good Girl."

Still laughing, he picked up the reigns in his frozen fingers and started to wheel Blue around and head back along the line toward the ranch. But as Blue struggled to step around in the deep snow, he noticed a faint grey shadow to his right up the slope. *What was that?* Nothing clear, it was just a smudge in the blurriness of the blowing snow. Then, it was gone. *Probably just wishful thinking.* But he had come this far, and it was worth checking to see if something was there. He tapped his heels into Blue's flank and trudged east slowly, step by step up the slope in the direction he thought he might have seen something. That was when he saw the bears— a sow and her two cubs.

Steele knew the bears were out of their den for a reason. The sow had probably not stored enough fat to last the winter. That meant she would be desperate for food to feed her cubs. Blue pricked her ears toward to bears but held her ground. Steele slowly reached for the rifle in its scabbard beside him. But it was not necessary.

The beasts were as startled as Steele and ran further up the slope to get away. But strangely, Blue continued to snort, whinny, and stomp her front feet long after the bears fled even though the danger was gone. *It's not the bears, it's something else. Blue, you got a scent?* She had gotten a scent. Steele trusted her and let her know it. But just in case, he pulled the rifle out and cocked it.

"Let's go girl," he said as he gave her the reigns. Blue went into a hopping cadence through the drifts that seemed both happy and purposeful. Then, after a minute, there it was. A lonely little cabin covered in snow. *Prettiest cabin I ever saw.* In truth, it was a wreck of a cabin, unfit for anyone except line-riders, squatters, and rustlers. But to Steele, it was home, refuge, safety, and it was his, at least so long as he was the line-rider. Like the vacant shacks Pop Steele and his family squatted in on their trek across Kansas to Colorado, Steele knew this shack was temporary too. Still, it looked like home—like every home he had ever lived in.

There was much yet to do before they could rest. Blue needed water and feed, the saddle needed to be stowed, Blue needed a quick brush, and the stove needed to be lit. He made quick work of it, and soon Steele was asleep on his bed while Blue was taking up the rest of the cabin and warming it so much with the heat of her body that Steele got up and put out the fire. Blue woke him up at six AM with another snort and a long-drawn-out fart that quickly filled the cabin. *Good thing the fire was out. Mighta' blown the place up with that one Blue!*

A week later, when Steele and Blue left the shack to return to the ranch, they rode directly to the line and paused before turning south toward the ranch. Steele dismounted and tied a red ribbon to the fence. It was a simple way to mark the spot for turning toward the cabin in the next snowstorm. Why no one had thought of it before, he did not know. Maybe they had not found the red ribbon or the left-handed glove which were lying under the bed for no reason. When he arrived at the ranch, he stepped down and was beginning to remove Blue's saddle when the foreman ambled up and asked him if he had any trouble finding the cabin in the storm.

"No sir. No problem at all. Me and my friend Blue over there just had a nice little ride through a little bit of snow. Ain't that right Blue?" To which, Blue farted again. "She farts a lot."

"Uh huh."

THE WAR

Steele liked riding line. He liked the solitariness, the time to keep up with schooling at night, the outdoors, and the freedom. But at eighteen, he felt the urge to move on.

It was still a time when young men factored in military service as a duty and obligation to mother and country. That was true even if his mother was already dead and Pop Steele had managed to avoid service in both WW2 and Korea. He caught a bus to the county seat in Montrose to enlist in the army, took tests, and signed papers.

He scored well on his tests. And because he had earned two years' worth of college credits through a correspondence course while riding line, he was offered Officers Candidate School. He accepted mostly because he would emerge as a Second Lieutenant in a much higher pay grade than an enlisted man. His acceptance of the OCS offer came despite his dread of having to give orders to people on what to do and when to do it. As head of household for his own family from a very young age, he had been the man in charge before. But being responsible for others' survival in battle, was another matter. On the other hand, becoming an officer meant that he would have more money to send back for the family in Nucla, and that won the argument.

He hoped the army would send him someplace exotic like Germany or Japan. But the ramp-up to the Vietnam War dashed those dreams. A little more than a year after completing his

advanced infantry training for combat engineering and OCS, he landed in Saigon on a Flying Tiger Airlines L-1049H Super Constellation. Soon he was in-country north of the capital city. It was mid-1964 when he was assigned what staff intelligence officer Major Morley called a gravy mission.

The mission was to take out a short tunnel that the Viet Cong had dug between a village in a clearing on the other side of a tree line that ended under the cover of the forest. The tunnel had enabled the Viet Cong to cross under the open ground that lay between the village and the trees undetected by American B-51 bombers and F 54 Phantoms. Once they had carried their supplies from the village through the tunnel to the exit in the trees, they could safely move north or south hidden under the forest canopy.

Just before the mission, Steele ducked inside the brown canvas flap of a hot tent surrounded by sandbags stacked eight feet high to get the latest intel at a briefing. The intelligence officer Major John Morley loomed over a table and dripped sweat onto a map. Pointing to the village, the Major assured Steele that there were no Viet Cong in the area and that the mission would be a cakewalk.

Steele looked up from the map to face Morley— "how do you know the enemy has left the area?"

"Because Charlie was there the day before, took supplies, and now they're long gone. They never come more than once a month. Our guy in the village told us," said Morley.

"Our guy?" quizzed Steele with his eyebrows raised.

Morley moved his eyes from the map to look Steele in the eye, stiffened, and straightened his tall frame to tower over him. He didn't like having his judgement questioned, so he replied or indirectly if not dismissively— "Yes, our guy. I picked him, and I trained him. You'll only need a squad of your combat engineers for this mission Lieutenant."

"What about a squad of infantry to back us up?That's the protocol — *sir*."

"Already ran it by the CO. He says he can't spare them. Too much activity in the north in the Iron Triangle. Besides, you guys are called *combat* engineers for a reason, right?" he asked as if to score one back against Steele for saying "sir" with a sneer.

Steele brushed off the challenge. "Well, if it's just one squad from my company, then I'm going with them just in case there's trouble and your guy in the village is wrong about Charlie." Steele was acting company commander—normally a role for a captain, but the army was getting short on captains as the war wore on. So, Lieutenant Steele inherited the job. The shortage of captains augured ill for his survival in the war and it was not missed by Steele.

"Your call Lieutenant," said Morley as he turned his back. "You leave in an hour," he said over his shoulder.

"One more thing," interrupted Steele, stopping Morley in his tracks. When do we get those new M14's to replace our M1's?"

"I'll let you know when I know," said Morley.

"And what about the C4 and the detonation cord?"

"Det-cord and plastic explosives are already on the Hueys. Anything else Steele?"

"Nope," he replied replacing his field hat and leaving without a salute. The day was more than half gone and he did not want to waste one more minute with Morley. With the work they had yet to do, they would have to bivouac near the village for the night.

The mission was two-fold. First, wrap det-cord around the base of each tree in and around the exit of the tunnel and for 100 yards north and south along the tree line and then lay camouflage to hide the explosives. The tree trunks were thin enough to blow by this method. And using det-cord would provide concealable ordinance capable of blasting the entire wooded area of small trees all at once. The explosion would create an open field so that Charlie could no longer move to and from the village without being detected. The other advantage of det-cord was that it was also a good defense for his team. Should Charlie decide to rush out from the tunnel and attack his defenses, Steele could detonate the charges and kill or incapacitate them. Steele had been given bad intel before. If the information saying that Charlie had left the area was wrong this time, their deployment of det cord and C4 explosives in the forest gave them a fighting chance. They could hit them in the trees as they readied for a sneak attack on his men who were positioned in a grassy clearing a mere hundred yards away from the tree line.

The second half of the mission was to send his tunnel rats into the underground labyrinth itself and then set charges to destroy it. Steele knew they could not complete both parts of the mission that afternoon with dark coming on, so he split up the work by ordering his men to wrap the explosives around the trees for their immediate defense. They would go into the tunnels the next day to set cratering charges. Once all that was done, they would blow the tunnel and the trees in one big boom and get the hell out of there on helicopters. That was the plan.

The Hueys flew the team in low to avoid detection, but Steele was able to glimpse the village on the other side of the trees before setting down. That meant the village could glimpse them as well. As soon as they hit the ground, he set up a perimeter of his fifteen men with M1's aimed at the forest and sent Joe Dort on a Thompson to the far right to set up cross-fire in case it was needed. Dort was the youngest and the newest member of the squad. "I'm from California," he said as if anyone cared. His blonde hair, penchant for calling fellow soldiers dudes, and lanky toned body identified him as a surfer. "You know what comes from California," the others would answer. "Queers and steers." A variant taunt was "fruits and nuts." He took all the teases in stride and was an affable young man who usually walked around with a smile; but on this day, he was visibly scared. It was his first combat mission.

Placing him on the flank isolated him from the others, and it was a dangerous assignment. But Steele had to pick someone to do it. The rest of the men were either in charge of explosives, manning M60 machine guns, or the grenade launcher. The others had combat experience with M-1 semi-auto rifles and were needed along the line. Steele saw the fear in Dort's eyes but reassured him by reminding him that the Thompson was a formidable weapon that would serve him well. "You'll be fine. Besides, it's not likely you'll even have to use it." It was an order Steele hated to give. He knew that guarding the flank was a position the enemy would attack with force if it came to that. The Thompson gave Dort a big edge. It spit bullets out of its barrel like angry bees made of lead.

After calming Dort, he sent five demolition experts into the tree line to start wrapping the trees with det-cord and then camouflaging it to prevent the enemy from discovering it. For added measure, Steele ordered forty sticks of C4 Explosive to be fused by the same det-cord wrapping the tree trunks. Steele was being inventive by using C4 like claymore anti-personnel mines. He had his men press pebbles into the soft putty-like texture of the C4 to act as shrapnel. The innovation allowed all the ordnance to go off simultaneously with the det-cord acting as a blasting fuse. That was unlike the anti-personnel Claymore mines which required individual activation like tripwires that would stay dangerous for decades after the squad left. Steele knew that unexploded Claymores with tripwires would remain behind in that forest long after this war was over. And Steele, always the protector, wanted no part in causing the death of a curious kid walking near his village years after the war ended.

After setting the charges, the team spliced three fuses to the string of det-cord woven among the trees—one fuse at the north end of the tree line, one in the middle, and one at the south to ensure that if one failed, the other two would do the work of setting off the entire interconnected string of explosives. *Redundancy is good,* he concluded. Steele assigned a man to each fuse a hundred feet away from the blast zone in case one or more were incapacitated, or their line was cut. The team finished just before dark, drew back away from the trees, and then dug into defensive positions for the night. There were neither stars nor moon.

It was three AM when enemy carbines and AK-47's rang out in response to a solitary M1 and Dort's Thompson firing at movement among the trees. The only features visible in the dark were dozens of muzzle flashes coming from the tree line near the tunnel exit where Steele's men had placed the deadly charges. Suddenly, a rocket-propelled grenade trailing fire roared out from the trees and headed directly at Steele who dropped to the ground. The missile slammed into a tree behind him. Bits and pieces of shrapnel from the grenade whizzed by, but he felt no pain and saw no blood. Steele recovered quickly from the near-miss and immediately yelled out, "blow, blow, blow."

Then he heard each man assigned to a detonator respond slightly out of unison in an unintended syncopation— "fire in the hole, fire in the hole, fire in the hole." And with that warning, they pulled their detonators and the night exploded with fire, death, and brimstone.

Whether it was only one of the three detonators that worked, or all three did not matter — the string of explosives instantly tore through the trees. The enemy threat, if not eliminated, was greatly diminished. Steele and his men saw silhouetted trees backlit by bright white explosions rupture their trunks like toothpicks with fire and sparks shooting toward the heavens. Human debris flew through the air with the rest of the detritus. No one cheered, and aside from a few dying screams and groans near the forest, it was silent for the next three hours — all the way to dawn. No one slept much less opened their reviled C Rations. Each man stayed as low to the ground with weapons at the ready and breathed shallowly into the thick grass to muffle the sound in case sappers were slinking toward them with knives drawn. But there was no more shooting. Morning light would be the next test.

As the sun rose, a band of low-lying fog lay over Steele like a falsely protective blanket. Still hidden beneath the mist, he rose slowly to a crouch and tried to peer over the fog toward the enemy line. With the sun rising behind his position, he thought he saw blurred movement ahead near the trees. He wiped his eyes and then saw a distant figure coming forward. He was dressed in black and had an AK-47 at his side pointed listlessly at the ground. It was Charlie marching brazenly toward his line of defense.

Steele sucked in and held his breath as he kneeled while aiming his .45 at the lone man advancing slowly across the field through the fog up to his waist. Steele's men, a few yards ahead of him, aimed their weapons at the man too, but they held their fire. As he came close enough to see the details of his face, the men could see that his right arm was missing from his shoulder and that his black clothing was soaked with blood.

Steele stood up above the mist, his feet, knees, and waist still hidden in the low-lying fog and faced the man who was staring past him with blank eyes. Steele raised his weapon to the man's head ready to fire as the man drew within a few feet. The man stopped, turned his eyes to Steele for a few seconds, looked down the barrel with disdain, and then returned to his empty stare. Steele let the pull of gravity drop his pistol hand to his side. The man walked past him toward the rising sun, his lower body and legs hidden in the mist.

They did not discover Joe Dort, the man on the flank

with the Thompson, until later that morning. Steele heard the commotion of his men on their right flank and arrived to see that Dort had taken a round. The bullet had furrowed through Dort's forehead, burrowed through his brain, and exited at a cowlick at the back of his head leaving a large hole and his brains exposed. Steele remembered Dort as the new kid that usually had a smile on his face. He was always making the other soldiers laugh. But he also remembered that he was the one responsible for ordering Dort to guard the flank with his Thompson. Dort wasn't smiling then. He was scared, and his lips trembled as he told Dort he would be fine and not to worry. Now his swollen facial features were barely recognizable, and Steele had trouble imagining his face as it was a few hours before.

The bullet that had crashed through his skull left bone fragments and grey matter scattered nearby. Death was still new to the Americans in 1964, and even though that would soon change, the shock of seeing one of your own dead on the ground shook the men—especially Steele. It was as if he was seeing the ghost of his older brother Jesse who was mangled years before in a head-on collision with a lumber truck. Or maybe it was like seeing his father who he almost killed with a blow to the head that left his skull crushed from forehead to cowlick and bleeding face-down on the floor.

"Eighteen years old," murmured twenty-year-old Steele as he paused over his body and tried to remember the way Dort's face looked yesterday. He let his pistol hang down loosely at his side. It shook as his arm began to tremble. Then, realizing he had lingered too long over Dort, he turned away under the concerned gaze of the squad, and then followed the path of the armless man through the mist and the tall grass. He walked that direction for a hundred feet before coming to a halt. There he stood looking at the sky while cradling his hand which was shaking so badly that he dropped his pistol. Then he kneeled quickly to find it beneath the fog among the blades of wet green grass.

When the men saw him disappear below the fog, they ran to his aid and found him flailing on his hands and knees wailing, "Oh god, Oh god, Oh god." Then, sensing that he had lost control in front of his men, he put a tight grip on his emotions and tried to steady his ship.

"Sorry boys, I just dropped my gun."

It was then that one of his men noticed a trickle of blood seeping out from below his protective vest and beginning to paint his pants bright red near his right trouser pocket.

STEELE WHIMPERS IN HIS SLEEP

Allie awoke to hear Steele whimpering in his bedroom. "Pop…Pop…you Okay?"

Rubbing his eyes in the dark room, he looked around to see where he was while he held his hand on his right side. "Where am I?"

"You're home Pop. In the bedroom. You know. Where you and Marija slept before she died."

"Oh. Okay. For a minute I thought…"

Steele's face took on a panicked look. He leaned over and yanked the chain switch on the bedstand light and held his right hand up to the light. When he was satisfied that there was no blood on his hand, he flopped back and heaved a sigh. "I guess I was dreaming."

"Dreaming of what Pop? You know you were kind of whimpering. Scared me."

"Wasn't anything. Just one of those bear in the woods dreams. Say, we got any sleep medication in the cabinet?"

"No, just some Tylenol."

“”I’ll take it.”

“Ok Pop.” And with that, Allie fetched him two extra strength Tylenols and a glass of water. “Could you make it milk?” Steele asked. “Sure Pop.” A minute later she returned with a full glass of milk. It was all he needed. Soon his hands released their grip on his sheets as he faded back in time again. It was three AM.

DR. COHEN

A single piece of shrapnel from the rocket propelled grenade had skirted under the lower part of his protective vest just as he was diving for cover. The piece of metal entered the small of his back and tore through soft tissue until it bounced off a rib bone and pierced his right lung. The wound was small, but enough blood was leaking into his lung to make him feel as if he were drowning. It was also losing air. By the time they loaded him on the MEDEVAC helicopter, he was coughing up blood and his lung was near collapse.

“Feels like a bad cold,” he offered to the medic who was splattered with foamy droplets of blood spraying out from Steele’s mouth with each cough.

“It’s all right son. It’s my job.”

Minutes later, he began to feel dizzy and could not catch his breath. He passed out in the helicopter four miles from the field hospital. After being triaged in a medical tent for a sucking chest wound, Steele was flown to the USS Repose, a hospital ship anchored at sea near the Mekong Delta. It was then that he had the first surgery. Steele was not fully conscious until the sixth day. On the seventh day he awoke in a sweaty panic while gripping the sheets on his bed. “Dort,” he screamed. "Dort's been hit," he yelled," as if his squad were still with him.

"It's all right Lieutenant," consoled a frightened nurse. "You're on a hospital ship now. You've been out of country for a week."

"No, no, you don't understand. Dort was hit in the top of his head. He's — dead." Steele uttered "dead" as if it was the first time, he admitted Dort's death.

"I'm so sorry. But you can't help him now, can you?"

"No — I can't," answered Steele, realizing the finality of Dort's plight. But it did not bring closure to his pain.

That night, Steele woke up with a frightful dream. It was about Dort. In the dream he relived every detail of that night starting with the sound of Dort firing his Thompson, the rest of the team opening up with their M-1's. That was quickly followed by the night sky lighting up with the explosions from the det-cord he had his men wrap around the trees in the grove that hid the tunnel to the village. The next night he awoke screaming with the same dream at the same time again. On the third night, the tending physician called Dr. Cohen.

In the morning, Dr. Cohen quietly opened the door to Steele's room. A light sleeping Steele awoke with a start gripping the chrome bars on his hospital bed and looking from side to side for a threat. Dr. Cohen was a woman. She wore a uniform, but her glasses, curly orange hair, red-lipstick, and the size of her breasts clashed with the military look. When not in use, her glasses dangled like an ornament from a long string of red, white, and blue beads. She held them close to her face like binoculars when she needed to read, but never wore them on her face. Steele later suspected she never wore them because she thought it distracted from her appearance.

As Steele's eyes darted around each corner of the room searching for an unseen enemy, he saw Dr. Cohen standing at the foot of his bed calmly smiling at him with her red lips and straight black eyebrows. Soon Steele relaxed his grip and slumped back down to a lying position. He looked at her name tag.

"So, you're Doctor Cohen?"

"Yes, I am."

"Another surgery?"

"No, I'm not that kind of doctor. Are you familiar with the Diagnostic and Statistical Manual of Mental Disorders Lieutenant?"

Steele had already suspected who she was and what she did but was determined not to acknowledge that he needed her kind of help. After all, he had survived his father's drunken abuse, a childhood moving from abandoned shack to abandoned shack, getting his father booted into the cold, the bloody dent he had hammered into his skull, and now Dort. He would survive him too.

"I assume you mean the DSM Dr. Cohen?"

"Yes, that's what I mean. I expected you might," she said as she went through his chart. "I noted that you took several classes in Psychology before joining the army?"

"Yes."

"And what interests you in psychology Lieutenant?"

"That's private."

"And by private you mean what Lieutenant?"

"I wanted to understand a few things about my family... and me."

"I see. You know it may be of interest to you that many of us are drawn to the field because we have issues that we want to understand about ourselves. What might be your issues Lieutenant?"

Steele ignored her effort to get chummy or identify with him and his interest in psychology. But over the next several days, Dr. Cohen coaxed Steele into telling his life story. She took copious notes, asked questions, and paid attention to every detail. Steele had a tactical purpose in the telling of his tale. He told the doctor his story of his survival thinking it would make her realize that he was resilient, and he did not need her help. But the doctor viewed the same information differently.

One day she looked up from her notes, held her glasses up to her face, and looked directly at Steele as if he were a specimen. Steele thought the move signaled some sort of an ending to their talks as he squirmed under the microscopic gaze that peered at him through her lenses. At the back of her notes was a folder titled "Autopsy report/Subject-Joseph Dort/ Serial No. RA197768092 Status: KIA." She made sure he could see that she had that report.

"You are an intelligent man Lieutenant Steele. But I'm afraid you don't yet get it, or you don't want to get it. Which is it?" she asked rhetorically to get his attention. Then, she proceeded to answer her own question. She began with his father's abuse and Steele's role in his banishment from the household.

"How did you feel about being the one responsible for banishing your father from your family—a family of nine young children did you say? That's your original trauma Lieutenant, isn't it? Should I call it your original sin, or should we call it the sin of your father?

Your bad dreams didn't start with Dort did they Lieutenant Steele?" Not waiting for answers, she connected the dots that Steele had not yet seen or simply refused to see. Each of the events that Steele described, she told him, was a brick in a road leading to Dort—the abuse, the dent, his mother's rolling pin, the bullet that creased through the top of Dort's head.

"Did it ever cross your mind that if you hadn't put that dent in your father's skull, he would have killed your brother Jesse? And have you considered that Dort's wound, which you said went from his forehead to the cowlick at the back of his head, is close to how you described your father's wound? See any connection here Lieutenant Steele? Quite a coincidence, don't you think?" Then she paused and let him ponder her words.

Then she asked another question. "Lieutenant, would you like to know what really killed Dort? Did he really have the wound you described—a bullet running from his forehead to his cowlick?

Steele saw where she was leading him. He was afraid to know and did not answer. He knew what he thought he remembered. He dreamt it every night—at the same time every night. But even before Dr. Cohen's probing, he worried that what he remembered about Dort wasn't what really happened to him. And if that were true, what would that mean about his sanity? As Dr. Cohen explained more, Steele allowed himself to feel that she had a point. Then he began to hope that she might be able to help him get some peace or at least stop the bad dream and the guilt. Guilt about his father and now Dort. *Were they related*, he dared to ask himself? Instead, she shocked him. She told him he needed to get back to his men as soon as possible.

"Why?" asked a now panicked Steele. I thought you said I need help with this," he said as he scooted himself upright and pulled his knees into his chest.

"And you do Lieutenant. We'll help you all we can, first by telling you that you have been injured, and it's real. And I don't mean the shrapnel. That wound will be completely healed soon. The wounds inside your head that started with your father may take years to heal — maybe a lifetime. We once called it battle fatigue, battle shock, shell shock. Now we know a bit more. Today we call it Post Traumatic Stress Disorder—PTSD.

"What we know now about trauma like yours is that patients do better by going back to their units, their men, the scene of the injury, and their routines as soon as possible. We call it *Front Line Treatment*. Those that go to the protection of the rear and try to pull the covers over their heads, do far worse. Facing your fears works better than trying to outrun them, or so the theory goes. To be frank, we're still working on this Steele.

"So, I'm your guinea pig?"

"Harsh, but fair enough Steele."

"Unfortunately, you never had the chance to face your fears about your father or his fears about you. He left before you could deal with him head on. A bit Oedipal don't you think? His fears about you I mean. Anyway, his banishment took that opportunity away—maybe forever, or maybe not. For your sake, I hope not. But you and I both know that your issues with him need to be sorted out someday. But for now, maybe you can face your issues with Dort. On my orders, when your medical team clears your physical injuries, you will return to your unit. Until then, call me any time. We'll talk. Oh, and one more thing. If you ever feel so anxious that you are losing control of your thoughts and emotions, try this."

Dr. Cohen held up both of her hands. She had pressed her index fingers against her thumbs forming an "O." Then she lowered her hands while still holding the "O," closed her eyes, and began a regular breathing pattern.

"Do you know what I am doing," she whispered in a distant tone?" Steele shook his head.

"With my fingers and thumbs, I am showing myself that I am in control. 'I can do this' it says. Then, by focusing on how I breathe, in one nostril and out the other, I narrow my thoughts to that simple task leaving no room for any other thought other than keeping my fingers and thumb in the "O" position. It's not by the book, and some say its experimental or just hooey, but some say it works. And it's way better than a bottle of booze or a pill."

And with that, she left him alone. The door closed behind her with a click of finality. Once he could no longer hear her high heels clattering down the hall, he practiced an "O" with his thumb and forefingers and tried to breathe in one nostril and out the other. Try as he might, he could not breathe in one nostril and then exhale out the other. *Impossible*, he thought.

Finally, after hours of trying, he concluded that the

impossibility of the task was the entire point. Every shred of his mental capacity was consumed in the hopeless effort leaving no room for another thought—*Clever.* Two weeks later, he was on a helicopter heading back to his men and the war. It was almost a year before he returned home.

SHEEP

With Vietnam behind him, Steele went about putting his future together. Gordon, the youngest in the Steele brood, was now ten years old. A younger friend of Steele's mother in Nucla had a mane of long black shiny hair. She had taken Gordon into her home soon after Steele joined the army. He was a towhead and she with her shiny black hair could not resist him. Together they looked like those black and white Scotty dogs with magnets under their feet — bound together but complete opposites. The second oldest to Steele was James the accountant. He had been managing the finances for the family. He was now twenty and making good money as a bookkeeper at a business in Montrose. He was still sending part of his salary home to help support his brothers and sisters in Nucla.

The two oldest girls had married, and each of them had taken one of their younger siblings with them. That left just one brother, Richard, and he was taken in by Steele's Aunt Sabra. She was Ginny's older sister and lived in Bazaar Kansas with her husband of thirty years. They were childless. So, they were overjoyed to have him. Sabra and her husband legally adopted Richard, and he became a Martin. That left Steele back on his own with no children to fend for, a few dollars in his pocket, and seeking his next chapter.

Flying Tiger airlines flew him to Los Angeles from Saigon. From there he took Western Airlines to Denver. *The only way to fly*, he thought — remembering their jingle. Still wearing his uniform as he strolled through Stapleton International, he noticed some people seemed annoyed at his presence. He ignored them. Setting his duffle bag down, he paused at a newsstand and then bought a copy of the Denver Post to check the latest news and peruse the help wanted ads. Soon he found something that looked interesting. “Sheep man wanted to run ranch.” There was no phone number—just an address on a rural road for a sheep ranch near Norwood, Colorado. The ranch was in the heart of the Uncompaghre sheep country, and not far from Nucla. Why anyone would bother to place such an ad in an urban Denver newspaper, Steele could not divine. But ten hours later, he arrived in Norwood on a rural route bus still wearing his uniform. He walked three miles with his duffel bag slung over his shoulder until he reached Mc Tavish Ranch.

“Ever worked on a sheep ranch son," asked Mc Tavish?

“No, sir.”

“Ever herded sheep?”

“No, Sir, only cattle.”

Ever sheared a sheep, lambed sheep, or treated one for foot rot?”

“No, Sir.”

“Well then, why are you askin’ me for a job as a foreman?”

“Three reasons. First, I’m an army veteran. Lieutenant Steele at your service.”

“Sheep don’t give a sheep about officers and they don’t salute. What’s the second reason?”

“Because I’ll work the first month for free, be able to answer any question you have about raising sheep after that month, and you can fire me if that isn’t true.”

“All right. But what’s the third reason.”

“Because I didn’t come here telling you I knew anything about sheep, so you know I was honest enough to tell you the plain truth. If you’re the kind of man that values that, I’m your foreman."

Mc Tavish smiled, put his left hand on his hip, tilted the brim of his hat up with his right and stood akimbo despite the stiffness in his back. After a pause, he reached for the white stubble of his beard and gave it a little rub while looking at Steele. A bit after that, Mc Tavish looked behind him as if something might be there — then back again at Steele.

"All right son, you got a deal. But why the hell do you want to run a sheep ranch anyway? It's not like it's a growing business. Been in decline in these parts since the fifties."

"Well, the Uncompaghre is my home. I like it here. But if I'm going to stay, you know I've only got a few choices to make a living. I can work cattle, bale hay for pennies, go down into the mines and die young, cut down perfectly good trees, raise sheep, or rustle wild horses. I'm thinking it's sheep for me with wild horses as a close second."

"You have a sheep ranch in Nucla?"

"Not yet."

"Well, if you're planning on starting one in this economy, you don't lack for balls. Where you stayin'?"

"Right here, I hope. Got an outbuilding?"

"Well sure, but it ain't got no runnin water, and it..."

"Does it have a door and a roof?"

"Well yes but..."

"I'll take care of the rest. Thanks for the job Mr. Mc Tavish. You won't be sorry. What time do we start in the morning?"

"Four dark thirty. I'll introduce you to Ganiz. He's taking the north herd up onto a high plateau near the Lone Cone for summer. My other shepherd will take the south herd to another place. You'll stay with Ganiz for the summer or so, then come back here and learn about the business side."

"What about that meeting in thirty days to see how I'm doing."

"Won't need it. I already trust you son. See you in the fall."

BASQUES

The next morning, Steele met his mentor. He figured that Ganiz Ibarra was about fifty-five years of age. But it was hard to tell in the early morning dawn by the dim light of a bare bulb hanging from a wire above the barn door. Ganiz wore a narrow-brimmed hat instead of the usual wide brim that cowboys used, and a long-sleeve shirt buttoned at the neck and wrists. His brown trousers ended mid-calf, and white stockings ran from the calf down to low cut leather shoes instead of boots. Later, he learned that after the day's work was done, Ganiz would switch to a beret for the evening by the campfire. *Jaunty*, thought Steele.

Two Border Collies were at Ganiz' feet with their heads resting between their outstretched paws. They barely acknowledged Steele and looked to be deep in thought. Ganiz spoke little English, and what little he did speak was reserved for niceties like good morning, hello, or sorry. He was better with Spanish than English since he came from the Spanish side of the Pyrenees. He would be Steele's teacher about working the dogs, moving the sheep, tending to their health, and shearing and lambing when those seasons came. Mc Tavish would teach him how to run the business of the ranch so that he could work a little less. Age and arthritis in his hips and knees had slowed him down.

Ganiz preferred sheep to people, especially Americans. He also preferred his Kangal Shepherds and Border Collies to most anyone. Mercifully, he introduced Steele to his Kangals before Steele got too close. The larger one was named Asaseno, and he equated strangers with wolves and coyotes unless they had been properly introduced. Thus, it was important that Ganiz show Asaseno that Steele was not a stranger but a friend of his, or at least an acquaintance of his. The smaller one was only one hundred ten pounds. She was called Arazoak.

"Que es el nombre de el perro grande," asked Steele in his best Spanish. "What's the name of your big dog?" he repeated just in case.

"Ah. Es Asaseno."

"Assasin?"

"Bai."

Steele didn't know what Bai meant, so he hunched his shoulders and raised his eyebrows.

"Bai es Si," rescued Ganiz.

"Ok. I understand — entiendo. Su Perro grande es un assasin."

"Bai."

Steele held out his hand to Asaseno but kept his fingers protected in a clench just in case. Asaseno sniffed his knuckles. It put him at ease for him to see that Steele was not in fear of him.

"And the smaller one — y la perra pequeña?"

"Arazoak." Then struggling with Spanish, he translated to English — "Trouble."

"Gracias,"replied Steele who was now scratching the head of Asaseno. It was another good sign that Asaseno allowed Steele to touch him. Soon his nose was pushed into Steele's crotch, and Asaseno uplifted his head hard to let Steele know how strong he was. Arazoak watched Asaseno and Steele from a distance and concluded that Steele could be trusted. Then she took a nap.

Steele was hopeful that he and Ganiz were going to be able to muddle through between English and Spanish and get past

Ganiz's general dislike of Americans. Steele was eager to learn what he could from Ganiz quickly since he had promised Mc Tavish that he would be useful within thirty days. His lessons began soon after Ganiz picked up his crook and strode off toward the North Pasture. It was late spring and there were just a few patches of snow left on the ground to cool the air. The high pasture was ten miles away.

"We're going to walk the whole way?"

"Bai."

"How are we going to keep all these sheep together?"

"You see."

As Ganiz opened the gate to the north herd's pasture, early questions that Steele had about the role of the dogs and the role of the sheepherders were quickly answered. Ganiz' main job was to decide where the herd would go. Sheep can only graze in one place for so long before they eat the vegetation down to the dirt, so, they needed to move frequently from one area to the next to ensure the sheep always had rooted grass regrowing behind them after they left. The movement of the herd from place to place was called herding. *That was easy,* concluded Steele.

As for the dogs, the border collies took direction from Ganiz and moved the herd where he wanted them to go. Meanwhile, the Kangals, Assassin and Trouble, guarded against predators and sometimes unwary strangers who go too close to the herd. The sheep liked Assasin and Trouble who often slept beside them at night. But they held the bossie Border Collies in contempt due to their rude manner of controlling them. The collies used two methods to dominate the herd. First, they would lower their head into a threatening position and then stare them down. Steele later learned the herders called that *giving the sheep the eye.* Their other method was to nip at their heels to keep them moving in the direction Ganiz wanted. They knew what he wanted by the direction of his walk, their experience on this same path the previous spring, and an occasional hand signal or whistle to correct their course.

Herding was lonely work done mostly in the wildlands—suited for a man like Steele. Soon days melted into days, and time was measured by the length of grass remaining for the sheep. Then he, Ganiz, the sheep, and the dogs would move on. As they moved from one feeding place to another, they sometimes came upon dilapidated camps with old wagons, pots and pans, and some large rocks arranged around a fire pit. They looked like props in a play or simply equipment left out in the elements to wither and fade. Steele asked why they were all abandoned. Ganiz explained as best he could.

"Cow people," he said — "Ellas odian las ovejas."

They hate the sheep?

"Bai."

Steele wondered what hating sheep had to do with abandoned camps. Ganiz went on. He explained that cows and sheep had contrary grazing habits—sheep nibbling the grass almost to the roots, and cows taking only the long grass. Nevertheless, they had to compete for the same pasture. Cowboys believed that sheep were a threat to their herds and their livelihood, so the cowboys got hostile. Fearing the armed cattlemen, the shepherds would set up fake campsites. Then they would settle down far away from their false bivouacs in case hostile ranchers and their hands came looking for them as they slept. Despite the threat, few shepherds armed themselves. Some had rifles to protect sheep from predators. But unlike the sheep men with their rifles, almost all cowboys were armed with rifles and pistols. And they were not shy about brandishing guns on other men to make a point. Shepherds figured avoidance was best.

Most of that overt hostility from cattlemen against sheepmen was history. The last serious incident happened twenty years before Ganiz arrived in Colorado. But while history fades, it does not die. Ganiz showed Steele a scar on his shoulder. A bullet from a rifle shot by a man he never saw grazed his shoulder. Six inches to the left would have hit his heart.

"Un accidente de caza," Ganiz asked rhetorically with raised eyebrows?

"Yeah," maybe a hunting accident agreed Steele as his eyes darted toward the surrounding trees which seemed to lean towards him and creep into the meadow.

Ganiz and Steele drank a a bit more wine than usual that night. Wine was not Steele's drink of choice at the time. Like most men on the western slope, he drank beer. But he was acquiring a taste for wine. And Steele was pleased that he and Ganiz were getting along. As the old man's eyelids drooped, he descended into a polite drunkeness. After that, he began to sing songs in Basque that Steele could not understand. But he knew they were sad. After an hour, Ganiz tired of singing. Then he told a story about the old days. He painted the image of a young sheepherder who was sitting on a rock at sunset watching his sheep much like the rock Steele was sitting on by the fire. His Basque father was sitting ten feet away drinking coffee when he heard the thud of a bullet tearing through his son's face and then watched him fall to the ground. After a one second delay, the sound of the rifle followed the bullet and roared out across the land almost in triumph over the boy's death. Steele wished Ganiz had not told him that story.

"Dort."

"Que," asked Ganiz? Que es Dort?"

Steele slept with his pistol that night. The next morning he went to put it back in his napsack and noticed his hand was trembling. *Must've slept on it,* he thought.

Later that month they moved the herd to higher altitude once again. They were following the season as it warmed and dried the lower meadows. On their way to the next pasture, they passed a stand of aspens in the mid-day sun. The chalk-white bark stood out from the purple sky. Steele watched as their silver dollar leaves shimmered when the mountain air blew by them flipping the leaves from heads to tails and back again. It was beautiful, and he thought to take a picture. But he had no camera.

Looking closer into the stand of trees, Steele saw random dark lines on the bark. But by cocking his head and squinting, he suddenly saw what he thought before was an accidental shape morph into that of a naked woman with large breasts. Believing he was imagining it, he stepped back to take it all in. Then he was awed to discover that none of the black lines on the white bark were random at all. Each tree had images carved into them. A few showed men and women having sex, but most seemed to depict family. It was a forest of living art that moved with the wind, sucked in the snowmelt after stinging alpine winters, and shaded the meadow in summer with its dancing leaves.

Steele asked Ganiz about the carved images. Ganiz explained. Basques in America were lonely men in a hostile place that was not their home. They came for the money they could take back to the Pyrenees — money to buy farms and raise their own sheep on their own land. Some made it, some did not. Most had families they had risked leaving behind to war, and they often carved images of them — a house, the face of a lover or wife, or children standing as if for a photograph next to their home in the Pyrenees.

Then he pointed to one in particular and then quietly stepped back and studied Steele's face to see his reaction as Steele leaned forward to inspect the image. It was the side profile of a handsome woman with dark hair pulled back tight and a hint of a smile. One eye looked out from the side of her face with the other eye hidden from view. Her nose was pronounced and aquiline. It was much like what an artist like Picasso might have carved had he, like Ganiz, been a Basque alone in a strange land yearning for family. Below her face were three smaller oval heads that faced front with large eyes opened wide and coal black irises.

"Nire emaztea da," said Ganiz. He added in Spanish, "Mi esposa y mi niños."

Steele understood. These were of his wife and children and not just one more carving on the sea of white-barked trees. He smiled at Ganiz and nodded in appreciation of showing him such an intimate portrait of his life back home. Below the images was a date, 1939. He asked him if he missed them.

"Do you miss them? Los Estransas?"

"Bai."

"When did you see them last? Cuando Viste?"

"1936."

"Why? Why not sooner?"

"Todos estan Muertos."

Steele's face dropped. "They are all dead?"

"Bai. Guerra Civil de Española." Franquistas los asesinó mi Familia."

"Franco's people murdered them?"

"Bai."

Then Ganiz went on to tell him the story of his family, and that they were killed during the Spanish Civil war. He had no family to return to. So, he stayed in a foreign land and never bothered to learn its language. *Why should he?* Most of the time he was alone with his sheep who did not care which language he spoke.

He's like a ghost upon the land of strangers, thought Steele.

By the end of the summer solstice, Steele had learned all

there was to know about herding sheep in the summer and fall seasons. A few months after that, summer came to an end and crisp fall air began to funnel through the green forest and the orange, red, and yellow aspen leaves, He had learned how to work the dogs and how important they were to the business of sheep ranching. And Ganiz had taught him how to treat all the health issues of sheep except for the maladies that would come with winter. Steele had arrived too late to experience the shearing season in early spring before he signed on with Mc Tavish. But the lambing season would soon come. When spring came around again, he would learn to shear the wool in anticipation of summer pasture and his year among the sheep with Ganiz would come full circle.

Sheep ranching, he learned, had its own calendar and did not adhere to spring, summer, winter, or fall. By the end of his first year, he began to parse time in sheep seasons. Ganiz, for his part, had not spoken so much to another human being since he left his family behind in Basque country. So, when Steele saw Mc Tavish, he made a point of telling him that Ganiz had become talkative.

"Downright chatty."

"Ganiz — chatty? I'll have to see this," replied a disbelieving Mc Tavish.

Then, Mc Tavish paid Steele.

"Here's your wages for half the year and the first month's wages that you said you would work for free."

"I said I'd work that month for free, and I meant it."

"So, you did. But you were already earning your way from day one, so I don't feel right not payin' you for it."

"I'll tell you what Mr. Mc Tavish. You know that dusty .270 Remington hanging above your door in your living room?"

"That old thing? That's a 1949 model 721."

Yes, sir. I know. Same family of Remington's our snipers used over there. I'd take that instead of money if that's all right."

"Well sure, but your pay is more than…"

"I'd be happy to take it as payment in full for that month."

"Well then, it's yours."

Steele stayed on with Mc Tavish until he died three years later. There was some commotion about whether he had a will or not, and no one seemed to remember anything about him having a family. His wife had died years ago, his parents were gone, and his only son had died in Vietnam. The Lieutenant in Steele felt a duty to get the man's affairs in order and went to Montrose to see what he could do. A clerk at the probate court told him that the ranch and all the sheep were going to have to go to the state coffers of Colorado. That's what happens when you have no will and no kin. The clerk called it escheating. *Sounds like cheating,* thought Steele. The clerk told him to get a lawyer to sort out Mc Tavish's affairs and maybe find a way to block the state from taking everything Mc Tavish had worked for all his life. He told Ganiz the sad news.

That was when Ganiz spoke up and delivered a crumpled piece of paper to Steele. Steele's eyes opened wide as he read the note. Soon he and Ganiz were in Mc Tavish's truck driving across town to see an attorney.

"Well, I'll be damned," exclaimed the lawyer. "Haven't seen one of these for years."

"What's that," asked Steele.

"It's a holographic will."

"Sorry, need a little more explanation. We're not lawyers you know?"

"Well, a holographic will is a will that you write out all by hand, sign it, and date it. You don't need witnesses for it to be valid. All it requires is that it was written all in the decedent's hand and reflects the intent of the man who wrote it. No typing allowed."

"You mean Mc Tavish's intent?"

"Yes."

"So, how does intent get proved."

"By the circumstances surrounding it."

All Steele knew of the circumstances was that Mc Tavish had given the will to Ganiz. Ganiz was standing in a corner of the room with his hat in hand waiting for Steele to finish his business. Steele turned and motioned to Ganiz to step up to the attorney's large desk.

"What did Mc Tavish say when he gave you this?" asked Steele.

"El dijo que las ovejas son de usted."

"What's that mean?" asked the lawyer.

Steele translated. "Mc Tavish told Ganiz that the sheep were his."

The attorney read the wrinkled paper and spoke aloud Mc Tavish's words that he had written by hand.

To whom it may concern.

> I'm feeling poorly and know my end is not far off. While I am still alert and conscious, I've made up my mind about how I want my property given out when I'm gone. I have no kin that's alive. But if I do, I don't know them and don't want them to have anything.
>
> I don't own much more than my sheep which I give to Ganiz. He has been with me from the beginning and he deserves to have them. I rent the land and the buildings, so there is nothing to give of the ranch and the land.
>
> Please pay my debts to the landlord and the feed store out of my savings which are in a box behind a book on my

> bookshelf titled *The Flock*, by Mary Austin. After you have paid them, give what's left along with my truck to Glenn Steele, my foreman. He's a good man just starting out."
>
> Jason Mc Tavish
>
> June 18,1969

"I'll be," muttered Steele.

Months later, the will was probated at the courthouse and declared to be a valid legal will after matching Mc Tavish's handwriting and signature on other papers. An accounting was made of the assets and Mc Tavish's debts were paid. Ganiz inherited the entire herd but had no place to pasture them. Steele inherited Mc Tavish's old pickup truck and $8,458.02 and bought forty acres of fenced land in Nucla that had a barn, a ranch house, and a two-room outbuilding in the pasture. So, Steele had land but no sheep, and Ganiz had sheep but no land. *Like skinny jack sprat and his fat wife*, chuckled Steele — he and Ganiz needed each other.

After a brief talk, a hearty arm swinging handshake, and the only full smile he ever saw on the face of Ganiz, Steele and the old shepherd owned a ranch together in Nucla with a large herd of sheep. A year later, the ranch was making a profit, and the gods seemed to be smiling on him. He had spruced up the ranch house just in case he might meet the right woman. If that ever happened, Ganiz would move into the cabin in the pasture. Until then, they lived together in the big house — Steele's house. The idea of it being his made him both proud and scared. Proud because he could see his name on the deed. Scared because he wasn't sure if he could keep it.

MARIJA

Marija roared into Nucla in late October riding a fiery red Ducati 750GT south from Leadville, a mining town high on a windy plateau so full of Slovenes that it felt like Slovenia to those who lived there. Her shiny motorcycle looked like a café racer that the Brits were fond of racing from pub to pub in the sixties. But it wasn't hers. It belonged to her latest ex-boyfriend in Leadville. She had ridden it southeast to Pueblo on a lark to see her artist girlfriend that she dropped in on sometimes along with several of her favorite cousins.

Her girlfriend's name was Elina, a dark haired woman with blood red fingernails. She had a one bedroom studio with a pleasant view above the Arkansas River. It was decorated with her erotic oil paintings mostly of women loving women. Her favorite depicted a redheaded woman who looked much like Marija. In it, the crimson haired beauty was locked in flagrante delicto with another woman with long black hair. But her subjects were not exclusively women. Some depicted men with women usually intertwined in random genders of three. Elina had a queen bed which she was happy to share with her friend. Marija stayed with Elina for over a week until she reeked of the linseed oil that Elina cleaned her paintbrushes in. But she did manage to sneak in a breakfast with her cousins at the All You Can Eat Buffet on the day she left. Pueblo was another town where Slovenian names could be found on every street.

Then, on another lark, she rode west through Salida, Gunnison, and on to Montrose. There she heard from a gas station attendant that the Uncompaghre was a wild and beautiful place to see, especially on a motorcycle. He offered to take her there on her Ducati. “You can ride on the back, hold on, and watch the view,” he said with a knowing wink and a sly smile. She batted her bright blue eyes at him and countered. She told him that would be just fine, but only if he was the one holding on in the back. He wanted none of that. So, she punctuated her solitary departure by laying down some fresh Goodyear rubber on her exit from the station. After leaving Montrose and riding for an hour and a half, she pulled off Highway 141 hoping to find a place to stop and get a drink, but the Ducati broke down on CC road across from the Steele Ranch.

Ganiz answered the knock at the door.

“Got a phone I might borrow?” she asked.

Ganiz stood expressionless then turned his head impassively toward the kitchen and called Steele.

“Steele, venga aqui. Es una señorita bonita.”

Steele met Ganiz at the door, saw Marija and nodded at Ganiz for the accuracy of his description. Then he adjusted his wrinkled pants and tucked in his shirt in honor of the marvel that had just landed on their doorstep. “Muy bonita.” Then he whispered—"damned gorgeous” into Ganiz’s startled ear.

She was dressed in leather from collar to toe, had a purple sash at her neck, long curly red hair, dark sunglasses, and pink lipstick. She looked as fast as her motorcycle, and both seemed built for speed.

“I don’t speak Spanish. Sorry to bother. I really need a phone. My bike just broke down over there,” she said pointing behind her toward the road.

“What happened to it?”

“Please. Do I look like a mechanic? How should I know? It broke.”

Steele ignored her saucy response, leaned out and looked

both ways on CC road, saw the shiny red motorcycle, the leaking oil underneath the engine, and took in the emptiness. It was a lonely place to break down.

"Sure, you can use our phone. It's on the wall over there pointing to the kitchen. But what, may I ask, were you looking for clear out here?

"A bar."

"You are pretty lost if that's what you wanted. I can offer you a beer if you like?"

"Sorry, I was looking for a glass of cold Chardonnay and a table to sit at, maybe with a pretty umbrella and some fresh air."

"Sorry lady. This is Nucla. No umbrellas here. Any kind of Chardonnay in particular?"

"Morgan?"

"How about Carlo Rossi red instead."

"If red is what you have?"

"Got plenty. Out here we have to order it by the case from Modesto. That's in California, he said as if it gave credence to the appellation. "We drink it because Basques like Ganiz here love it. You from around here?"

"No, I'm from Leadville. Not much of a place. No fancy wine there either. But we're close to Aspen so, you know, we always have any kind of wine we want. Brings in the millionaires from Texas, Idaho, and Montana. Really hate the Texans even though they throw a lot of money around town.

"My grand folks make their own wine, she announced with a smile," as if to soften what she had just said about Aspen and Texans. "My folks are old school. Can't say I like the home-made stuff though." She rattled on frenetically. "They get grapes from a town called Ignacio five thousand feet below, and then make wine in fall before the cold sets in. They ask me to help.

But I ask them why bother with home-made. You can buy it in Aspen. Oh, and here's this little secret," she said as she lowered her head and whispered as if to shield the news from Ganiz. "My folks make their wine from Red Riesling, but we just call it red. Some of the uppity people in Aspen hear Riesling and tell me our red grapes are really white. I always say "fine" just to make them stop. How do they know anyway? It's one of the few grapes that survives the altitude in Ignacio down the mountain from Leadville. Got a directory?"

She sure talks fast, thought Steele still wondering why it was important to educate him on Red Riesling. "Sure, in the drawer by your right."

Steele watched her leather bound hips moved from right to left to clear the way for her to pull out the drawer and bit his lip.

"What do you do around here anyway."

"Sheep. I wanted to say rodeo. Sounds tougher. But it's just sheep. They're kind of quiet— friendly but quiet."

"So, you have sheep in your back-yard?"

"A couple thousand — in my back yard."

She missed the joke on the back yard, but upon hearing him say "thousands," she put down the phone and asked, "can I see them? I just love animals," she added in a voice that was almost a coo.

"Don't you need to make a call?"

"It can wait," she smiled.

Steele looked out the front window to see the motorcycle still leaking oil from a tossed rod on the apron of CC road and then said, "sure, I'll show you."

Ganiz had been sitting in a dark corner of the house watching Marija. He had seen enough. "La Señorita es demasiado rápida—too fast," he muttered under his breath.

After spending some time walking among the sheep and fussing over the Border Collies, they headed back toward the house. Assassin and Trouble, were laying in the shade of the cabin watching the flock from a distance. The only acknowledgement they gave to Marija were some low growls as she and Steele strolled by. When Marija saw the cabin, she pushed her dark sunglasses low on her nose and scowled.

"What's that old place used for," asked Marija.

"The cabin? Oh, it was here when I bought the place."

"Kind of creepy all alone out here in the pasture don't you think?"

"Never thought about it like that. I'll give you that it's one way of looking at it. But my way is that it's kind of like an old shepherd watching out for his flock. Or maybe just an old rustler's cabin."

"Rustlers?"

"Yeah. There used to be rustlers in the Uncompahgre. Long time ago."

"Oh."

Steele offered Marija a chair at a table covered with a checkered plastic tablecloth that flapped in the breeze. Steele started to get up and fetch some red wine, cheese, olives, and crackers. But Ganiz was ahead of him. He was exiting the screen door balancing a tray full of food and drink. As he walked carefully toward the table, the taut spring on the screen door yanked it shut with a bang. Ganiz startled at the sound of the slamming door and almost dropped the tray. Gathering himself, he made his way to the table, set down plates for each of them, and then set a cutting board full of cheese, fruit, and crackers. Marija sat in a small sliver of shade coming from the roof line leaving Steele to sit in the full sun. Though it was October, it was also the third day of an Indian summer, so the air was warm but laden with a faint smell of sheep dung. Ganiz placed two water glasses down and filled them with Carlo Rossi red out of a carafe. It was as if he had made a living for years as a waiter in a restaurant though he had never been in one in his life. As he poured, Ganiz looked askance at Marija. Then, after topping off her glass, he turned to Steele and whispered a warning as he cupped his hand over Steele's ear.

"La Senorita esta una buscador de su oro."

"She is a gold miner," whispered Steele?

"No. Ella quiero su oro."

"She wants what?"

Frustrated, Ganiz stood up and left but not before saying "stupido" out loud to Steele.

"Always wanted to learn Spanish," announced Marija as the screen door slammed behind Ganiz again as he sulked into the kitchen. "What's that he said about gold? There's gold around here?"

"I thought you didn't speak Spanish," replied a surprised Steele.

"I don't. I stayed at a place in Mexico once called Casa de Oro—'House of Gold.' That's how I knew about Oro."

"Oh. Well, to answer your question, Naw. Just me, Ganiz, our dogs, and some Sheep. No gold around her that I know of."

"Yes, I see. A lot of sheep. By the way, how much does a sheep cost?" Marija then took a sip of the wine waiting for Steele to answer but quickly had to suppressed the urge to spit it out. Her face betrayed the look of someone who had imbibed lemon juice by mistake. Steele didn't answer her question, but asked one of his own to distract her.

"How do you like the Rossi?"

"Lovely. Just lovely," she said with a voice that was suddenly raspy and dry.

Marija and Steele made noisy bed-shaking bone-rattling love that night while Ganiz sat on the porch smoking his favorite pipe to the sound of a howling coyote. As the yowling of the wild dog faded, Marija's primeval moans flowed out an open window into the pasture until they melded into the dung covered soil. Ganiz listened and ached in silence for his long-dead wife.

In the end, Marija turned out to be quick at almost everything. She died less than a year after they married. And in the days following her death, it struck Steele as strange that he could not remember much about her. It was as if his time with her was always on fast-forward. *Maybe its grief blocking my thoughts.*

Of course, he had photographs. There was one taken of her in front of the ranch house, one with her standing beside her ex-boyfriend's motorcycle, and another of her standing alone beside a bridge in Ljubljana flashing a V sign with her fingers. That was on their honeymoon trip to Slovenia to see the homeland of her grandfather and grandmother who raised her in Leadville. Then there was that photo of her standing next to the wall of a church in a small village called Ambrus. On the wall were the names of the fallen during the second world war. Her family name Brankovič was there in great numbers but most dated to 1945.

"Why did they all die in 1945? asked Steele?

"Tito," she answered tersely. "His partisans slaughtered them all after the war."

Steele struggled to visualize her lips moving as she spoke and could not recall the sound of her voice other than it came out in low tones and she always talked fast. She spoke as if she each of her sentences was trying to outrun the other. One night he paused in their bathroom and stared at the stool where she would sit while fixing her face and hair in front of the mirror. The impressed features of her buttocks were still visible on the leather seat and gave credence to her former presence in the house. Another time he found her perfume bottle and sniffed at the aroma. But it was dead. He could not conjure how it smelled on her when it blended with her skin. Other memories were captured as moments in time on the emulsion plate of his mind like still pictures, but the lens was blurry. Far fewer images were imprinted on his brain as moving pictures. Steele thought that was odd. After all, she was all about moving.

Going through the specific odds and ends of what he could remember about Marija, he recalled how she filled out her motorcycle leathers. He fondly recalled the flush that he felt when he first saw her fitted tightly into the black skin of a slaughtered animal. And among those few clear memories was the sight of her removing her helmet and shaking her long red curly hair with the sun at her back at his front door on the day she arrived. *Jezebel,* he thought.

But he could not remember her face because all there was to see was her dark silhouette against the daylight and her hair snaking out like Medusa and crowned by the glow of the sun. And he still felt a warm tumescence whenever he remembered her hips moving from right to left as she cleared the way to open that drawer in the kitchen on the first day they met.

What he lacked in visual recall of Marija, he did not lack for memories of her food. Steele's food habits were plain. His penchant for torn toast with milk with sugar was testimony to that. But he could still smell the delicious the aroma of Marija's Potiča baking in the oven. He treasured the hand-written recipe that Marija's grandmother had given her that showed how to make it. The notes gave step-by-step instructions along with secret ingredients that she kept hidden from everyone except those she loved. *Food doesn't lie,* he thought —he believed it to be true. It seemed to Steele that it was the only authentic thing she brought with her to the ranch other than Molly and the throaty moans that erupted against her will from the depths of belly when they made love.

After Potiča, the next strongest memory he could remember, was the image of her bloody hands gripping his as she strained to deliver Molly at the hospital. Before either one of them knew whether it was to be a boy or girl, Marija made Steele promise to name her Amelia if it was a girl. But if it were a boy, Steele could name it. She seemed not to care. Why the name Amelia was important to her, Steele did not yet know. But it was one of the things he could remember with ineluctable clarity.

MOLLY

Amelia was born at two AM on the Fourth of July. She slid out into the world looking as pink as Marija's lipstick and screaming her annoyance at being ejected from the comfort of her mother's womb. Tight fisted like a boxer, she pissed on the nurses as Marija lay pale on the gurney after her birth. In the commotion, Steele noticed that Marija was lying in a river of her own blood that was flooding her gurney. He looked toward the doctor for reassurance. He seemed to be unconcerned until a nurse yelled "pressure drop," and the alarm on a monitor began to blare making it hard to think. In the chaos, the doctor announced "girl," but Marija probably never heard him. She bled to death within minutes of Amelia's birth. She died with the hope that Steele would honor his promise about the name Amelia —it was the only way Marija could fulfill her own promise to a grandmother when she was on her deathbed.

"You must promise me Marija," begged her Grandmother Amelia. "Promise me that you will name your first girl Amelia in remembrance of me and your poor dead mother who was Amelia too."

And as Marija's Grandmother lay dying, she exacted another promise.

"You must make Potiča every Christmas in honor of me and place a slice on my grave and another on All Saints day too." She punctuated her demanded in mock anger with her old finger wagging in Marija's face.

"I will, Babiča. I will. I promise. Every Christmas and

always on All Saints Day."

Grandfather Franz stood in the corner of the room wringing his hat in his hands with tears in his deep blue eyes helpless as he watched the life fade from the eyes of his wife of sixty-eight years.

Grandmother Amelia and Grandfather Franz had narrowly escaped torture and death by partisans loyal to Tito during the war. Marija's parents were not so lucky. Her father Tomas Brankovič was shot outside their farmhouse among his hogs. They left him dying in pig dung. Her mother, also named Amelia, was shot near her rose garden in front of the house. Her body lay tangled and askew among rose buds and thorns. They killed them because Marija's father had once been in a scouting group called the Sokols when he was a boy. Tito partisans, always quick to believe a rumor, suspected the Sokols of political ties to Nazis and Nazi sympathizers. Some were, some were not. But soon it was dangerous to belong to any group. As the war progressed, mere suspicion of collaboration was as good as probable cause. Killing became easy.

Grandfather Franz and Grandmother Amelia Brankovič had relatives in Leadville who had emigrated at the turn of the century as part a first wave of Slovenes to America. They came for the mines in Leadville and Pueblo. Fifty five years later, Franz and Amelia Brankovič followed in their footsteps to the safety of America with grandbaby Marija in tow. Once there, they raised her in their old age as their own child amidst a throng of Slovene expatriates—a place where the smell of Potiča often mixed with the pine scented air—especially at Christmas.

Steele sat beside a table strewn with Gideon Bibles and Books of Mormon while a volunteer pastor tried to console him with comforting quotes from the old testament. Steele stared blankly at an unread copy of the Montrose Daily Press until the pastor left. He was grieving the death of Marija in the bereavement room, and had no time for his words. A clerk interrupted his thoughts by handing him a birth certificate with the feisty newborn's footprints recorded in smudged ink.

Steele thought the baby probably kicked the document causing the smear. It showed the name of the child as "Amelia Ginny Steele." On the next line he read "Marija Amelia Brankovič Steele and Glenn Steele, Mother and Father." The clerk was a helpful young man. He informed Steele that the death certificate would be mailed from the county coroner as if that would be consoling news. Steele gave him a blank stare before turning away.

The maternity ward agreed to care for the baby for the rest of the day. Steele picked up Amelia at sunset, put her in a bassinet he had purchased at K Mart, and drove south in Mc Tavish's old pickup toward Nucla. The truck-bed was filled with bags of diapers, baby oil, baby formula, and Desitin. It was two of everything that the pimple-faced checker at the drugstore said he would need for a new baby. As he drove down the two-lane highway toward Nucla, fireworks exploded on both sides of the road lighting up the visage of a bedraggled Steele and the smooth face of the bright little baby beside him. Steele winced at each of the popping sounds of the fireworks. But he let it go, though he felt a twinge of old pain in his side. He had more pressing things to do and had no time for sad memories of dead fathers, dead soldiers, or rocket propelled grenades.

As they drove through the rocket's red glare, Steele worried how he and Ganiz would manage the ranch and a baby. Before he left Montrose, he hired the Blessed Hills Mortuary to take care of Marija's body. They would arrange for her burial in Nucla. But there was no space in the cemetery beside his mother Ginny and his brother Jesse, so Marija would have to be buried in another row behind them.

Steele reflected on how she had come into his life on a speedy red motorcycle but departed almost as soon as she came.

As he drove south with Amelia, Steele shivered beside the open driver side window as warm summer air swirled through the cab. Within a week, he was calling her *Molly*.

MOLLY AND EMILY

Sixteen year-old Molly and her best friend Emily giggled as they tickled each other in the oven room in back of the Columbine Bakery. Emily's parents had finished their pre-dawn baking of bread, croissants, and muffins, and the ovens were still warm to the touch. Her parents had carried their aromatic delights in on trays to the front room where they filled the glass display cases and served their early morning customers coffee and treats. The buttery smell of their warm baked goods escaped their chimneys and enveloped the whole town.

The aroma drew customers ranging from cowboys, to sheepmen, to miners. The girls often helped Emily's parents with their business. They worked mostly in summer when they were not in school and before the winter lambing season had begun at the Steele Ranch when Molly would be needed to help out. Emily's parents could not afford to pay them for their work. With people leaving Nucla for better jobs in other places, business had been slowing for years despite the bakery's buttery scent. Fact was, there were fewer and fewer people in town to tempt with their wares. But Molly didn't care about the pay. She just wanted to be near Emily.

This was the summer of their sixteenth year, and it was going to be special. They were going to summer camp. Molly was so excited with anticipation that she had butterflies in her stomach and was sick almost every day anxious for their departure date arrive on August 12th. A charter bus would take their girl scout troop from Nucla to Grand Junction, then Denver, and finally Boulder where it would turn west toward

Aspen Camp at the foot of Long's Peak. For months the girls had pored over the brochures and the pictures. There were images of lush green meadows, cabin tents where they would spend their nights, lakes, streams, hiking trails, and Long's Peak which hovered more than fourteen thousand feet above the landscape like a forbidding giant. Emily worried that the canvas covered cabin tents were too fragile to keep bears out while the same thought excited the always adventurous Molly.

The only bad thing about the camp was Mrs. Kratchner and her two daughters. The good thing was everything else including the nice assistant scout mother whose name was Nancy Parker. Kratchner was the scout mother in charge of troop 108 and she lorded over her position like a military officer. Worse, she considered her daughters Becky and Priscilla as her lieutenants, ignoring the fact that it was Mrs. Parker who was second in what Kratchner called "command."

"Spies," asserted Molly. "Little miss bitches," retorted Emily who was uncharacteristically harsh with her words when speaking of Becky and Priscilla. But many of the parents approved of Kratchner's strict manner because, if nothing else, she would keep them on a tight leash and that would keep them safe. Steele wasn't so sure that her controlling nature was good for the troop. *After all,* he thought, *camp is supposed to be about new experiences and high adventure*. More than that, he trusted Molly's common sense over the thinking of an idealogue who equated obedience to her with godly behavior. Three days before departure, Steele woke Molly up for work at the Columbine Bakery and she threw up on his shoes. "You sick honey?" he asked as he looked down at the slop covering his feet.

Three days after that she was holding her duffle bag next to Emily waiting for the bus to arrive. Mrs. Kratchner was a heavy-set woman who always dressed in one of her tent-like calico dresses with side pockets from K Mart. She was stalking up and down the line pushing the girls into place and busily ushering them into a straighter line. Molly had her back to her while talking with Emily and did not see her coming. Kratchner grabbed her by her shoulders and forcibly turned her to face the front. That was when Molly threw up on her dress. A sneering chorus of whiny eew's issued from Priscilla and Becky to punctuate the event. Ellen, who was standing behind Molly, tried but failed to contain a guffaw by routing it through her nose. She pretended it was a sneeze. Molly muttered "gesundheit," with the acid taste of stomach bile still on her tongue.

The bus trip took over six hours. As they exited the bus Molly looked up and saw Longs Peak holding court over the meadows, rivers, creeks, lakes, and forests below. "The air is so sweet," whispered Emily as she leaned close to Molly's ear and touched her shoulder. They assembled next to the bus as the driver unloaded back-packs and duffel bags into a pile. Kratchner started calling out names and numbers. Molly and Emily were assigned to tent number 10. Happy to be together, they did a patty-cake to the chagrin of Kratchner. But then she called out two more names for tent number 10—Becky and Priscilla, and the patty-cake ceased causing Kratchner to crack a cruel smile.

The highpoint of the week was a hike to a place called Chasm Lake at the foot of Longs Peak. But the hike had to wait until the troop acclimated to the 8,500 foot altitude for several days and only after attending an outdoor safety class put on by Mrs. Parker. She was the assistant scoutmaster who was also a forest ranger in the Uncompahgre. Until the scheduled Chasm Lake hike, the girl scouts would have the run of the highly civilized nature trail built by the ranch, other local trails, creeks, and lakes close by Aspen Camp. For the trip to Chasm lake, they would take a shuttle bus to the trailhead. Then they would hike the trail of 4.5 miles, gain of over 2,000 feet of elevation, and rest at the foot of Longs Peak.

In the meantime, Molly and Emily contented themselves with staying as far away from Becky and Priscilla as possible. And for their own reasons, they stayed away from everyone else as well.

The meadow in front of Aspen Camp was disappointing. Though verdant green and inviting, the water that fed it was underground. There was no river or creek to swim in as with most mountain meadows. There was, however, a local trail that led to Finch Lake. The lake was sometimes crowded since it was less than five miles by road from the Ranch. But Cony Creek which fed it from higher elevations to the north, was never crowded and had no direct access by road. It was covered by forest and had deep pools of cold mountain water swirling around white granite boulders as it tumbled down from the peaks toward Finch Lake. All they had to do was hike a half mile up Cony creek from the lake and they were alone together in the wilds.

Mrs. Parker gave her talk on wilderness safety on the first day. She talked about dangers from wild animals, what to do if lost, the danger of lightning storms which came most afternoons in the Rockies in late summer, how to build a shelter and start a fire. At the end of her talk, she asked questions.

"So, Priscilla, what do you do if you see a black bear?"
"I don't know. Run?"

"Probably not a good idea. Anyone else have an answer?"

Molly knew all about black bears. Steele had taught her. "Stand your ground and look as big as you can."

Priscilla smirked until Mrs. Parker said "very good" to

Molly.

Mrs. Parker went on. "We didn't talk about this. But, just for fun, what if it's a grizzly bear instead of a black bear?"

Molly shot her hand up again. "There are no grizzlies this far south in the Rockies, Mrs. Parker."

"And how do you know that Molly."

"My daddy told me."

"And your daddy was right. Ok, now class, the next question is what if you are approached by a mountain lion?"

Priscilla and Becky shot their hands up thinking the answer was obvious.

"All right, Becky this time."

"Run really fast, faster than the lion," she answered with a confident smile.

"No. That's not what you should do. Anyone else have the answer."

Emily responded. "Stand your ground, look really big, and maybe pick up a big stick or a rock to hit it with?"

"That is correct. And where did you learn that?

"From Molly's daddy and you," she smiled.

"All right. Now, despite talking about scary animals, what did I say about lightning?

Molly piped up again. "You said it was the most dangerous thing in the Rockies and comes every afternoon."

"Yes, Molly. Almost every afternoon."

Every day for the next three days Molly and Emily hiked to their private spot on Cony Creek. And sure enough, in the afternoon the clouds would form, and they could hear the distant sound of thunder often coming from Longs Peak which was not far away. If they saw a flash of lightning amidst the dark clouds, they would count the seconds: "thousand one, thousand two, thousand three" until the roar of thunder rolled over them. Steele had taught Molly that thunder travelled a mile every five seconds. The closest it had come to Molly and Emily then was twenty five seconds which meant it never came no closer than five miles. But the third day brought darker clouds. Emily saw a flash of lightning and calmly began to count. She had not gotten to five when the thunder crashed over them. Molly and Emily froze and looked into each other's panicked eyes.

"We should've gone down the mountain an hour ago," complained Emily. "What do we do now?"

Molly looked around quickly for a low spot away from the creek and trees. A gully was thirty feet away. She knew they had to get as far away from water as possible and made a quick decision. She grabbed Emily's hand and dragged her to the bottom of the gully. Then she told her what to do.

"Stand on the balls of your feet in a low crouch."

"That's silly. How will that help?"

"I don't know, but it's what Steele said to do!"

As she barked commands to Emily, she could hear Steele's words coming out of her own mouth, and it was exactly what he had taught her. Soon, fat drops of rain came down like solitary messengers from the dark clouds hovering above. Heavy globules of water splatted individually against the ground for a few moments. Pit...pat...pit...pat, pit, pit, pit. Then it rose to a roar as the clouds above let loose their load.

"Molly," shouted Emily over the din of the falling rain "We might as well be in the creek. Everything is wet," she complained as water draining from elevations above formed a temporary creek that flowed down the gully and swirled around their ankles and feet.

Ellen was right to complain. Other than staying in a crouch and keeping their contact with the ground to a minimum, there was nothing left to do to protect themselves. As with the bears and the mountain lions, there was nowhere to run that the bolts would not chase them down. Lightning began to strike trees just feet away from where they cowered severing large branches that fell to the ground in flames. Soon the strikes and the roar of the thunder that followed were no longer separate. They joined together as one and shook the ground through the balls of their feet as icy water gushed over them.

But just as the storm came to them suddenly, so too did it drift away after just a few minutes of violence. The deadly lightning strikes slowly crept south toward the lake below and left only dark billowing clouds behind along with a few rays of sun to poke through. Thin shafts of light lit up the creek and give the girls hope that it was over. But Emily felt it first and began to shake.

"It's getting cold Molly."

Hail has its own kind of roar. It is loud like rain, but heavier, harder, colder. In minutes, it smothered summer with winter, and the landscape seemed covered in snow. But it wasn't snow. It was ice— four inches deep, and the temperature dropped thirty degrees in seconds. Molly and Emily were still crouched on the balls of their feet which were now buried in hail ice at the bottom of the gully. If anyone had stumbled upon them, the girls would have looked silly as they huddled and shivered in the ditch. The lightning had passed quickly, followed by hail, but now they had a new worry—freezing cold.

They stood up from their crouch to the sound of crunching of ice below their shoes. Their hair was dripping wet, and their t-shirts and shorts were soaked.

"So, did Steele tell you what to do when this happened?"

"No. He missed this part," she answered as she broke into a shivering tooth rattling smile while holding her crossed arms close to her body. "But I do know this. We need to wring out our wet clothes, warm up, and then get moving. We'll freeze here." First, they stripped. Soon the tree branches around them were strewn with their wet clothing.

"Um, how do we warm up?" asked Emily now standing naked except for her shoes and with goose-bumps all over her body.

"We hug."

Molly stepped closer to Emily and faced her with a smile and wiped a wet strand of Emily's hair from her face. After a few awkward efforts at a hug, they leaned against each other pressing their soft naked bodies together. Soon it became more than an embrace as they frantically sought to have every inch of their nakedness touching the other. That was when they kissed for the first time, felt love, and explored it with gentle touches of their hands until fresh rays of sun warmed them and turned their wet bodies into the color of gold.

When Mrs. Parker came around the next day to gather the scouts for the hike to Chasm Lake, Molly and Emily peeked out of their tent and declined.

"We're still feeling the altitude," they said.

"Oh, I'm so sorry. It's a beautiful hike, but I understand. Altitude sickness is not fun. Take care of yourselves and get some rest. You'll feel better tomorrow."

Becky and Priscilla pushed past the girls and left the tent all to them and mumbled "good riddance" as they boarded the bus. Soon the bus chugged up the mountain road toward the trailhead for Chasm Lake. When the whine of the engine disappeared into the distance, Molly zipped the tent flap closed and laid down with Emily.

THE MARRIAGE OF MOLLY AND MORGAN

Eighteen-year-old Molly Steele sat cross-legged and nude among the wildflowers and lush summer grass surrounding an isolated alpine lake too small to have a name. She basked in the morning sun with Emily lying beside her wet and naked drying off from her swim. The sharp tips of the emerald grass teased Molly's skin as she gazed at Emily's body and marveled at the sleekness of a woman's form and felt a familiar flush. Molly leaned over Emily and pressed her sun-warmed lips upon hers. Emily's lips were still chilled from the lake. Then Molly brushed the back of her fingers gently across Emily's nipples and smiled when they became erect. Soon they embraced and sank deep into the grass in an erotic swoon as lake water gently lapped the shore.

They had been the best of friends through elementary school, and girl scouts. It was on their summer camp at Aspen Camp that they first kissed. But as they descended deeper into the warm depths of eroticism, they became frightened. So, both pretended to believe that it was just practice for when they would kiss the boys. But they never kissed boys and they learned ways of being together that boys could never vie for. So, they stayed together in secret and pretended to like boys and even date boys. Then, soon after a broken young man came home from a distant war, Molly married him. His name was Morgan, but he wasn't really a man at all.

Morgan had all the trappings of a man including the apparatus and conduct that qualified him as such. He shaved, he talked dirty if he had to with the other boys, and even ogled girls just to affirm his gender. But he was not like the other boys. His weak masculinity was obvious enough to him and to others that he felt the need to mask it by letting everyone know that he was an artist — a bit different than the others with thin delicate fingers, but nothing to worry about. Maybe he was what they used to call a milquetoast. A harmless asexual oddity that fit no category and could be ignored because he did not constitute a threat. *I'm not queer*, he often told himself. Thus, when Molly was drawn to him for her reasons, and he was drawn to her for his, it had nothing to do with sex — it had to do with keeping secrets.

Morgan wasn't queer even if Molly was. He just wasn't interested in girls. Try as he might by thumbing through his father's Playboy magazines under his covers with flashlight at night, nothing stirred him. In his mid-teens he gave it up. But his lack of interest in girls never translated into an attraction to men. Far from it. The gamut of male behaviors that defined masculinity was abhorrent to him even if it was constantly thrown into his face. "Be a man," his besotted father would urge when a bully would beat him at school. But if being a man meant acting like the men that beat him, Morgan wanted none of it. So, he buried himself in his art and worried about what would become of him in this world when he seemed to have no gender at all. Because of all that, it made sense to him — if to no one else — to join the army.

Molly and Emily worked to keep their love hidden while also vowing to stay together forever. At first, Molly was alarmed that she was not like the other girls who lusted after boys. Then, while she was taking a class on Greek history in junior college, she read about a Greek isle called Lesbos where the women there were like her. On that island, there was an infamous woman called "The Poetess," just as Homer was called "The Poet." She wrote poems about her love for women. Her name was Sappho. And it was liberating to find her. It validated her being, and it linked her erotic feelings toward Emily to ancient times. *It's normal*, she thought with joyful relief. She listened intently to her teacher as she read "Summer" by Sappho while girls in the classroom tugged their dresses over their knees, and boys snickered under their breath.

Slumber streams from quivering leaves that listless
Bask in heat and stillness of Lesbian summer.

Breathless swoons the air with the apple-
blossoms' Delicate aroma From the shade of
branches that droop and cover.

Shallow trenches winding about the orchard, Restful
comes, and cool to the sense, the flowing Murmur of water.

But as deep as her love for Emily was, it never tarnished her daughterly love of a plain talking man named Steele. Nor did she have any antipathy for men in general. She just had no desire to have their sex thrust into her. Competing with men, however, was another matter entirely. She relished it. And when it came to beating bullies, she lived for it. That may have been Steele's doing. He never lavished the typical girl toys on her, nor did he ever call her princess, or shy away from teaching her how to clean horse apples from the stable.

Her nickname may have been Molly, but her birth name was Amelia. Amelia fit Molly's femininity in every way. But once Steele learned that Molly was a common nickname for Amelia, like Dick was for Richard, he started using Molly. He figured that was a harmless change to the promise he had made to Marija that she might approve of. After all, Molly was a feisty name that matched a fiery spirit even if it muted the feminine softness intoned in Amelia.

Despite being grounded in who she was, she knew Steele would be befuddled by her love for Emily — not rejected — confused and maybe worried too. So, she did her best to hide it. When a local boy named Morgan came back home from the Army without finishing his tour of duty, Steele wondered what triggered his sudden discharge before his tour was up. He suspected, but he never asked. It was not long after his return that he became Molly's way of hiding who she was from Steele. And Molly became Morgan's way of looking like the stud that had caught the eye of the prettiest girl in town. So, they married.

Emily made her home near the bakery. She had become the town baker when her parents retired and passed the struggling business on to her. Soon after she took over the bakery, the Steele ranch began to have fresh bread home-delivered once a week, but only on days when Steele was not there. Meantime, Molly and Morgan had taken to living in the bungalow out in the pasture separate from the main house. The bungalow had two rooms — one for Morgan and one for Molly. It was as if they lived in separate abodes, and neither much cared about the goings on of the other.

If Steele happened to be back from his Rustler's cabin on the mountain where he tended to his demons for weeks at a time, Molly and Emily escaped to the wide-open spaces surrounding Nucla. There were plenty of spots in the nearby woods for them to picnic without raising eyebrows. "A girl could have a girlfriend — right?" Molly would ask. And there was always Estes Park, and hotels in the big city of Denver on the other side of the Divide where no one would know about their love — particularly Steele. The only time they were ever caught happened when Steele walked too quietly into the stable when they were kissing in the shade.

"What'chu' doin' girls?" he asked without being particularly alarmed.

"Oh, Emily was just showing me how her new boyfriend kisses. He kisses pretty good."

"New boyfriend? Somebody I know?"

"Oh, probably not. He's from Silverton," answered Molly.

"He got a name?" asked a smiling and unsuspecting Steele.

"Yes. Of course. His name is — um — Bill. His name is Bill," stammered Emily.

"Good kisser eh?

"The best," replied Emily with a show of confidence that convinced Steele that there was nothing to it. Then he went on with his business in the barn, found the tack he was looking for, and wished them well.

"All right then, practice makes perfect."

MORGAN STANDS TALL

Molly and Morgan married a few years after he returned from the war on Grenada. They called the conflict Urgent Fury. What was urgent about it, Morgan never thought to question. They were told the mission was to prevent the spread of communism. When the conflict ended in victory, the president said: "our days of weakness are over. Our military forces are back on their feet and standing tall."

Morgan was the last person who should have gone to Grenada. As a shy teen, he would ride his horse to rugged haunts in the Uncompaghre carrying an easel, camping gear, and food for a week. There he roamed the territory and painted mustang horses in wild places often near the Lone Cone, an extinct volcano. Sometimes he painted Steele's new colt, a grey roan that Steele kept in a corral in his sheep pasture. Morgan liked to catch her in mid-air as she jumped and frolicked with the sheep. Other times, he painted wild sorrel colored horses with pale riders in landscapes covered with ice-blue snow. The army cared little for those talents. And if it weren't for the fact that he could shoot the tail off a rabbit without a scope at over 100 yards, it might have washed him out of basic training in the second week. But, like the celebrated pacifist Sergeant York of an earlier war, he was deadly with a rifle—so they kept him.

Morgan had his reasons for signing up for a three-year tour in the first place. Being in the army validated his manhood and kept wolves at bay about who he was. He never expected to be in a shooting war any more than Steele thought he might go to Vietnam. And like Steele, Morgan did not come home with his mind all in one piece. Steele sensed a kindred and troubled soul in Morgan. That made him want to protect him just as he had protected his own family after his father was banished. More than that, he saw Morgan as one of his own men in the army. Years before, he had failed to protect Dort, that other young man under his charge who died manning the Thompson. Saving Morgan would give him a new chance to succeed where he had failed with Dort—maybe even be redeemed. But Steele never told Morgan about Dort. And Morgan never told Steele about the enemy soldier he killed on Grenada.

America led the assault with elite troops in their attack on the island. Pundits had argued the war was really about erasing the stigma of the loss in Vietnam. Thus, losing to some ragtag guerrillas on a tiny island was not an option for the military so they sent their best. Navy Seals and Army Special Forces attacked from the west. Army Rangers marauded from the south. And Marines splashed ashore on the eastern side of the island. But for a few fanatical holdouts, the war was all but over in three days with 19 Americans and 122 guerillas and civilians killed. Morgan's group came ashore later on the fourth day with a combat engineering group out of Fort Bragg, North Carolina. Their mission was to disarm any booby traps and mines left by the guerrillas and make the place safe for civilians.

Soon after their arrival, they were sent to a grassy soccer field which lay in view of the turquoise waters of the Caribbean. It did not have the look of a war ravaged countryside. Morgan Le Conte, Tony Sforza, and Dick Manning were ordered to clear the stadium of possible explosives and booby traps. American military planners had worried that Cuban combat engineers deployed on the island to help the guerrillas would leave mines and booby traps behind. But they did not lay mines and only a handful of home-made booby traps were ever found. So, Morgan's group of combat engineers had nothing to do.

Nevertheless, they were sent off to do busy work. Morgan heard one lieutenant smoking a cigarette with some other officers say, "it'll be good training for em.'" They had their orders. When they arrived at the field, Sgt. Sforza led his team of three on to the field on what they thought would be a useless task.

"Fuck, piss, shit, hell," ranted Sforza as he ambled across the field toward the bleachers holding his M16 rifle in one hand casually at his side. Proud of his long string of swear words, he added—"we fly two-thousand miles to a shitty little island that's supposed to be littered with land-mines, and all we get is blisters on our ass from a six hour flight. Ok Le Conte, you take the southern end of the stadium, Manning you take the north end, and I'll take the middle bleachers."

Morgan Le Conte looked beyond the green grass to the blue Caribbean waters with amazement. It wasn't Colorado, but it was beautiful, colorful, paintable. He was in mid-artistic thought when a rifle shot rang out and dirt flew up near his feet. "Shooter," he yelled as he and the others hit the ground. But there was no cover other than the short-bladed grass on the field. Worse, the location of the enemy fire was obscured by the stadium which bounced the report of the rifle in multiple directions.

"Anyone see where it's coming from?" yelled Sforza.

"No."

So far. it had been a single shot and no more. All three soldiers hugged the ground and scanned the landscape trying to locate the shooter. Morgan cradled his weapon in the prone shooting position just as he had during training at Fort Bragg and won his Expert Marksman Badge. Then he saw it — movement at the south end of the grandstand.

"Shooter — south end," he yelled and then trained his sights on where he had last detected movement a hundred yards down range.

"Covering fire," screamed Sforza as he stood up to run to the other side of the stadium to outflank the shooter. Morgan and Manning began firing at the general area where Morgan had seen the shooter seconds before.

But just as Sforza got to his feet, a second shot rang out and a bullet tore into his thigh. Morgan heard the thudding sound of the bullet hitting then ripping through Sforza's leg and then saw him hit the ground holding his wound with both hands. Then he saw the sniper do something strange. The shooter stepped out into the open to taunt the Americans and hurl insults in French Patois language at Sforza who was writhing in pain on the ground. The shooter jeered them with both his arms in the air and his macho courage humiliating the pinned the Americans pressing their faces down into the thin grass. His taunt lasted but a few seconds. But when he dropped his arms to reach for his weapon and turned to dive back into his protective cover, Morgan squeezed off a round before he got there.

Morgan rolled over on his back with his weapon laying from his crotch to his nose on top of him and squinted at the bright tropical sky. "I got him. He's down," he said in a voice pregnant with disbelief. Morgan's whole body trembled in shock, surprise, accomplishment, and fear. *God, did I kill him?*

"You sure you got him?' asked a wary Manning a few feet away. "Is he dead?"

"Maybe. I think so. Might be just wounded." He rolled back over to his stomach and quickly pointed his weapon again at the downed soldier. "He's down. I can see his helmet from here. He hasn't moved. Only one way to find out. Covering fire," he screamed, "I gotta' go look."

Morgan wasn't volunteering to check on the soldier out of courage. He was doing it out of fear—he had a dreaded feeling that he had killed. Manning shot short bursts of fire in the direction of the downed man as Morgan ran low in a crouch.

But Manning wasn't much of a shot, and couldn't see his target since he had smashed his glasses when he hit the ground for cover. Morgan zigzagged across the field counting his steps to decide when to zig and when to zag and create a random pattern that was difficult to aim at. Burdened with having to dart this way and that, it took 30 seconds to reach the soldier who lay face down. Morgan kneeled by the body. Then, after pointing his weapon in all directions to ensure the downed man did not have companions nearby, he yelled "clear" to Manning who then raced to aid Sforza writhing on the grass and still clutching his wound with both hands.

Morgan could not see the soldier's face and was not sure he wanted to. But he had to know if he had killed. Gingerly, he pushed the barrel of his rifle under the man's shoulder and lifted it to turn him over hoping he might be alive. By using his rifle to move him, he was at the ready to shoot if he had to. Though small, the body was dead weight. Morgan struggled to lift his shoulder with the point of his rifle, but finally he raised it high enough to roll him over. As his face came into view, Morgan jumped back and immediately threw up. *Oh god, it's a woman!*

Gore spurted from the severed carotid in the girl's neck where his bullet had struck, and Morgan's face was drenched with a pulse of her hot blood as the dying girl looked up to see who had killed her. Her youthful eyes were dark brown, her eyebrows were arched and thin, her skin was soft and dark, and her lips were heart-shaped and delicate. On her wrist was a Mickey Mouse watch. On her forearm was a tattoo. It read, "Angélique aime D' Andre." Morgan locked his eyes on hers in a touchless embrace, and he tried to span the widening gulf between him living and her dying and tell her he was sorry. She squinted at him and looked as if she wanted an explanation. Then her eyes faded, turned dull, and then they saw nothing. Hurling his rifle away, Morgan sat beside her with his hand on her shoulder crying. He patted her as he sobbed while the last of her life force drained into the black volcanic ash beneath the grassy field. *Who will tell D' Andre*, he worried? Soon after that, the Army sent him home on a Section 8 discharge.

Morgan's artistic bent and war jitters kept him from holding down much of a job after he returned. So, following the wedding, Steele offered to let Morgan and Molly move into the two room cabin on the Nucla ranch. It was an arrangement that was supposed to be temporary—just until Morgan could get on his feet and get a good-paying job. Ranching cattle, herding sheep, bailing hay, and mining were the basic choices for work in the Uncompaghre, but he wasn't good at any of them. What he really wanted was to paint horses, and he was getting better at it. He had already sold five paintings to a bank up north in Delta, and more were hanging on every wall of the main house where Steele lived, and the outbuilding where he and Molly were staying. A bank in Montrose was thinking about buying some too. But so far, it was not enough. He was still looking for steady income a year after the wedding when Leon Posey crashed into their lives.

LEON

Leon Posey was everything Morgan was not. Leon was evil—a bad man. While Morgan was off saving America from communism, Leon was busy beating an unconscious man lying helpless on his back in an alley behind a bar. Before passing out, the man looked into Leon's ferocious eyes as his fists continued to crash into his skull. Later he said he could see no soul behind those black eyes—only darkness. Another of his victims disappeared after he beat Leon at cards. Since his body was ever found, the town sheriff lacked the evidence to arrest him. He also rationalized that no sane man would murder another over a game of low stakes poker. Thus, he reasoned, it couldn't have been Leon. Leon may have been cruel, violent, and even evil, but he wasn't crazy.

One night Molly and Morgan had a fight over his failure to find work. The marriage was a marriage of convenience, but, economically, each was supposed to pull their load. Doors slammed and angry words rippled through the night. In a pique, she took off for town in the truck while still fuming, and after finding the Family Buffet closed, she wound up at the only place that was open at midnight—the Badwater Bar. The Badwater was Leon's private haunt where he reigned supreme over roughnecks like himself. Molly knew that, but didn't care.

As she walked through the entrance, she was aware that she was out of place. Although she wore jeans and shit-kicking boots just like the male patrons, she filled them out in ways men noticed even if that were not her intent. But like all attractive women, she knew when eyes were on her. She might have been lesbian, but she wasn't unaware, and a part of her even enjoyed the power of the tease. *They can look, but they can't touch,* she taunted. Her simple white top was Clorox white and her long blonde hair was woven into a horse braid that swung from side to side as she strolled toward the bartender and a stool. Her earrings glinted of silver muted by turquoise and flashed her presence.

"What'll you have lady?" asked the stubble-faced one-legged bartender with a patch over one eye who sat on a raised stool while sporting a leering grin and a bellybutton protruding out from an overstretched t-shirt with the words *Second Amendment* emblazoned across his chest.

"A martini," she said, pausing to raise her finger to signal there was more. "A Martini in a glass splashed with dry vermouth, swirled, then emptied. After that, fill it with Stolichnaya vodka and shaved ice, shake it until very chilled, and top it with an orange twist—not a slice, a twist. I'm having a rough night."

Normally, she drank wine; but one time when she was in Denver with Emily, she saw a city lady order a martini just like that, so she was trying it on for size.

The bartender put his elbow on the bar, raised himself up from his high stool to stand on one leg, and leaned over as if he had a confidence to betray or some advice for a lady having a rough night.

"Sorry lady, for Vodka we got Smirnoff Blue, *jet fuel* as they say on the other side of the tracks. We're short on Vermouth, we don't stock oranges, don't shave our ice, and I don't have no shaker. But I can get you a slice of lemon I keep in a bucket for the boys over there drinking Coronas and some ice cubes from the bin."

"Well then, a Smirnoff Blue on ice with a slice," she said with a coy smile.

It was no surprise that Leon Posey left the pool table to his friends and strutted across the bar like he owned it, and sat down next to Molly. And no one was shocked when he invaded her space by pulling the stool closer and putting his face near her left ear. She knew who he was. Everyone in town knew who Leon was—a bully. She looked straight ahead with the look of a woman having to suffer a fool as Leon went into his routine.

"You play pool?" was the best he could muster. Molly took a sip of her martini, ignored him, and waited a moment before swallowing and saying “Ah” to her drink. Then she set her glass down hard on the bar.

“Yeah, I play pool,” she answered with her silver earrings flashing as she turned her head toward him with a look of defiance and disgust. Then, to punctuate her claim, she pushed her stool away from the bar scraping the wooden legs across the raw timber flooring and jumped off with the clunk of her boots. That left Leon still sitting alone as she strode over to the pool table. Leon tracked her from the bar as she measured a cue stick by its heft; he watched as she carefully rubbed blue chalk all over the felt tip of the stick that would launch the cue ball into the triangular set of multi-colored orbs at the other end of the table. When she was finished with her chalking, she held the tip close to her ruby red lips and blew sending blue dust spewing across the table.

“Eight ball,” she announced as the game they would be playing. “You breaking, or am I?” she asked, hoping he would defer to her.

“By all means,” Leon said with a perfunctory bow, a sneer, and a wink at his friends leaning on their cues. They were partially hidden in the dark away from the bright light shining down on the table.

“Laadieees first,” mocked Leon.

Molly had learned pool from Steele, and Steele was one

of the best eight ball players in Vietnam between 1963 and 1966. He taught her well. Other than winning, there were two things she liked best about pool. First, it was a man's game where grunting men smoked, drank beer, cussed, talked of women, and scratched their privates. And she loved beating men —especially when they underestimated her. Second, she loved breaking. While most of pool is a game of subtle eye, hand, and arm coordination measured in micro-fractions of an inch, the breaking of the rack of balls stacked in a triangle at the opposing end of the table with a single white cue ball was athletic. And even more than the sporting aspect, she loved the dramatic shock of the cue ball crashing into the prow of the triangularly grouped balls. The break set the tone for the rest of the contest, and you could often measure the game of your opponent by their skill at the break.

Molly leaned over the table to place her cue ball and line it up knowing full well that her move aroused the lustful attention of those behind her. She didn't care and stayed focused on her game. She slid the hardwood cue stick back and forth over the fingers on her left hand with an even tempo to get a feel for the direction, weight, and stiffness of the stick. Then, on the third stroke, she thrust it forward in a heaving lunge that plunged the felt tip low on the white ball to create backspin. That was followed by a loud *crack* when it slammed into the balls at the other end. After impact, the cue ball stopped going forward and then spun back to her and slunk away from the chaos it had created on the other end. As the colored balls scattered in all directions, some went in. Plop went one ball into a scrotum shaped leather pocket. Then, plop, plop, went a second and third. Leon's face betrayed a moment of shock but quickly reformed into his look of cocky superiority.

"Lucky," he said, strutting around the table as if to survey a battleground.

"Yeah, just luck," she responded, not letting him get away

with ignoring her skill, and fully enjoying seeing the cracks in his well-manicured facade. "Bet five dollars I can run the table from here," she challenged.

"Ten," said Leon anxious to show he was still in control.

"On."

Since two solid colored balls had already gone into pockets on the break, but just one striped one had gone in, she called "solid" to take advantage. Thus, she only had five solid balls left on the table. Leon, on the other hand, would have to sink six striped ones if she lost her turn by missing a shot. If she did miss one shot, she would lose the bet that she would run the table, but not the game. But if she could pocket those five, she could then go after the eight ball for the *coup d grâce* and win both the bet and the game.

"Solid seven into the right corner pocket," she announced firmly as she tapped the corner pocket for effect. But before hitting the seven with the cue ball to knock it in, she surveyed the table. *Where do I want my cue ball to stop after it knocks the seven ball in? Gotta be there,* she concluded. *"There"* was behind the six ball which she would call for the side pocket after dropping the seven in the right corner pocket. She leaned over the green felt to line up her shot and gage the amount of backspin she would need to bring the cue ball back behind the six ball. Unlike the break, this part of pool was all finesse and touch. Molly calculated that she needed a soft kiss by the cue ball to nudge the seven ball in, but a lot of spin to bring the cue ball back to the six. A hush came over the table as she made a delicate move to pocket the seven and then spin the cue back to the six. *Easy Molly, Easy,* she cautioned herself. When the tip of her cue stick gently met the cue ball, it made an airy hollow sound and a small puff of blue chalk from the felt tip billowed up toward the light. Then the cue ball inched forward toward the seven ball even though it was spinning in reverse. At the instant the cue ball touched the seven and wheedled it into the corner pocket, the cue ball's spin took over and the ball came back to Molly exactly at the spot where she wanted it to be — right behind the six ball in perfect position to knock it into the side pocket.

Then, to Leon's amazement, she proceeded to run the entire table filling all the pockets with balls in minutes except one—the eight ball. The run caused shock among the stunned observers murmuring in low tones in the gallery. Unfortunately, the eight ball was lined up along the bumper cushion. It was a hard but not impossible shot for one who had practiced it. But if she could not sink the eight ball, it would be Leon's turn. And Leon played the game every day.

Steele had taught Molly the shot. It required the cue ball to kiss the rubber bumper on the perimeter of the table first, slightly compress it without yet touching the ball, then a millisecond later, bounce away from the bumper and touch the ball on the rebound. If done correctly, the cue kissed ball would slide down the line into the left pocket. Everyone in the room knew how bleak were the odds against her. A few guffaws came from the audience, confident she could not make the shot. That was all she needed.

"Left pocket," she asserted as she cracked her stick defiantly over her target.

At the sound of the eight ball plopping into the leather bottom of the pocket, the room went silent as the cue ball rolled to the center of the table and stopped ending the game with Molly the winner of both the game and the bet that she could run the table.

"Ten bucks," she demanded holding out her left hand with her body in a svelte akimbo taunt coupled by an annoying smirk on her face.

Leon ignored her demand and counteroffered. "Twenty says you can't beat me again," he said in desperation with his eyes darting from side to side.

"Nope," the deal was ten and I gotta' go. Hubby's waiting for me with bated breath," she lied while still holding out her hand.

"That ain't fair, he whined. You're not leaving without giving me a chance to make it back." His complaint earned a few obsequious "yeah's" from his cronies.

"Never heard of that rule," she sassed. Then, while pointing her finger inches from in his nose, she asserted, "the rule is *loser* pays, and I never heard of any other rule about losing except when it comes from a loser." Leon's face quickly took on an evil look as he pondered the word that dare not speak his name — *loser*. Beaten at his own game in front of his vassals, he slapped her taunting finger away. Then, in a reckless retort to his slap, Molly leaned back, grabbed the cue ball, hit Leon on the face, knocked an unlit cigarette out of his mouth, chipped a tooth, and cut his lip. As she turned to walk out of the bar, Leon dabbed blood from his lip, grabbed her elbow, jerked her back, hit her on her cheekbone with a closed fist, and threw her onto the pool table. Molly now lay face up, dazed, and surrounded by Leon and his cronies each leering at the accidental beauty that had landed in their turf. Still smarting with rage over being called "loser" by a woman, Leon jerked his belt off and threw his body on her while she hit, scratched, and kicked. It was no use.

Ripping off her jeans, Leon raped Molly as the others leered in an act that was less about sex than the utter humiliation of another human being. Molly's head bobbed with each of his punishing thrusts — the swinging light over the table illuminated each shuddering bounce of her face. Helpless to stop Leon, she floated away from the present and watched every detail from afar as if she had died. But she found comfort in a firm resolve. She would never tell anyone except Emily about the rape—not even Steele.

Molly arrived home crying, bruised, and disheveled long after midnight. Morgan greeted her at the door expecting to

continue their fight. Instead, he saw bruises on her face and arms and his mood shifted quickly to empathy and a concern that soon elevated to anger.

"Who did this to you? Who did this?" he repeated, not yet knowing that she had been raped and neither of them knowing that she was also becoming pregnant?

"Leon did it," she sobbed. "Leon Posey."

"He hit you. What the hell for?"

Molly did not answer. She simply crossed her arms across her chest and set her jaw in a defiant pose.

Morgan was not a man who could easily conjure courage or anger, but he felt both now. As a man who rarely felt such emotions, Morgan leaned into the moment and recklessly imagined himself as manly and capable enough to defend Molly from Leon. His relationship with her may not have been a real marriage, but that did not mean he did not care for her, love her, or feel that he had no duty to protect her. Self-consciously wallowing in his rare outburst of masculinity, he left Molly crying on the bed. Then he threw on his jacket, stormed out to the truck, and drove to the Badwater where he knew the town's bully would be waiting for him.

Barging through the door like a confident streetfighter, he yelled "Leon, you're a pathetic excuse for a man. She's a woman you know!"

Leon was leaning over the pool table with a young girl who was chewing gum and hanging on his arm. He had a cigarette hanging out of his mouth looking at ease.

"Yeah. She's a woman all right. But me—me pathetic?" challenged Leon in a calm voice — "me pathetic?"

The light shade over the pool table was still swinging side to side under a ceiling fan, and Morgan could see marks on Leon's face when the shade swung its light over him. Molly had fought him and scratched him. Seeing it helped soften his pique at her for whatever her part was in this. But Leon was now in his sights and justice was on his side. *You don't hit women,* he repeated to himself. Defending that maxim made him feel strong. As Morgan strode toward Leon, the bully straightened, spit out his cigarette and smiled in anticipation of what he knew was coming — a fight.

"Bring it on, boy, bring it on," he said as he nodded his head up and down with a menacing look from the whites of his wide-open eyes.

They circled each other for a moment.

Then Leon taunted. "Hey boy, I sure had fun with your wildcat wife tonight. I know she had fun too. You know, I think I'm in love with your Molly. Yes sir, I think I'm in love. I might even take her from you punk cuz' you don't deserve such a sexy hot woman like her."

Now Morgan knew what had really happened to Molly. It was more than an altercation. It was a rape, and he felt another boost of rage. He reminded himself that he'd killed on Grenada even if his enemy then was a seventeen year old girl. *Man girl, no matter—she was trying to kill us,* he rationalized. But this time, he could not use his skill with a rifle, and he was facing a full grown six-footer. It was man to man.

Morgan had never won a fistfight in his life. He had only been in beatings where he was the victim and loser. So, like the amateur he was, he telegraphed a roundhouse punch that the street fighting bully easily ducked. Leon countered with a heavy-fisted left jab to Morgan's nose which ended with a loud crack of cartilage and red blood that sprayed all over the green felt on the pool table. Morgan was stopped with one punch and stunned at how quickly his manly rage abandoned him. His anger was now replaced by the cowering fear he always suffered. He held his face as his eyes watered from the blow to his nose and was bewildered at how a single strike from Leon— a jab no less—

could have vanquished him so quickly. Blood trickled out from between his fingers.

Leon turned his back on his wounded victim and casually walked over to pick up a cue stick from the rack as if to select the right one for a new round of pool. He took his time to pick out a big one as Morgan blubbered in pain behind him. Then he sauntered back to Morgan, wound the cue stick up, and brought it sideways into Morgan's left knee splintering the joint. Morgan felt pain so intense he was breathless as he wobbled off balance and grabbed at the pool table nearly falling down. Just when he turned around to see what Leon would do next, he saw him wind it up again but swung it around to his right knee. That dropped Morgan to the ground to his hands and what was left of his knees. Morgan's defeated eyes turned blank and looked straight ahead. They bore witness to his quick, humiliating, and utter defeat. After a purposeful and dramatic pause, Leon looked back to ensure his friends were watching. Then he donned a menacing grin and completed a coup d'état. Slowly raising the cue stick high overhead, he brought it down on Morgan's skull killing him and said:

"Die you little queer."

When Sherriff Posey arrived ten minutes later, Morgan was lying eyes wide open in a puddle of blood. His skull had a long bloody dent in it where it had been crushed. Leon was shooting pool when the Sherriff walked up behind him and asked,

"You do that Leon?" pointing to Morgan.

Turning from the pool table to look down at Morgan while wiping away some sweat on his brow from his exertion, and then back to the Sherriff, he answered.

"Yeah dad, I did that. He had it coming."

Sometime around dawn, Steele got a call at the ranch from the Montrose County Coroner to come up and identify

Morgan. As the coroner pulled Morgan's body out of a locker, the cloth covering his head slipped off to display his crushed skull. *Forehead to cowlick*, he noted before he added, *Dort*. Steele's mind began to race uncontrollably back in time. At noon, Steele went to the Badwater Bar just to see for himself where Morgan had met his end.

As he entered, the bartender looked up from his Playboy Magazine and asked, "What'll you have.?

"Jack Daniels straight up," answered Steele as he walked over to the pool table where the coroner had said he found Morgan.

"I thought you didn't drink whiskey?"

"I don't."

The Badwater had sloshed a bucket of soapy water over the blood but didn't bother to scrub it. The dark red stain was still there on the raw wood floor for all to see. Steele downed his drinks and stayed the afternoon near the spot where Morgan had died. His eyes faded into a dull stare that could only see the past, and his past was looking ominously clear through the bottom of each passing glass. In his stupor, he barely noticed that a tremor in his hand was creeping up his arm.

By the time Morgan was buried, Steele couldn't raise his arm to remove his hat because of the shaking, and a dream began that would not stop. The dream and his trembling were making Steele useless to himself and to the ranch. He knew he had to get himself to a safe place to sort out what was wrong in his head. He remembered what Dr. Cohen had told him about facing his fears on the hospital ship in Vietnam. But the pain was too much. He had to escape. A week after Morgan's funeral, he asked Molly to drive him up to his getaway cabin on the mountain. He thought it would only be for a short time, and that he would be back for Posey's trial for murder. But the weeks turned into months. Molly made weekly trips to bring him groceries and visit with him. But after five months, she began to cut her visits short and not even get out of the truck after he unloaded the supplies.

"See you in a week," she offered flatly when he finished unloading.

"Yeah. See You," said Steele huffing from the exertion.

She had her own reasons now for wanting to stay away. The first one was that she had still told no one except Emily about her rape by Posey. The second was that she was pregnant from Leon and beginning to show. She did not have the courage to reveal either secret to Steele, especially in his mental state. Because of her guilt, she complied with his requests for whiskey by the quart as part of his supply package knowing that he was descending deeper and deeper into alcoholism and depression. She didn't respect his drinking and neither did he. The difference was that she had begun telling him so.

As he sank into oblivion, his dream began to change. Dort was fading away and being replaced by the bloody, wide eyed, crushed face of Morgan. Other times he saw the grizzled face of his father lying in a pool of blood motionless on the floor of their old house. His dream was morphing into a triumvirate parade of mayhem worthy of a carnival house of horrors.

LEON GETS OUT OF JAIL

Twelve months after killing Morgan, Leon Posey walked out of jail. Jurors at the trial for the murder of Morgan only heard the redacted evidence submitted by his father Sherriff Posey. And they never heard the damning evidence he omitted. Absent from the evidence was the rape of Molly — something she had only told to Emily. Sheriff Posey likely never knew about it either. Leon and his henchmen knew, but they were not about to come forward to incriminate themselves. So, his cronies sat in the courtroom gallery and snickered, fully confident that their hero was castrating justice all by himself.

In the end, Posey was given the lightest sentence possible. It was just 12 months for voluntary manslaughter because his sentence was mitigated by Leon's claim that Morgan was a "homo" and had propositioned him. A year later he sauntered out of the Delta Correctional Facility with a toothpick in his mouth wearing a white tee shirt with the sleeves rolled up and sporting a sly smirk. The day after that he knocked on Molly's door.

Molly answered the way most people do on the western slope with a smile expecting someone she knew.

"Hello pretty lady," was his opening remark as she swung the door wide open. Seeing her rapist, she put her shoulder into the door to slam it closed, but Leon straight armed it before it hit his face.

"That's no way to treat the daddy of our child," he taunted.

Leon had done the math in jail, and both he and Molly knew the ugly truth. Allie was his, though everyone else assumed it was Morgan.

"You gonna' invite me in, because, you know, I've been thinking about you for a long time since we last met and had such a fine time at the Badwater? You haven't forgotten me, have you?"

Molly glanced to her right toward the secretary desk three feet away. Then, looking back at Leon, she cooed, "Why no Leon, I haven't forgotten." Leon was disarmed enough by her unexpected tone that a smile came across his face just as Molly took one quick step to the desk, flipped up the roll top, grabbed the single-action revolver out of the pistol drawer, cocked it like a gunslinger, and stood her ground with the seven-inch stainless steel barrel pushed against Leon's nose. Then she edged forward gripping the cocked .45 with both hands and her index finger on the trigger ready to fire.

Backing away with his arms raised he said, "now that's no way to treat the father of your child."

"You mean the dead father of my child, don't you?"

He had enough sense to know this was not the time to push it further. He walked backwards to his pickup with his hands in the air, got in, closed the door, started it up, and then rolled down the window.

"I'll be back," he shouted as he peeled out on the dirt driveway in a cloud of red dust. "Allie's mine too."

BACK AT THE RUSTLER'S CABIN

Back at the rustler's cabin, Steele had been awaking in the dark in a cold sweat. His dream had been repeating loop to loop for almost a year—ever since the murder of Morgan at the Badwater. Then one night in the middle of the tenth loop, Steele was startled by cackling coming from the CB radio. It was Molly calling him from the ranch, and she sounded desperate.

"Pop. I can't explain. But you gotta' come home. Over. "

Slurring his words in the same ugly way he heard his father talk, he asked why.

"Pop trust me. You have to come home. Over."

"You gonna' uh, you know, uh pick me up," he asked almost incoherent?"

"Can't leave Pop. You'll have to walk down the mountain and then flag down the bus on Highway 145. Sorry Pop. Please come. Please come soon. Over."

Steele heard Molly turn off her microphone with a piercing click. He had never heard Molly sound so desperate, and the fact that she could not get away had an ominous tinge that cleared his head. He put on some unwashed clothes lying near his bed, slid his Model 1911 Colt in his belt behind his back, and stuffed a fresh fifth of whiskey into the side pocket of his coat. He had taken to wearing his old fatigue jacket that had his name on it. The name tag was white once, but now it was dirty brown.

He peered into the dark to see if there was anything he missed. It was three in the morning. If he walked fast, he could flag down the noon bus coming up the grade from Dolores.

He reached the highway at the base of the mountain just before noon. When he saw the bus, he stepped out into the highway and waved his hands trying to get it to stop. But the bus kept up its hard earned speed and veered across the center line to avoid him as it whizzed by causing Steele's white hair and beard to fly in its wake.

A hundred yards past him up the road, the driver relented. The bus slowed, then stopped, and the door swung open with an impatient clunk. Steele trudged as fast as he could toward the yellow wreck of a bus idling in wait for him as the engine's valves ticked and clattered. He paused for breath at the open door with his left hand gripping the grab bar as the driver glowered at him to step in and take a finally take seat. With a heave and a groan, Steele pulled himself up to the first step, then to the second, then into the aisle way. The piqued driver yanked the lever that closed the door, hit the gas, and sent Steele stumbling as the bus lurched forward. His right hand reached for the safety of a seat-back to keep from falling. He smelled of alcohol.

"Jerk," he muttered as he lowered himself slowly down into an open seat. The engine strained as the bus pushed up the grade against a headwind. He noticed that most seats were filled with Basques. Steele let himself slump into a cracked leather seat. *They don't make em' with leather anymore*, was his last thought before his head toppled sideways with his mouth wide open and his dusty stubble glinting in the noonday sun. As he drifted off, he barely felt his pistol digging into his back or the fifth of Jack Daniels in his pocket as his mind dreamed again of a long-ago battlefield he could no longer escape.

The dream started as it always did at three AM— Pop-pop-pop off in the distance, and then the telltale ka-ching sound of an empty clip ejecting from an M1 Garand followed by short bursts of fire from a Thompson sub-machine gun off to the right just before the night erupted with the sound of fifty enemy rifles, and bullets pattering against the leaves and ground like a midwestern rain.

He awoke from the dream startled by the driver shouting "Rico."

The driver was announcing both their arrival in Rico, and the fact that his shift was over. He and the replacement driver both lived there and swapped shifts each day. All the passengers had to get off and stand outside in the wind until his replacement arrived. The driver was anxious to get everyone off the bus so that he could get home.

"Everybody off now," he said. "Now, *Ahora mismo*" he snarled thinking all Basques spoke Spanish.

He continued to growl as if their slow exit from the bus was delaying his first beer. Then, in an act he would regret, he put his hand on Steele's back to hurry him out of his seat. Suddenly, in a blindingly quick move, Steele's hand shot out, grabbed the hand of the driver, rotated outward, then down in a clean Aikido move, and forced the driver to his knees. Steele was in no mood.

"Not polite to touch people that don't want touchin'" he growled as his eyes invaded the pained gaze of the startled driver. Before letting him go he launched one last grievance against him. "They're Basque, not Spanish so next time it's *orain* when you want to say *now*, not *ahora*."

Turning away and taking a deep breath, he grabbed the chromed seatback frame and pulled himself upright. He winced a little from the pain of lying on his pistol. As he stood up to exit the bus, he reached into his jacket pocket to feel for the bottle of Jack Daniels. He pulled it out and gave it the kind of sneer one gives to an enemy and then put it back in his pocket. As he walked by the Basques standing outside the bus, they smiled and nodded approval of the way he had handled the bus driver.

The new driver arrived, and the passengers reboarded the bus. Steele took a seat and fell quickly back into a deep sleep. The engine again struggled for power while gasping for air in the high altitude and struggling against a stiff wind sliding down from the Rockies. With sleep came the dream of a grassy clearing in Vietnam. An M-1 was firing off in the distance followed by a pop- pop-pop... and a ka-ching when the clip ejected, followed by a short silence that gave way to the Thompson firing short bursts into the moonless forest. It was then that the tree line lit up with fire from the SKS Carbines and the five AK-47's. After that came the exploding det-cord and the C4 explosives, the screams of the dying, the armless man carrying the AK-47 through the low-lying fog, and the grotesque face of bullet torn Dort staring up at nothing. That was how the dream had gone for years. But now it was Morgan's face staring at nothing, not Dort's. Other times it was his father's face looking confused beneath his dented skull. Soon he would hear the M-1 and the pop-pop-pop to signal that the dream was starting again—from the beginning.

Steele awoke an hour later and watched the terrain pass by the window. After Placerville came Norwood. After Norwood, came Nucla. As he neared his ranch, the ragged volcanic point of the Lone Cone near Norwood was catching the last rays of sun.

It was dark when the us stopped in Nucla. It was October 1.st

SECRETS

Exiting the bus, he ambled into the Badwater Bar and found a payphone. Nucla was a town of unique but unrelated facts—everyone was armed, and it still had working payphones. He waved off the bartender who asked; "what'll you have?" Then he dropped a quarter into the payphone and called his daughter. "I'm back."

Ten minutes later Molly arrived in the 1953 blue Chevy truck. The pickup had gone by various names as it aged. First it was just *truck* or *pickup*. Then it was the *old blue truck* for a time. But after it reached twenty or so years, it got a human name. Steele called it Mc Tavish after the old sheep rancher who gave it to him years before. Rolling onto the dirt parking area, Molly reached for the vertical handbrake mounted next to the floor shifter and yanked it while Mc Tavish was still moving. The rear tires locked up and slid sideways kicking up dust under the security light hanging by a wire from a tree. Just before it stopped its slide, Molly swung the driver door open with a loud crack followed by a long metallic groan.

Malcolm, a Border Collie, was asleep in the bed of Mc Tavish and barely roused during the commotion. He opened one eye when Molly yelled out for Steele inside the bar. But when Steele answered, Malcolm opened both eyes, and his ears lifted to attention. Then they pricked toward the direction of Steele's voice. When Steele answered from the exit door with an "on the way," Malcolm leaped out of Mc Tavish, bounded to Steele, and jumped all over him while nipping at his hands to punish him for his long absence. His joyful greeting kicked up a cloud of dust under the red neon sign that read "Badwater Bar."

"He remembers me," said Steele dryly. "Sorry it took so long for me to get here, I was..."

"It's OK Pop it's ok." Her eyes were watering as she reached toward him. "I'm so glad you're back," she said while standing on her tiptoes to give him a full-frontal hug. "God I've missed you. Are you feeling any better yet?"

"Well, after living alone in the woods for most of a year and staying drunk most of the time I should be."

Steele was a loving man deep at heart, but never good at hugs, and he guarded his emotions with relevant, if inconsequential, small talk.

"Sorry I, uh, well I had to take a bus," as if it were news.

He patted her on the back clumsily during the hug and said what he thought was the most appropriate thing to say.

"Still got Mc Tavish and my dog Malcolm huh?"

"Always and forever," she taunted while leaning over at her waist and toward him with both her hands in her back pockets as if to pounce. Then she jumped up, threw her arms above her head, clasped Steele behind his neck, and landed a big kiss on his stubbled face. After that, she stepped back away from the light to wipe a tear.

Standing toe to toe, there was a short silence until she spoke: "let's go home Pop" which she then repeated in a hush with the tone of the sacred, "let's go home."

Malcolm ignored Molly's hand signal to jump into the bed of the truck and laid flat on the ground, head between his paws, defiantly staring her down. Molly stared back for a moment, shook her head, and then she and Steele got into the cab and took their seats. Steele left his door wide open and made a clicking sound to Malcolm who then jumped over his lap and landed in the small space between the two of them on the bench seat and then quickly lay down with his head on Steele's thigh and his butt pushing against Molly's leg. He was not scolded.

Molly was the prettiest girl between Norwood and Grand Junction. She had the look of her mother Marija but had the mostly kind spirit of her father who raised her alone with the help of Ganiz. Her only flaws were small but dangerous in this tough region of miners, cattle ranchers, and sheepherders. She was fearless, feisty, and took no bull from men on any topic from riding horses to hunting, especially from "real men" who were really just bullies and braggarts masquerading as men. There was no pursuit claimed by a man that she was unwilling or unable to do, pretty notwithstanding. There were times when that put her on a collision course with men like Leon Posey who had something to lose—their God-given birthright of superiority over women.

When they got to the ranch, Molly and her father went inside. Malcolm preferred to sleep on the porch so that he could watch the door where his people came and went and to spot threats to the sheep in the pasture. He curled up next to the chair that Steele used to use and went half-asleep. Ganiz snoozed in the cabin deep in a dream about his homeland in the Pyrenees. Inside the house, Molly sent Steele to a chair at the kitchen table. It was covered with a red and white checkered tablecloth. After he sat, she went straight for the stove, pulled out a pot, poured in two cups of milk, and turned the burner on low.

"You want a drink?"

"No, I quit."

"When."

"Today," he smiled.

After a pause, she smiled back, got a happy wiggle in her walk, got some sugar and cinnamon ready, and started the toast. It was an old ritual Steele had retained from his days riding the line. He had shared it with Molly as she grew up. It was a poor man's dessert, a shared pleasure, and now a bond between father and daughter—torn buttered toast, cinnamon, sugar, and warm milk. She needed to share it again with Steele tonight. Soon she would tell him the good news, the bad news, and the reason she called him to come home on the CB radio. She looked up from her chores at the stove and met Steele's eyes. Steele looked back and he felt his back tensing as he braced for the news he knew was coming. Molly took a breath, set a dishtowel down on the cabinet, crossed her arms over her chest while still standing, and then blurted it out.

"You're a grandfather, Pop."

Steele froze with a spoon dripping warm milk and toast rising midway up toward his waiting mouth.

"I'm a what?" he asked as he dropped his spoon into the bowl with a clank and splattering milk all over the table.

"You're a grandad," she repeated with joy on her face for Steele and a hint of deep sadness for herself. "A baby girl. Her name is Allison, but I've already taken to calling her Allie."

A huge grin spread across Steele's normally stoic face as he shook his head in surprise and disbelief.

"God damn. Good god damn." Then, thinking of Morgan—"Did Morgan know?"

"No Pop, Morgan never knew."

Steele's face took on the distant look of a man holding a tragic thought. Molly noticed and cut him off before he could follow his tendency to wallow in guilt. "It's not about you Pop. You did nothing wrong. Stop! After a pause, she added a note of caution. There's two more things Pop," as her eyes began to water up, and she began to crumble.

"There's things that're hard, really hard," her sentence ending in a gulp. She waited while choking back tears before blurting out the second truth to her father. It was the one she had told herself she would never reveal to him.

"Allie's not Morgan's, it's Leon Posey's."

Steeles eyes opened first in wonderment and then in disbelief. He knew Leon by reputation, and by that reputation Molly and Leon together was not a possible thing in his mind. He looked at her, unable to disguise his incredulity. Molly knew Steele needed more and prodded herself to let it out.

"He raped me, dad. Leon Posey raped me the night he killed Morgan. It's why Leon killed him. Morgan tried to protect me. And it's why I couldn't tell you before calling you on the CB to come home so I could finally tell you in person. I was ashamed. "

Molly fell into her father's arms and sobbed as Steele tried to digest the news. But there was still one more truth to tell. She gathered her strength as Steele held her tight. Steele sensed there was more to come, and felt his left hand begin to shake on Molly's shoulder blade as they embraced. It had been just a few weeks since Molly had pulled the pistol on Leon after he got out of jail and threatened Molly and Allie. And it was now more than a year since Molly's rape, Morgan's death, and Steele's effort to escape his demons in the mountains. And Molly was now working hard to gather the courage to tell Steele the final piece of bad news and why she needed him to come home from the cabin.

"Here it is Pop."

And with that, she went on to tell Steele what happened after she pulled the gun on Leon.

"He got a lawyer to file a paternity suit to prove Allie was his. When that took longer than he had patience for, he threatened to take her by force. He said if he couldn't have me and the baby, then he'd take the baby. So, here's the final piece. Two days ago, Leon broke through a window, and took Allie to who knows where. I couldn't call the sheriff, because, well you know, his father. So, I called you on the radio early this morning.

Now he has Allie god know where somewhere in the night right now Pops. "

The final revelation was now complete. Molly was spent, had no more tears, and Steele did his best at resting his shaking right hand on her shoulder. Both fell silent with their foreheads bowed and touching as if deep into a redemptive prayer. Then they sat down across from each other at the kitchen table holding hands.

The rush of facts poured over Steele, and his mind raced over all the details of Molly's confession. The revelations did not make sense. How could a man get just 12 months for the murder of Morgan? He choked on Molly's rape and felt helpless about Allie being kidnapped by Molly's rapist. His mind rushed back to the day when he saw the crushed head of Morgan covered in blood and his unsmiling face tilted over to the side on the coroner's table. Steele struggled for the second time in a year whether to fight or flee and shuddered under the weight this second salvo of bad news. He needed a drink. But Steele dug deep to find the man he once was before the whiskey, the guilt, and his nightmares forced him to his knees. Steele put both hands underneath the table and pinched his thumbs hard against his index fingers. Then he straightened himself in the chair and began taking deep meditative breaths. *In one nostril and out the other,* said a mantra in his head.

"You Ok Pop?" asked Molly.

Steele did not allow the interruption and continued his breathing until he felt the calm he needed for what was ahead. N*ever did like the taste of whiskey anyway*, he thought as he pulled his bottle from his pocket and set it on the kitchen counter. Then he resolved that neither he nor his family would lose another year to Leon Posey—*not this time.*

"I'm good Molly. I'm fine."

Steele felt the flex of an inner strength strong enough to

force Morgan's murder, Dort's death, and his father's ejection from the family into a box and close it. Then he carefully buried those three horrors in a deep corner of his mind to clear space for a mission. He martialed Molly's rape, and Allie's kidnapping to the forefront of his mind. Now, having forced his distractions into retreat, he redirected his thoughts to calculate a strategy of war just as the Army had trained him to do. He pulled his hands from beneath the table and set them down to rest. He had not yet noticed that his left hand had stopped shaking even if Molly had.

A BABY IN A CRIB

Steele quickly ran down a checklist and asked Molly questions.

"Would he hurt Allie?"

"No. I think in his twisted mind he thinks he actually created something good in the world, or at least he thinks Allie's his property, and he can't let it go."

"Good, that's an edge. Any idea where he went?"

Molly shrugged, but Steele was just going through the motions of asking. He already knew. Leon would go to the place where all the rustlers, moonshiners, killers, and mean men in this territory had gone for a hundred and fifty years —Disappointment Country. That was where Leon's on and off Ute girlfriend had been squatting in a shack near the old Lizzie Knight cabin. They had been occupying it long before Leon killed Morgan last year and kidnapped Allie. *He'll need that Indian woman to care for the baby,* he thought in silence. Since Leon had no other woman that would put up with him other than his woman in the Disappointment, Steele was all but certain he would find Leon there.

From the kitchen table near his cold half-eaten bowl of milk and toast, he looked up and saw a painting of a horse in a meadow with the Lone Cone looming in the background. It was his favorite and Morgan had given it to him as a gift. To the right hung the 1949 Model 721 Remington .270 caliber rifle that Mc Tavish had given him for his first month pay on the job as foreman with Ganiz. Steele stood up and lifted its familiar weight into his hands. *Good balance, and a clothesline trajectory,* he reminded himself.

"How's the roan," he asked Molly?

"She's a bit cranky from not getting enough time on the trail, so she's raring to go."

"Saddle her up Molly; I've got some miles to put in tonight."

He could have just driven down Hwy. 141 with the horse trailer in thirty-five minutes and parked beside the road when he reached the Disappointment. But he didn't want the lights on the truck to announce his arrival in the desolate place where a headlight could be seen for ten miles or more. He also wanted to settle into the horse, and collect his thoughts while riding slow along the old Indian trail. It was twenty-six miles on the path he planned to take. That would put him in Disappointment Country by dawn. Arriving then would give him time to scout the cabin, confirm that Leon and Allie were there, and then figure out a plan to get Leon out in the open.

He opened the breach of the .270, checked it as he always did, and laid it bolt open on the table with one box of cartridges. *One box will do.* Then he unfolded a map of Colorado and put his finger on it. *Disappointment Valley*, said the map, but his father called it Disappointment Country and sometimes, just called it the Disappointment. It was the same place no matter its name.

"How's the mule," he asked?

"Mule's good."

"Fine. Fix her up with the panniers for Allie, and add some formula, a basket, and a bottle."

"What about Leon," she asked?

"Leon won't be needing anything."

Molly knew Steele needed no more encouragement. But with a furrowed brow, she said this for herself. "You get him daddy. You get him good."

At ten o'clock, Steele climbed aboard the roan bathed in the weak light from a solitary forty watt lightbulb screwed into a rusty fixture over the entrance to the barn. Moths flew in frantic circles around the bulb creating flitting shadows on the ground. With the mule in-tow, he smiled at Molly and headed southwest toward the Disappointment at a walk. He looked up to a moonless sky, thankful for starlight. At 6,000 ft. of elevation, the stars were all the light he and the roan needed to see the trail. With the soothing rhythm of the horse's gait interrupted only by occasional snort of vapor from the roan or the mule into the cool night air, he began his calculations. At a walk, the roan would cover the twenty-five miles downhill to the Disappointment in about six hours. That would put them at the abandoned line-rider's shack where Leon was holding the baby between 4 and 5 AM. But Steele still needed a plan to separate Leon from the baby and the woman and get him into the open. He didn't know Leon, but he knew his type. He was a bully. *Bullies are easy,* he thought. *They carry more fears than most men, and they'll do anything not to look weak or scared — another edge.* The next question was exactly how to use that edge.

It was four-thirty in the morning when he came within sight of the shack. He tied the roan behind some of the sparse cover of bushes on the creek bank. The shack lay on the other side of Disappointment Creek near where it forked away from the Dolores River. By starlight, he could see a wisp of white smoke from the chimney. The ground between Steele and the shack was exposed with no cover except for a lone pine standing two hundred yards from the shack on the shack side of the creek. He left the .270 in the scabbard on the roan. Then he checked the clip on the .45 and chambered a cartridge before crossing Disappointment creek which was flowing at low ebb. He paused at the lone pine on the other side. Then he trod carefully in a low crouch across open ground. As he moved slowly toward the cabin, he mused on the sadness of the place. The whole country was called Disappointment, the creek that divided it was called Disappointment, and the river the creek branched from was called Dolores which meant sorrows.

As he got closer, he slowed down, and carefully scanned the ground for anything that might snap with a misplaced step. As a boy, he preferred playing Indians over cowboys and practiced gliding across the ground without making a sound. Once his drunken father saw him playing Indian and beat him for it. *I bet Leon Posey was a draft-dodging, boot clomping, spur ringing cowboy. And you would have preferred him to me*? he asked the ghost of his father.

As he got within twenty feet of the shack, he became a slow-moving statue. Even if Leon might have looked right at him in the dim starlight, his glacial movement would not have given him away. Twenty minutes after he crossed the creek and the lone pine now two hundred yards behind him, he was crouched under a window with his pistol drawn. Steele removed his hat and raised his head just high enough to peer through the vintage wavy glass pane into the one-room shack. By the flickering firelight, he could see Leon in bed lying on his side with his woman at his back, her arm hung over his waist. She was against the wall. A Winchester Model 94 lay within arm's reach of Leon. He squinted to see if it had a scope. *No*. Near the fireplace was a wooden rocking crib. When a flicker of light lit the baby's forehead, Steele smiled, lowered his head from the window, put on his hat, and moved away carefully again to avoid stepping on anything that would make noise. What he observed through the glass clinched his final plan.

Recent advertisements for the retro Winchester Model 94 ran through Steel's head — "the gun that won the west," it said. It appealed to men who smoked Marlboros and wanted to look tough or look like 19th-century cowboys sporting thick cowboy mustaches. But the lever-action that harkened back to tough cowboy days of shooting Indians was designed to eject spent cartridges out the top where a scope would have to be mounted. Few 94 owners bothered with a scope that was hindered by its design. Besides, you never saw a cowboy hoisting a 94 with a scope out of their horse-mounted scabbard. It just didn't look tough and Leon was all about tough. It gave Steele one more big edge because his .270 had a Redfield 3X9 scope, the scope of choice in Vietnam for snipers.

Steele figured Leon to be a late riser because of his late hours at Badwater Bar. So, part of Steele's plan was to roust him out of bed early without enough sleep. As he returned to the roan and the mule munching on grass beside the creek, he pulled the .270 out of its sheath and detected the first bluish glow of the sun rising over the Uncompaghre Plateau. He ambled across the creek again to the lone pine on the other side and clicked the safety to off with a round already in the chamber ready to fire. Then he waited for the first shafts of bright morning light to hit the front door and windows that Leon would have to peer through with the sun in his face. When that moment arrived, he pointed the rifle at a granite rock about a foot wide and ten feet left of the shack, lined it up in the crosshairs of the scope, and squeezed the trigger. The rock exploded into white dust and the bullet ricochet with the signature sound of a deflected round.

The .270 is louder than most rifles, and it awakened all occupants of the valley within three miles in an instant. A startled Leon hastily grabbed for his 94 Winchester and knocked it to the ground. Frantically wiping sleep from his eyes, he stumbled buck naked to the side of a window to see who was doing the shooting. Squinting into the morning sun, he saw nothing but open ground and the lone pine. He yelled without opening the door.

"Hey, you damn jackass. There's people over here."

Before Leon got to "here," Steele squeezed off another

round into the air while staying hidden behind the pine.

“Shit you idiot, you wanna get shot. I’ll shoot you if...”

Boom went the .270 again as it tore through the valley at supersonic speed. Still ranting under his breath, Leon jerked on some pants without underwear, boots without socks, an unbuttoned shirt, and grabbed the 94 off the floor. Since he could not remember if he had left a bullet chambered, he cocked it just like John Wayne always cocked his before shooting an Indian and wasted an unspent bullet that went clattering across the raw wooden floor. He was armed, ready, and pissed. He peeked out the window again and now saw a figure standing two hundred yards away next to the lone pine and holding a rifle pointing straight up to the sky.

"What the?"

Leon threw open the door and yelled at the distant figure next to the tree.

"You wanna die, mister," he said while lining up Steele in his sights with the bright sun in his eyes?

“I heard you raped a woman, stole her baby, murdered her husband, and had your daddy get you out of jail,” yelled a distant Steele.

“I did my time,” hollered Leon.

“Not enough,” snapped Steele. “What kind of man does that? I’ll tell you, he ain’t no man at all. He’s got no huevos, no brains, and probably can’t shoot.”

Predictably enraged, Leon jerked the trigger and shot five feet over and to the right of Steele. Steele leveled his weapon at a deliberate pace and leaned against the tree for support as Leon re-cocked and fired off another wild round.

He was starting to re-cock for a third shot when the .270 round tore through his right knee and knocked him to the dirt. Steele calmly reloaded four cartridges into the magazine and chambered another round.

Sounding surprised. "You shot me you bastard," as he groveled for his rifle lying in the dust.

Leon struggled to get back up and leaned on his rifle for support. After standing, he raised the 94 and pulled the trigger, and he heard nothing because he had forgotten to re cock after his last shot. Just as he looked down at the rifle to cock it, another round went through his left knee and he dropped to the ground landing on his splintered joints. As he screamed in pain from the second shot, his rifle flew out of his hands and clattered in the dust after falling five feet away and outside of his reach. He looked up to see Steele coming inexorably closer with his rifle trained on Leon's heart. Soon Leon was shaded by Steele's shadow; Leon's woman was standing in the doorway with both hands over her mouth.

"Knees feeling a little bit like Morgan's right now Leon? You killed a good man, and you raped a good woman. Your left knee there, that was for Morgan. Your right knee, that was for Allie. And this is for raping Molly."

He pulled the chambered .45 out of his belt, clicked off the safety, pulled back the hammer, and aimed it right at Leon's head.

"Please, please, please don't kill me," he blubbered with a stream of mucus dripping from his nose and down his chin as he raised his arms in supplication and to block the sun-glare forming a brilliant halo behind Steele's head.

"Please."

"You had your chance to be a man for what you did to Morgan, and fess up for what you did to Molly, but you got your daddy to get you off. You're no man Leon; you're a fake cowboy who can't shoot. Out here a man that can't shoot doesn't count for much no matter how many women they rape or how many men they bully or kill. Hell, even Morgan could shoot."

Leon hung his head low while swinging it back and forth. A thick drool hung from his chin and blew side to side in a light breeze. He wondered if he would feel the bullet burrowing through his brain.

"I told you why I shot your knees to hell. This one's for raping my daughter."

Steele held out his .45 straight arm without a bend in his elbow and pressed it against Leon's head. But as he held it, his arm began to shake, just as it had when he saw Dort's face after it was deformed by a bullet to the top of his head. With that awful image in mind, he lowered the pistol away from Leon's skull. It was pointing at the ground when Leon's visage grew into a mocking smile. Steele saw the look, lifted his pistol arm from the ground, and fired three bullets into his groin just missing his femoral artery. Steele grabbed Leon by his long greasy black hair, pulled his head up, and leaned down to speak in his ear in a deliberate low tone. Leon cupped his crotch with his hands in disbelief that the bullets had ripped away most of his penis and both testicles.

"I can't fuck no more," he repeated in shock and surprise thinking Steele might care.

"I want you to listen real careful. Dumb as you are, this will be easy. Last I heard, kidnappers, get twenty-four years in this state, and I doubt your daddy will want to intervene once he learns you're also a rapist—a murderer maybe, but not a rapist. Either way, I expect you to be gone from Colorado tomorrow, with or without your woman. And if I ever see you again, you won't just be a cripple, you'll be dead no matter what you tell your daddy. You leave and never come back! Never!"

Steele turned away from Leon and looked up at the woman.

"You hear that? Never."

She nodded, her hands still over her mouth, and her eyes

filled with fear. Steele saw the back end of a rusty red truck sticking out from behind the shack.

"That yours," he asked the woman?

She nodded.

"Then load him up and get him the hell out of here. When you get to a doctor in the next state, tell him it was a hunting accident. Then he looked at Posey as he went on with what to tell the doctor. Tell him somebody mistook him for a doe."

Steele went into the line shack and swaddled a still sleeping Allie. Then he picked her up gently, crossed the creek, walked her back to the mule, and placed her into the canvas pannier. Then, with Allie sleeping to the rhythm of the mule's careful steps, they slowly rode the Ute trail back to Molly at the ranch.

THE DEATH OF GANIZ

Ganiz had stopped herding sheep long before Steele retreated again to the mountain to deal with the perpetual demons that still swirled in his head. The burst of strength Steele felt after he rescued Allie from Posey did not last six months. His nightmarish dreams returned when Allie was still a baby and those dreams had become a steady stream of terrors he could not escape. Whiskey never cured it, but it softened the sharpness of his pain, and he preferred to be alone in the rustler's cabin on the mountain where Molly and Allie did not have to see him drunk like his besotted father Leon Steele always was. He had no desire to inflict those same scars on them. So, he mostly stayed at the cabin but talked every day with them on his CB radio sprinkled with occasional visits. Over the hard years that followed, Allie went from a baby, to preteen, to a teenager. She and her mother would come up dutifully in Mc Tavish once a week to deliver a home cooked meal and to check on him. On those days, he honored them by staying sober even though they all knew he would be drunk on every other day. Still, he was encouraged by his once a week sobriety. He started to believe that maybe he could be sober for two days a week instead of just one or maybe even three. That would free him to visit the girls while sober more often. But to do that, he would need a horse. The old roan back at the ranch was now too old, and was little more than a pet for Allie. And that was when he started thinking about the wild herds down below in the Desolation.

Ganiz had his own wounds from the old country, but he dealt with his terrors differently. He rarely drank, but when he did, he drank until he could not stand up. In his stupor, he sang sad songs in Basque from the seat of his rocker on the cabin porch. Once or twice a month, the girls would hear him belting out songs into the pasture as if someone were out there to hear him. Along with his singing was his accordion which he played well.

Why he only sang his songs in Basque he did not know. Years before he met Steele at the Mc Tavish Ranch, he had learned most of his songs in English. That was during his first years in America when he cared that he was understood by Americans. Later he did not care and spoke only to his sheep during the long summer season on the mountain herding his sheep. Yet sometimes, when he had drunk too much, he still sang in English—but only when the ranch house was empty. After each song, he cried.

> "Be quiet, Maria
> Didn't you see my wink?
> When you drink, your eyes wink with mischief
> Shamelessly—so shamelessly
> I could drink you with no problem
> From that full glass"

And each time Ganiz sang that song, he drank to his Maria.

Old Ganiz had been ready to give up herding for a long time. The horror that had ripped out his heart when his family was murdered in the Spanish Civil War had never eased. Now, without work to distract him, he reminisced endlessly on his past, not that differently than Steele when he replayed his tragedies—what had been lost, what might have been, but wasn't. One day on the cusp of winter, Ganiz rocked his chair steadily on the porch of the cabin next to the house. As he mused on his life, the rockers made a lonely rumbling sound punctuated by nocks and squeaks as they rolled over the uneven gaps in the porch planks. Deep in thought as he rolled forward and back, he was deaf to those sounds. His focus was elsewhere.

His eyes were fixed on the heavens as flighty snow clouds whirled about the peaks off to the east. His new Kangal Shepherd Arrate had now old. Asaseno and Arazoak had died many years before. Sixteen year old Arrate now lay curled beside the rocker. If Arrate had already died, it would have been his last dog. He would not have gotten another. He had outlived all his canine friends that came before and only Arrate was left. But instead of outlasting Arrate, he knew his last dog was about to outlast him.

God makes it hard to know when a man will die. Should a man get another dog even when he is old? What then will happen to the poor beast if his master dies before him? It is a great responsibility to have a dog. And a man should not get one when he is old. Maybe I waited too long to get you Arrate? What do you think? Do you forgive me? But then, when is a man old? Was I too old when we came together? What man believes his age unless he is in front of a mirror that cannot lie? And even then, some men do not believe their reflection. But I admit, I have seen an old man looking back from the glass, and he is me. Though it does no good to wish for what is not, it would be good if the dog and the man could die together. Perhaps god will correct this error. It is unfair that god puts this burden on men at the end of their days. I worry. Who will take care of you Arrate? Allie maybe? Molly? Too bad Steele will not be up to it. He is good with dogs. Always was. Poor man. I hope he is better someday, but he is running out of time too. He was a good friend.

Ganiz checked his watch as the afternoon sun began to

set. *Thirty five minutes until the rural bus stops in downtown Nucla.* He eased out of his chair and stepped toward the Ute trail that would take him to town. As he passed the ranch house, he saw the living behind the windowpanes. Warm yellow light painted the faces of Molly and Allie as they chatted across the kitchen table over hot chocolate. The heat of a log burning in the living room fireplace spread to the kitchen where the girls rested their elbows on a red and white checkered tablecloth. The house looked soft and feminine even as the air outside was hard and cold. It was the dead season. More snow was coming. As Ganiz walked down the trail to town, he heard the smooth sound of yesterday's fresh snow slithering under his boots. *Strange how new snow slithers, middle aged snow squeaks, and old snow crunches.*

As he boarded the bus, he noticed it was full of Basques. Lambing season was in full swing and employment and pay were running high. Men decades younger than him were barking his language. Their day's work was done, and they were eager to get to their favorite bars where they drank too much beer and talked of the homeland late into the night. Ganiz felt odd. He was of these people, but not of their generation—theirs was another world. *Someday, your world will go away too,* he counseled. It was fifty miles to Naturita by bus, then a walk to Mc Tavish's old Ranch where Ganiz had spent most of his working life. He was glad to exit the bus and the ribald chatter of younger Basques behind.

Ganiz was about to take his last walk. He had lived long —longer than most of the billions and billions who had lived and died before him. *It is true,* he thought as if thinking it for the first time. *Life ends,* he mused as he stood at the sharp edge of time. *But it is different here at the precipice—even if it is the same.*

From Naturita, he walked to the former ranch of Mc

Tavish. His old sign had been taken down by the new owner and cast aside. The new sign said "International Land and Development Co. Inc." *It should have said something about Mc Tavish and his ranch,* he thought. *These people have forgotten how to remember.*

A "no trespassing" sign with two bullet holes in it swung from a chain that spanned two metal poles set in concrete on either side of the entrance. It was padlocked. The poles were painted red which underscored the intimidating words on the sign. It warned vehicles, hunters, and hikers to stay out of what used to be The Mc Tavish Sheep Ranch.

Ganiz was unmoved by the message and lifted the heavy sagging chain and groaned as he bent over far enough to get under it. Once in the pasture, Ganiz looked up into the last of the fading light to find the path leading west to the wild upper pastures on the Lone Cone. This was the path he had taken with Steele more than forty years before. And this was the trail that he had travelled with his herd of sheep, his dogs, and thoughts of his family. Though he wore a wool coat, the cold bit his bare face telling him that the night would be cold. Not crisp—cold.

The old man trudged forward leaning on his stick with one hand, and clenching the collar of his coat tight against his neck with the other. As he trode further up the sheep path cut through tall trees, he saw silhouettes of pines on the horizon backlit by the dimming glow ahead. Soon, the only light left was starlight. It painted the snowy pathway with an icy incandescence that guided him through the black forest to the high country. Though he wore muffs over his ears, he could still hear his feet squeaking through the snow. The sound of each lonely step confirmed his solitary presence on the mountain.

Soon he came to one of the fake camps the Basques of yore used to mask their real camping location from hostile cattlemen. It was the place that Steele had asked about years before and where Ganiz had scared him with his stories of armed cowboys shooting sheepmen from the cover of the surrounding forest. Though the hour was getting late, Ganiz paused only for a moment to reflect. Then he moved on. He had another destination.

Sometime after midnight, Ganiz came to a grove of aspens. His chest was heaving as he struggled for air at the higher altitude and from the stress of the ten mile walk uphill in snow. Stars littered the sky like glittery embers from a campfire. He leaned on his stick and felt mortal as his breath rose into his face and steamed into his watering eyes. When his breathing finally settled down, he pulled out his flashlight and shined it into the stand of chalky white aspens growing out of the frosty white snow. The light revealed a cemetery of Basque images carved into bark. Then, after a solemn pause, he began to chant an incantation to his family.

"Ahh. Amala," he moaned for his wife.
"Ahh. Ander," he moaned for his son.

"Ahh. Nerea," he moaned for his daughter.

"Ahh. Ganiz," he moaned for himself.

Ganiz fell to his hands and knees and cried above the snow until he could cry no more and his hands were frozen. Then he sat and warmed his fingers in his coat pockets. There, he had a dream. It was of a stone house high in the Pyrenees with the sounds of his chattery wife and children wafting out an open window with a lace curtain blowing back and forth on a fresh breeze. He sat outside on a whitewashed step drinking in the familial sounds on a budding spring day surrounded by wildflowers, fresh green grass, and the bleating of sheep. A rivulet of melted snow water gurgled a few feet away as it danced down the mountain. He felt blessed.

They didn't find him for several days. He had told an unsuspecting Allie he was going to go and see his family.

"In the Pyrenees?"

"No. In another place. The place where we all go."

"Where is that?"

Ganiz was not a religious man. But with his hand on Allie's shoulder, he pointed to the sky with his stick. Allie thought he meant heaven. But what he really meant was that he would join the universe as dust just like his wife and children before him. Becoming lifeless motes after living a sentient life had a cheerlessness to it. Yet, there was also a truth to it, and in that truth was its own kind of comfort, bleak as it was.

"You know how sparks and cinders rise and swirl above a campfire?" he asked.

"Yes. They're pretty."

"Those are the souls of those who came before us," he said.

"Oh."

Days later, young Allie repeated to Molly what Ganiz had told her and asked her what he meant? Molly did not explain, but she knew immediately where they would find Ganiz. After her call, Search and Rescue found him frozen to death high on the Lone Cone right where Molly knew he would be. Fresh snow rested on his cap and eyelashes as he sat propped up against a leafless tree trunk. Carved into the white bark of the aspen just above his head was the image of a handsome woman named Amala with two small children and a date—1936.

MAVERICK

The week before Ganiz died, Steele was back at the ranch on a rare visit watching Allie bouncing in the saddle as she rode the grey roan in circles around the corral. Lately, Allie had become fixed on learning to ride. So, Steele began to come down the mountain to the ranch for her lessons. But he had to rely on Molly for transportation with the truck. And though Molly never complained, the trip to and from the cabin was a long one over a rough dirt road. That said, Steele was pleased to be doing something constructive for a change. His more frequent visits to the ranch pressured him to stay sober, at least during the lessons with Allie. Molly liked that. But though he smiled and seemed steady as he taught Allie how to ride, he was always anxious to get back to the cabin where he could self-medicate again on his own terms without witnesses.

On this day, Steele watched with grandfatherly pride as Allie squealed with joy while trotting the old mare around the pasture near the Ganiz' cabin. Ganiz was still among the living and sat in his rocker on the porch watching it all. First, he smiled at Steele and then he smiled at Allie who had a joyful look on her face as well. Steele knew where this was leading. He would need another horse at his cabin on the mountain. Molly could not transport him back and forth on his whim. And even if the roan had the heart, she didn't have the legs to make such a long trip to or from the mountain. Besides, day by day, the roan was becoming Allie's, not Steele's.

The idea of rustling a wild horse had always appealed to Steele. It was an entry on his to-do in life list. He wondered what was so exciting about it and where the feeling came from. *It's illegal you old fool. Yeah, but the government is going to cull the herd anyway. Why not just take one and save them the trouble?* He couldn't blame his obsession with rustling on his rebellious nature. He had never been rebellious in his life. Irreverent, stubborn, insubordinate maybe, but not *obstreperous,* a word he had learned in correspondence school for college. *No, it's something deeper. Maybe because it's fitting—me living in the Rustler's cabin, after all.* In the end he decided that he just wanted to do it. It didn't need an explanation.

Steele knew from riding the line and working with cowboys that there were three ways to capture wild horses. The first one required a skill he did not have—roping. While he had been around cattle for a time as a line-rider, he was no cowboy. Besides, roping was the most dangerous method of capturing a wild horse. Once a horse is roped, it thinks it's about to die so it does everything it can to escape. That means using teeth, hooves, and body to attack the predator at the other end of the rope. *Not my style,* thought Steele.

The second way was to build a large corral and funnel the horses into it by building a chute. Chutes are fences that are wide at one end, then narrow when it gets to the corral. The mustangs can be driven in from the wide end and then they be forced through the narrow end and then trapped in the corral when the gate is closed behind them. *Too much work building a corral, chute, and gate for just one man*, thought Steele.

The third way was to construct a water trap. *That's it,* he thought. Early in the morning, Steele rode the roan down the Ute trail to the Desolation to scout for a water trap. He knew what he was looking for. A small source of water in a dry area that could only be reached through a narrow canyon with steep sides. From his line riding days, he knew of just such a place. He had once chased a calf into that canyon that had escaped from a section of fence when was riding line. He remembered seeing unshod hoof prints in the same area which meant that wild horses frequented the water source.

By noon he had found his canyon and went to work building a crude gate to shut the door on his quarry. Once a small group of mustangs had gone past his gate seeking water, he would close it trapping the horses inside. It was high noon in the middle of summer when he finished building his crude gate which was a lattice of local wood and branches. *That was the easy part*. Now he had to wait.

Steele made camp downwind of the trap on a small rise where he could observe any movement by the wild herd below. He erected a low profile tent for shade and was prepared to wait for days. Horse-flies bit at his neck drawing blood as he sat in the sun. The blood mixed with sweat trickling down his back and soaked into his shirt. Soon he was passing the time with his bottle of whiskey which rarely left his side. After sunset, he fell over drunk in the tent, passed out, and slept until nightfall. Like his bottle, his dreams were never far away. Soon he imagined he was flying over a battlefield in Vietnam, running from his drunken father, pleading with Dr. Cohen, sponging Morgan's blood off the wooden floor of the Badwater, and then being chased by rustlers.

He scrunched into a fetal position as ten riders came up behind him at a gallop. His horse was old and slow and seemed to be stepping into molasses. But the riders behind him were relentless and undeterred by the sweet sticky goo. Their horses were chomping on his horse's tail when he woke with a wide eyed start. Then he realized it wasn't rustlers. It was the low rumble of the wild herd coming up the grade for water.

Steele climbed stealthily down the knoll toward the entrance of the water trap. A dozen of the herd had already gone in for water and passed his gate. The rest were grazing lazily nearby under a moonless sky. A breeze was blowing into his face keeping his scent hidden from the herd. Steele crept up a shallow gully to stay out of sight as he made his way to the gate. Quietly as possible, he dragged the gate shut behind the dozen or so horses that had passed through into the canyon and secured it as best he could with rope against the canyon wall. Now came the hard part.

Steele chose the water trap because he had no skill with a rope lasso where he might single out a horse from the herd. But he only wanted one horse, and he had trapped a dozen. His dilemma now was how to single one horse out of twelve without a rope. Steele had thought it through even though he had no idea if it would work. His plan was to release eleven, and keep one. *Easy.* Steele stepped into the canyon but stayed close to the gate and waited for the horses to come trotting back from drinking water from the spring and rejoin the herd. It didn't take long. When the twelve mustangs saw Steele and the gate blocking their path, their instinct was to run—but run where?

The sides of the canyon were too steep on all sides to climb. The only escape was the entrance which was closed by Steele's gate so they began to mill in confusion while snorting, neighing, and pawing at the ground. Steele did his best to isolate one or two of the horses from the circling band. Three mustangs decided to rush the gate while the others held back in fear of Steele. As the three ran towards him, Steele opened the gate just wide enough to let them by, then jumped forward waving his hands to keep the others back. Using that method, he soon whittled the numbers down to just two horses behind the gate. One was a fierce stallion, and the other was a small mare. Steele decided to gamble. He gave the Stallion room enough to get close to the gate while keeping the mare at bay. Sliding along the rocky wall of the canyon with his back to it as he moved toward the gate, the stallion was snorting aggressively fifteen feet away. Suddenly, the horse reared and threatened with his hooves. Steele then lunged for the gate and threw off the rope that held it shut it giving the stallion a way out of the trap. The stallion did not wait for it to fully open. He charged at Steele then crashed into the gate bashing it open with his shoulder and nearly breaking it.

When the wild mare saw the Stallion running free toward the herd she dug in her heels and galloped toward the gate in hopes of following the Stallion. But Steele blocked her path by waving his arms and then lashed the gate shut before she could escape. Having secured the wild mare, Steele fetched his roan and his tent from the knoll. Then he opened the gate and went in. After closing the gate behind him, he pitched the tent near the entrance but inside the canyon and hobbled his roan next to it. That was the first night the wild mare had slept near a human. But it would not be her last.

The next morning, Steele wrestled the flimsy gate from the entrance and dragged it ever deeper into the canyon closer to the water source and the Mustang. The wild horse kept her distance as Steele moved the gate toward her, and she was forced to back up. She watched Steele with a wary eye as he reduced her space inch by inch. After an hour of manhandling the gate, Steele managed to shrink the space into a small corral. It wasn't round; it was square. The canyon formed three sides of the enclosure and the gate the fourth. Now the horse had no choice but to be close to the human that shared her limited space.

Steele had watched his pop gentle a new horse when he

was eight years old. Pop took a position in the center of a corral and lowered his head to take a non-threatening pose. He had told Steele before he went into the corral that wild horses have three responses to a threat. Charge and attack, stay still, or run. This horse ran. But because the mare was trapped in the corral, it could only run in circles around him in her effort to escape. Steele watched his father in the center of the corral as the horse went round and round.

After an hour of this, his pop gently stepped into the path of the circling horse forcing it to go around in the opposite direction saying "Whoa, Whoa," in a gentle voice. Once it reversed his course, his pop went back into the center of the corral and took the non-threatening pose again.

This he did several times until all he had to do was take a step and the horse would reverse course. And in so doing, it was unwittingly submitting to his Pop's control. Finally, his father forced the horse to make eye contact by blocking its path completely, again saying "Whoa, Whoa." Once it gave in to that and allowed an eye to eye connection, the horse was on its way to being gentled. But the final step for its first day of training was to wait for the horse to risk venturing forth to explore the human in its midst.

When that happened, the horse was ready to be touched by his father, and it was the signal for him to begin rubbing and massaging her flank. His father explained that the massaging of the horse's coat was meant to mimic the tongue grooming it had received as a colt from its mother. All during the rubbing, Steele could hear his father saying that soothing word: "Whoa, Whoa, Whoa." From there, the horse was soon ready to tolerate a loose halter, a saddle blanket, and a light saddle. Steele learned his father's lesson well. Soon the little mare was gentled enough to bring her back to the ranch.

ALLIE GROWS UP

Allie was part Molly, part Steele, and part Steele's mother Ginny. Steel thought it was peculiar some traits get passed along directly from parent to children and others seem to skip a generation? Allie's grandmother Marija could be seen in her sleek figure, and her penchant for things that went fast. So far, that trait had been limited to galloping a horse at breakneck speeds down Indian trails strewn with rocks. Steele was relieved that there seemed to be no trace of Leon Posey in her either except for her smoking.

For her part, Allie saw Steele as a blend between a grandfather and father. The honorific "Pop" worked for both his roles. And to her, Ganiz had been a warm but distant old man from another time and another place. She thought he was like a lonely old dog that might have curled up on somebody's porch and was allowed to stay. Yet, she loved his stories. He rarely spoke, but when he did, it was about the Pyrenees. Allie imagined them to be a happy mountainous place filled with sheep, families living in stone houses, and snow. He never told her of the murder of his wife and children. He knew it would destroy the happy version of the place that Allie loved to hear him speak of and that he preferred talk of as well. He was content that his family tragedy was a secret that only Molly and Steele knew.

Soon after Steele was diagnosed with meningioma cancer, Allie and Molly had performed their intervention by fetching him from the rustler's cabin high on the mountain. They knew he wouldn't want to come down. But their argument finally won the day, and he relented. Once back at the ranch, they both knew that he would want to stay in the cabin in the pasture—not the main house. He had reasons for that. He still drank too much and though they all knew it, he didn't want them to see it. And he didn't want to be a spectacle as he slowly wasted away from the disease either. He had always preferred the cabin in the pasture to live in anyway. It was as if he thought he didn't belong in a real house. *No, that's not it,* Molly thought. *It's as if he thought he didn't deserve a house.*

As for Steele, he tried, but had never been able to explain his strange relationship with the cabins in his life. Maybe they were just the only places where he felt safe. After Ganiz passed, Allie moved into the cabin even though his dog Arrate still slept on the porch next to Ganiz's rocking chair. She and her mother had been bumping heads over her smoking inside the main house. The cabin seemed like a good way to get her nasty habit out of the family abode and resolve the conflict, at least until Steele came home. Then it would be his again.

Now, with Steele back at the ranch and needing the cabin for himself, Allie would move back to the house. She and her mother worked out a compromise on her smoking. Molly would allow Allie to smoke in the main house but only if she sat by an open window with a fan blowing the smoke outside. Molly never liked tobacco smoke and still remembered the smell of it on Leon's breath when he shoved his tongue down her throat on the pool table. She often wondered what would have happened had she bitten it off when she had the chance. She only hesitated because she knew he probably would have killed her if she had. When Leon killed Morgan shortly after raping her, it only confirmed her fear. She saw how Leon pleasured himself in the pain he inflicted on others.

Allie perceived Molly as her no-nonsense mother and plain talking friend. There was also a strange part to their bond as well. Just as Molly had never known her mother, Allie had never known her father. Hidden from most people, including Steele, was the fact that Allie had two mothers—Molly and her lover Emily. But unlike Mother Molly, Mother Emily was soft, doting, and indulgent. Steele was more like Emily than Molly except when the family faced a threat. Then he was decisive and deadly.

But it was Emily she went to when she was hurt and needed solace. It was Molly she went to when she needed hard advice. And that was why she chose Molly to announce that she wanted to find the man that fathered her and stare him in the face before he died of pancreatic cancer in a hospice in Phoenix. It was also one of the reasons Molly and Allie had driven up the mountain together to fetch Steele. Molly, with Allie's help, aimed to persuade Steele to come home and deal with his cancer there. But Allie also wanted to let Steele know that she was hell-bent on facing Leon, but not do it behind the back of the man who had raised her. And if she were able to talk him off the mountain, she hoped he would go with her to see Leon and keep her safe when she did it. And there was no better man than Steele to keep her safe.

PART II: IN MY END IS MY BEGINNING.

WAKING UP AT THE RANCH

On his third day back after being fetched from the mountain cabin, Steele again awoke in a soft bed after another long night of hard dreams. They seemed to have spanned his whole life—from his father's horse trading days, to the horse in the house, riding line, Vietnam—all of it. But he was also confused. *Last I remember, I was drinking a toast to Ganiz sitting on his rocking chair on the porch out in the pasture. Damn it was cold out there.*

In his groggy half-awake state following his dream, he felt the lingering presence of his father who had appeared early in the night somewhere out in the dark. In that dream, his father's voice had been kind, and Steele now awoke with a sense of missing him or at least missing the man who had appeared in the dream. As he wakened further, Steele finally recalled how he had gotten from the cabin porch to the main abode. Molly had helped him walk from Ganiz's old rocking chair out in the cold over to the ranch house.

Once inside, Molly and Allie had put him in the bedroom he had shared with Marija years before and covered him with blankets to warm his chilled body. He had not slept in the room since Marija died in the hospital after giving birth to Molly forty-one years ago.

As the sun rose, he held up his hands to the morning light coming through a lace curtain. He noticed his right hand had stopped shaking and, for no particular reason, a peace had come over him. He wondered if it had anything to do with his dreams. *Or maybe it's because it was our room long-long ago Marija? No. Probably not that.*

Despite his usual headache, he yawned lazily and allowed himself a morning stretch. That done, he threw one leg over the side of the bed and hurled it toward the floor. As usual, he used the inertia of his falling leg to pull his torso up to a sitting position. Then, after getting his other foot down to the floor, he stayed sitting for a moment and waited for the dizziness caused by being upright to stop and the headache to diminish. That was when Allie passed his open door as she shuffled toward the kitchen. The smell of Molly's first batch of morning coffee was already wafting down the hallway.

"Morning Pop," offered a cheerful Allie, happy to see him in the house but eager to get to her coffee.

"You know it's my birthday?"
"Yeah Pop. You're 68," she answered and then shuffled on.

Steele arose to splash cold water on his face in the bathroom sink. Then he dampened his cottony white hair with another splash to mash the wayward wisps flat against his balding head. Then, with one more swoosh of water over his face and his long white beard, he was ready for coffee and dripped water from his face and hair all the way to the kitchen.

Molly was already sitting at the table with her glasses tilted over her nose reading the morning paper. Allie had just finishing pouring her cup.

"Straight up, eh Allie," observed Steele.

"Yup."

Steele poured his and sat down with the girls.

"Been out in the rain Pop?" teased Molly.

"No, I uh..."

"Hey Pop," queried Allie. "Ever considered having your DNA tested?"

Damn these young people talk fast. "Nope."

"It'd help me."

"How's that."

"You have cancer. I researched the kind you have. Sometimes it's hereditary—depends on the gene. It'd be good if I knew if I carry the same gene."

"Yes, and it would also tell you if I'm the source of the Indian blood in the family."

"Yeah. That too Pop. I'd like it better if it came it came through you—not Posey," she said matter of factly.

"Me too," answered Steele. "And speaking of Posey, it would also help if we could get him tested. I may be your grandpa, but Posey is your bio dad, and he's got his own kind of cancer you need to know about. Tell you what. Why don't Molly and I both get tested? That'll answer all the questions about our DNA. Then we'll ask Posey. Maybe this late in his life he's less of an ass even though I doubt that. *Naw, he'll always be an ass.* With all three of our DNA results in one place, we can compare you to me, to Posey, and to your mother. Then we'll know if the Indian came from my side, Marija's side, Posey's side, or Molly's milkman."

Molly's eyes were still filled with sleep, but they shot daggers over her cup of coffee toward Steele. "Not the milkman Pop—not Morgan either. I've only been with one man in my life, and that wasn't my choice.

There seemed to be a subtle admission in Molly's words that forced a sudden silence. No one spoke for almost a minute until Steel changed the subject. "I see a road trip for the three of us coming up soon."

"Oh goodie," said Allie squirming with teenage excitement at the prospect. "Arizona?

"Yeah. We'll all go to Phoenix first to see Posey. Then I'll go on alone to Black Canyon where my Pop was last sighted."

"When," needled Allie?

"Before the snow sets in hard."

"That's next month."

"That's right." We'll go in November," confirmed Steele.

And with that, Allie left the table, went to her desk, opened the window above her computer, lit a Marlborough cigarette, turned on the fan and went online to order three DNA tests. One for Steele, one for Molly, and one for Posey.

"So, when will the cabin be ready," asked Steele sensing a lull?

"You mean the bungalow, retorted Molly?
"No, I mean the cabin in the pasture that you prefer I call the bungalow."

Molly responded curtly. "Clean sheets going on later this morning. It's all yours after that."

"I haven't been around this much estrogen for a long time. I'll have to get used to it."

"Geez Pop. It's only been three days that you've been in the house. And by the way, you look the better for it. Maybe you could use a little more estrogen!"

"You might be right. I am feeling better now that you mention it," he conceded, remembering the calmness in his hand. "Sorry."

Changing the subject, Molly asked: "You really think Posey will take the test?"

"We don't even know if he'll see us yet," offered Steele. "Allie is taking care of that. But if he does, remember he smokes. All we need is one of his cigarette butts or even a cup he drank from."

"Have you considered that Posey does not want to see you or Mom," shouted Allie still sitting at her computer in the living room?

"I think that's pretty likely. I never heard of a rapist that was anxious to face their victim, and I'm the one that took his manhood and his legs, so I doubt he'd want to see me in his condition—crippled, sick, and defenseless. You—that's another story. He wanted you once—meant to take you away. But one thing is for sure, you're not going to see him alone."

"Found something else Pop," shouted Allie over the noise of the fan. Her face was ghostly blue from the glow of her monitor as her cigarette smoke blew out the open window.

"I hope it's good news this time," Steele shouted back.

"No, it's more of a question," she answered in a tone that was quizzical and guarded at the same time. "You know how you said that Morgan was killed—a blow to the top of his head with a cue stick?

"Yeah. You want to hear that story again?"

"No. But it says here he died of a severe concussion and asphyxia after he was hit in the face. Says Posey hit him with his fist and then hit him in the throat with a cue stick. Morgan choked to death.

"Who says?"

"The Montrose Daily Press. I got from my genealogy website. The article is titled 'Coroner Report on Nucla Incident."

"Well, it's wrong—Dead wrong," he said with a tinge of defensive anger. Then he remembered what Dr. Cohen had asked him long ago after Dort had been killed. Soon Steele had his thumbs and index finger pressed so tight under the table that they turned a bloodless white.

POTIČA

After being back at the ranch from the getaway cabin for two weeks, Steele was sure he had figured out the so-called secret that Emily and Molly were lovers. Now he was starting to get impatient with Molly to get the announcement over with, so they didn't all have to dance around the issue. It wasn't exactly hidden. After all, he had interrupted them kissing in the barn when they were just girls. Sure, they said they were practicing for boys. And Steele believed it then. But there were other things that were not hard to notice.

First was her odd marriage to Morgan. Steele liked Morgan, but it was obvious that he was an asexual man and maybe even homosexual. And Molly never showed interest in dating men even though many men had pursued her before and even after she married Morgan. And then there was the strange fact that Emily made weekly deliveries of bread to the ranch even though a sign in her bakery window sign said "Sorry, We Don't Deliver."

Beyond that, there was that time he saw Molly walking with Emily along the Ute trail behind the cabin in the pasture. It wasn't just that they were holding hands. They were swinging their hands together with abandon and there was a joy in their walk and on their faces. And if that was not enough, Allie blurted it out in plain language when he asked who the grown woman at the door delivering the bread was. "It's her lover Emily pop," she had said.

"Emily is her lover," he had asked Allie incredulously?

"Uh huh. But nobody is supposed to know."

Steele decided that if Molly wasn't going to reveal herself, it was time to do something about it. So, he got in Mc Tavish and drove to the Columbine Bakery in downtown Nucla. Before he left, he pulled some papers from a file he kept on Marija and put them in his coat pocket. Winter seemed to be peeking around the corner and the fluffy down coat felt warm.

As he pulled up alongside the bakery on Sixth and Main, he noticed that most of the outdoor tables were empty. *Maybe the cool weather,* he thought. When he pushed on the door, it protested with a metal on metal screech. The aluminum door frame was slightly bent and scraped the metal door as it opened and closed. Along with the metallic screech, a large bell tied to the door handle with a red-ribbon jangled and announced Steele's entrance. The room smelled delicious to a man like Steele who thought sugared toast drowned in warm milk was food from the gods. He paused just inside as the door shut behind him with another screech and took in the sweet smell of baked yeast, butter, and gluten before sauntering over to the counter where a girl with short cut black hair stood behind the counter and smiled. A small vase holding some Columbine flowers was next to a jar filled with tips.

"Hello Emily."

"Hello Mr. Steele. You're back from the mountain I see."

"Yup. Over a week now. Say, where do you get Columbines this late in the season?"

"Oh, those?" she answered in a feminine but sing-song voice. "Well, mother thought it was important to find a way to grow them in late summer since we're called the Columbine

Bakery. There's a nice lady up the hill who likes to garden. She gives them to us. She says it's something about keeping the seeds ice cold until August. The seeds think its spring when she plants them in August, so, Voila— Columbines in October."

"Emily, do you know why I'm here?"

"Um, maybe you want some Basque sheepherder bread?"

"No. I'm having a picnic for my birthday tomorrow. And, I have this recipe that I would like for you to make. It's called Potiča. Every heard of it?"

"Yes. From Molly," she announced excitedly. "She said it's something special about her mother, her grandmother, and her great-great grandmother. They were all named Amelia, you know?"

Steele reached into his pocket and took out the century old hand-written recipe and handed it to Emily. "This came from Molly's grandmother. Above the Slovenian words, Marija had translated the original into English. Do you think you might be able to decipher it and make some for the picnic tomorrow?"

Emily put her fingers over her mouth as she read the recipe and held back tears. Molly had mentioned Potiča many times and always in connection with the mother she never met. It was more than bread. It had become a talisman for Molly and connected her by a thin thread to an unknown past. Now Emily had the power to link Molly to her mother with her skill as a baker by making the Potiča of her dreams.

"Yes, Mr. Steele. I can do this. Oh wait. I don't have any walnuts. Will pecans work?"

"Pecans are even better. And you are coming too—right?"

"Oh, Mr. Steele, I..."

"Don't you think it's time you joined the family Emily?"

Emily's hands and fingers suddenly went slack and her eyes turned sad as Steele's question washed over her. Her hands lay on the counter as she hung her head and started to cry. "Oh, Mr. Steele. I would like nothing better. But..."

"Sorry Emily. The time for buts is past. It hasn't been a real secret since I walked in on you two in the barn. It's time."

Emily swallowed hard, lifted her head, and managed a smile. Then she took in a large breath before accepting the invitation with an affirmative tone. "All right then. I'd be happy to attend your birthday picnic Mr. Steele. And I'll bring Potiča when it's still warm from the oven." As Steele's effort to include her sunk in, Emily pressed her hands together in front of her bosom and fought to contain her excitement. She looked much like a little girl who ached to say something out loud but couldn't out of fear. But then, a small smile displaying a hint of courage began to grow wider and wider on her lips, her body relaxed, and she stood a bit taller. Suddenly, she stepped around to register to face Steele and without any warning threw her arms around his neck and kissed him on his cheek.

"Well, I uh..."

"Thank You thank you Mr. Steele. Oh, and how about a chocolate birthday cake to go with the Potiča?" asked an upbeat and more confident Emily.

"Naw. I haven't liked chocolate much since I was a kid. Potiča is it. Can I take one of those?" pointing at the Columbines.

"Any one you'd like Mr. Steele." She put some water in a paper cup, fit the stalk of the columbine through the sipping hole and closed it over the cup. "There, that should keep it fresh until you get back to the Ranch. Oh, and two more things." She handed him some fresh sliced baguette bread in a crinkly bag. "Enjoy some sugared toast and milk Mr. Steele."

"Thank you," offered a surprised Steele as he opened the door with another screech while holding a warm bag of sourdough and sniffing the bag. A rush of crisp fall air rushed by him into the bakery chilling the customers next to the door as he held it open. Then he remembered. "What was the second thing you wanted to ask?"

"Where is the picnic going to be?"

"Those picnic tables in Naturita down by the San Miguel river. You know them?"

"Yes, Molly and I used to go there and skip rocks. See you there Mr. Steele."

Still at the door, it was Steele's turn to pause. He had some things of his own to mention before they parted.

"Emily—I forgot. I have two more things of my own. First, make an extra loaf of Potiča for your customers to sample. They'll like it."

"Sure. What's the second thing?"

"Start calling me Pop."

Arriving back at the ranch, Steele wasted no time getting to the toaster to make his sugared milk and toast while the bread still had a hint of warm. He put the columbine in the cup on the sink and then dropped two slices of bread into the toaster. Then he filled a pan with milk and turned the stove on low to warm it up.

"Hi Pop," offered Molly as she came through the back door and walked into the kitchen. "Where'd you get the columbine"

"From the Columbine Bakery, where else would you find a columbine this time of year?"

"True. Picked up some fresh bread, eh," she asked in a tone that was probing and wary?

"Yup. And I asked Emily to make you some Potiča too."

"You saw Emily?"

"Well, it's her bakery. So, I expect so. Yes, I saw Emily. Gave her your great great grandma's recipe too. She says she can deliver it tomorrow."

"What about your birthday picnic? We won't be here."

"That's what I mean. She's delivering it to our picnic by the river." Said she'd stay for my birthday and have Potiča with us."

Molly bit her lip as she tried to decipher what Steele was saying between the lines.

"What are you saying?"

"Whaddya think I'm saying?"

"Are you saying what I think you're saying?"

"Damn right I am. Everybody from Ganiz to Allie knew you fit better with Emily than Morgan. Everybody but me it seems. But now that I'm in on it and seeing you two together, I think so too. Soon, tears began to run down her face and splat on the floor interrupting the loud silence that had fallen over them. "That OK with you Molly?"

"I think you know that it's more than ok daddy, as she wiped a tear."

"Daddy?"
"Yeah. When you do things like this you rate more than just Pop."

"Guess this means we'll be seeing Emily a lot more around here?"

"If you don't mind, I guess we will."

"About time too," scolded Steele. "And no more secrets in this house. Deal?"

"Deal, Pop."

BACK TO THEIR BEGINNINGS: ROAD TRIP

"So, what's the plan Pop?" asked Allie.

"Well, I've been thinking so get out your maps. Here's the deal. It's shortest to go straight to where my Pop was last seen in Black Canyon, and then let you two go on to Phoenix. You could pick me up on your way back after looking up Posey. But I'm not keen on you two seeing him alone. He may have been gelded, and we know he's laid up with the cancer, but still…So, my plan is we go to see Leon— get it done. Then we go on to Black Canyon. Whaddya' think?"

Molly gritted her teeth. She would grudgingly support Allie's need to see where she came from. And she would go with her to protect her from the beast that raped her. But that was it.

"Sounds good to me, piped Allie. Except for one thing."

"What's that?"

"I think I just found where your pop might be buried," she announced as she held her finger on a place on her map.

Steel went grey and silent as a panic settled over him over the news about finding his grave. Graves are final. The questions he still had about his father could not be answered from a coffin. Shocked by the news, he waited to see if he could weather the storm in his head. By now he had mastered Dr. Cohen's techniques to stay in control. Sometimes they worked. He pinched his index finger against his thumb on both hands then talked himself into a safe place. The pinching of his finger against his thumb had become his secret weapon along with deep meditative breaths and self-talk.

Calm down, calm down. Isn't that exactly what you hoped to find when you went to Black Canyon? Find where he's buried? What did you think? He's still alive? Dumb thought. He'd be over a hundred now. He was sick with alcoholism when they kicked out of the house." Having gathered himself, he consciously used his calm voice to ask Allie a question:

"And why do you think you found his grave Allie?

"I looked in the only place I hadn't searched before—the message boards. Its where researchers of specific surnames like "Steele" make random notes on their findings. And that's where I saw the post. The message said they were on a trip through Northeastern Arizona and saw a grave marked 'L. E. Steele' in a cemetery on an Indian reservation."

"Can't be him. My father never used a middle name."

"How do you know. I know lots of people who never use their middle name even though they have one—don't even use an initial for it. Did he ever tell you he didn't have a middle name?"

Steele had no argument. Just because he had never heard him use a middle name didn't mean he didn't have one.

After all, his father was a secretive man who seemed to hide his past. He had not even told his wife Ginny the names of his own parents. It was as if they didn't exist. Steele accepted Allie's argument then cursed in disbelief at the unexpected news. *Good god damn. An Indian hater buried among Indians? Can't be.* He peered out the window toward the cabin and Ganiz's old rocking chair. He imagined Ganiz calmly smoking his pipe while gazing at the pasture. Then he imagined Ganiz suddenly looking up at him with a light smile on his face. Warmed by that image and self-soothed once again, he asked: "where is this place?"

"Fort Apache. It's in the White Mountains not too far from Black Canyon, Phoenix, and the San Carlos reservation where they kept Geronimo."

Steele pondered the news then quickly adjusted the plan. *We're still going to the same area. The news of where this L. E. Steele might be buried don't change anything.*

"Here's what we'll do then. We bypass Black Canyon and go straight to Phoenix together. Then, after we finish with Leon, we go east to Fort Apache, and we look for whatever we can find out about my father. Then we'll be done. No....Then I'll be done, I hope.

"But who's going to manage the ranch," asked Molly?

"Emily," retorted Steele. "Start of lambing season is still a few weeks away. All Emily has to do is feed Fergus and Arrate and check on things while we're gone."

"Does Emily know about this?" Molly asked with a tinge of pique that Steele was talking directly to her lover instead of going through her. *Ridiculous,* she scolded herself—suddenly ashamed of her thought. *It's just Steele being Steele, and that's not all bad.*

"Yup. Talked to her this very morning."

"All right then, it's settled. Road trip," repeated Molly as she and Allie gave high fives and then patty caked like little girls.

"I figure we leave in two weeks, get up late, cross the state line to Utah, then Monticello, and south to Mexican Hat. It's a bit longer, but we'll take in Monument Valley along the way. I think I know a place to get lunch. I mean if it's still there. Then on through Monument valley, Flagstaff, and Phoenix. I'm guessing eight hours total, so we'll stop in Flagstaff for the night, get up the next morning and be in Phoenix before noon. We're not in a hurry, right?"

"How do you know about that lunch place, queried Allie with her nose wrinkled? My map shows Mexican Hat in the middle of nowhere."

"Yeah. It's off the beaten path—a small spot on a spit of sand surrounded by a River. Before your mother was born, Ganiz and I fixed Marija's broke down motorcycle. You know, the one she rode in on from Leadville. Then Marija and I—we took it for a ride and wound up there around lunch time for no particular reason. It was her idea. She was always wanting to go somewhere. Didn't seem to matter where," he added while staring off at something out the window toward the pasture.

"Who sat on the back and held on," probed Allie with a wink?

"I had more bugs on my goggles than she did if that tells you anything." he answered proudly with a laugh and then left it at that.

Molly had gone quiet when she heard about the lunch

place. She always listened to every word Steele had to say about her mother, the odd places she had been, her girlfriend in Pueblo with the pictures on the wall, and the boyfriend's motorcycle that had brought her to Steele. She circled Mexican Hat on her AAA map and scribbled—*must see.*

"What happened to that old Motorcycle after Marija died," Allie asked Steele as if it were an idle curiosity? "Was it fast?"

"Like a blazing bolt of lightning followed by a trail of rumbling thunder." He hovered on the thought, his words, and the image—that shiny red beast splitting through dry desert air and gritty desolation with the two of them hanging on for life and hurtling to nowhere at all. For Marija, it was speed for the sake of speed, a hurrying without aim. It was life winking at death—her life. It had nothing to do with getting somewhere. A line from someone Steele could not remember popped into his head: *"I'd rather wake up in the middle of nowhere than any place on earth." But who wants to live in nowhere?* queried Steele. Then he remembered his love for a cabin at the end of a dirt road that led nowhere on a mountain with no name.

Steele was a practical man whose actions mostly needed a purpose—a practical beginning, a productive middle, and a predictable end. But for Marija, he sometimes allowed himself to set practical notions aside. And he learned to share her thrill of acting on a whim and riding wayward winds to god knows where. And along the way, he learned to love her. *That was her gift,* he mused— *that, Potiča, and Molly*. Then he snapped out of it and tossed one back to Allie. "Ok, Allie. Now it's up to you to see if you can weasel a visit out of Leon at the hospice. We have two weeks."

Dear Mr. Posey,

We met seventeen years ago when I was a baby girl. You tried to steal me from my mom, but my Pop stopped you. You remember Molly Steele. I am your biological daughter, the one you kidnapped. Pop Steele is my dad. I learned you have cancer. Since we share genes, it is important for me to learn about your illness as it may affect me too. I plan to be in Phoenix in two weeks. Will you see me then? I have questions.

Allie Steele

Hello Allie,

I'm going to guess this is not easy for you. You know who I am. You know what I've done. Not that it will do any good, but I'm sorry about that. I'm not that same person. But you will see that soon enough. Yes, I will meet with you in the hospice chapel. It is private, quiet, and we can be alone.

Leon Posey

Three days later, Allie went to the mailbox and found the DNA kits: one for Steele, one for Molly, and one for Posey. Allie walked into the kitchen with the kits where Molly and Steele were having their second cup of coffee of the morning. Allie had already taken her test several weeks before. She already knew that 1/16th of her DNA had come from an indigenous source. Now it was time to find out who those genes had come from.

"Got em."

"Got what," asked Steele?

"The DNA kits. They just came in the mail."

"Oh those."

Steele hadn't told the girls, but he was worried. Up

until now, the primary suspects for the indigenous genes were Steele's grandfather or grandmother. *Pop never said a word about them. Was he hiding something?* The news that his father was buried somewhere in Indian territory suggested a connection to indigenous roots—or it hinted at nothing more than the closest cemetery to where his days ended. But it was sounding more and more like one of Pop Steele's parents was Indian. *He did have high cheekbones and his hair was black and straight.* Yes, the genes could also have come from Posey's side. *We'll find that out soon enough.* But Steele worried about a sinister outlier. What if the indigenous blood came from that "ex-boyfriend" who had lent Marija the red Ducati? Then he fretted when he recalled that Molly was born almost nine months to the day of Steele's first time with Marija and not long after her arrival on the ex-boyfriend's motorcycle. *Was she already pregnant when she knocked on my door?*

Allie spread the three kits out on the kitchen table. Steele couldn't help thinking they represented straws in the game of drawing straws—two long, one short. It wasn't really a game. Long straws would mean a good outcome. A short straw meant a bad one. The long straws might prove the indigenous blood came either from Posey's side or Steele's side. Steele could accept that. But the short one might point to the boyfriend of Marija. Infidelity wasn't what Steele was afraid of. What perplexed him was that the tests could blithely prove that Steele was not Molly's father nor Allie's grandfather. That beloved title would then default to a mixed blood boyfriend of Marija's from Leadville. *What was it that Ganiz said about her,* thought Steele. *Oh yeah:*

"La Señorita no es moral!"

"Pick one Pop," asked Allie with an innocent smile, wondering why Steele had sweat on his forehead when it was so cool outside.

"Naw. You pick for me. You'll have better luck than me.

"Pop, the kits are not about luck, they're about science.

They're all the same. You can't argue with standardized tests."

Steele said nothing but fretted. *That's what's worrying me,* he thought as he secretly pinched his thumbs against his index fingers under the table. *No edge*. After gathering his nerve, he opened his kit. Molly and Steele followed the directions and spit saliva into their test tubes. Allie took control of the kit she would use for Leon and put it in her backpack. Then she sealed Molly and Steele's test tubes in mailers, took them to the mailbox, and raised the red metal flag to alert Buddy, the postman.

Allie plopped back into her chair at the table and slurped the last dregs of her coffee. "We'll get the results in a few weeks."

A quiet settled over the room. All three had something to solve with the road trip and their DNA results. Steele, of course, wanted to close the book on his abusive father, and his guilt over his part in his banishment from the family. He wanted to understand why Dort's death, Morgan's death, and Posey's bullet to his groin all connected to his pop. But he also wanted to be sure that he was Molly's father instead of it being some boyfriend of Marija who was with her days before she arrived at his door. For her part, Molly wanted to find connections to the mother she never knew. And Allie wanted to meet the man whose rape of her mother created her.

ON THE ROAD

Mc Tavish was built in 1953 and was going on 250,000 miles but had never traveled further than fifty miles from the Ranch. Nevertheless, Steele had held it to a rigid maintenance schedule and believed it could make the 1,200 mile journey to and from Phoenix. The engine, transmission, and differential were fine, but the exterior, the hinges, springs, and the seats were another story. It had never had shelter in so much as a barn and had spent its whole life outside through rain, wind, hail, and snow on the western slope of the Rockies. "Patina," was the word Steele would use to describe the faded blue paint. It was at that age when vintage truck aficionados would approach Steele asking if he wanted to sell the old thing. But it's never easy to sell something with a name. And so, Mc Tavish had a place in the Steele family for life.

Steele wondered what to bring. Clothes were not the issue. It was about which weapon he should carry to a hospice, and whether he should bring one at all. *It's a damn hospice Steele,* he scolded. But then he went on. The army .45 was too large and bulky, and the .270 rifle was out of the question. Years earlier he had traded the Red Ducati to a neighbor for a pocket pistol he didn't really want or need. The trade was about clearing the old Ducati out of its resting place in a corner of the barn where it took up space. He hadn't ridden it since Marija died soon after their racing jaunt down to Mexican Hat. As for the pistol, it had never been fired even for practice. But now it had a purpose. So, he loaded the magazine with .38

Special cartridges, walked to the far end of the pasture, and fired ten shots hitting a fencepost with all ten rounds from thirty feet away. *That'll do*, he thought as he reloaded the magazine, slid it back into the pistol, set the safety, and dropped the loaded weapon into his pocket. *That'll do.*

Molly and Allie were not fussy clothes horses, so they were packed almost as soon as Steele. Molly called Emily at the bakery and gave her last minute instructions about taking care of the ranch for the week. Emily was excited, not about them leaving, but about Potiča. Customers were beginning to ask for it and some were coming from far away towns based on word-of-mouth about an exotic nut-bread called Potiča. Emily was even thinking about selling Potiča by mail as part of an annual Christmas delicacy. Molly put her hand over the phone and gave the news to Steele who quickly donned a wide grin. "Told her so."

"Let's go girls." urged Steele as he leaned over to give Fergus a last chuck on the chin as the early morning light lit up his brown eyes. "Be back soon boy. You be a good dog." Fergus's ears dropped. He knew what that phrase meant. Arrate raised his eyelids to half open then shut them closed again after seeing that no food was involved in the commotion. At his age, he slept most of every day and night. Steele got into the driver's seat and started the engine. Allie got into the middle, and Molly rolled down the window on the passenger side. As they turned onto the highway, Allie popped up and down in her seat like the teenager she was saying "Road trip, Road Trip, Road Trip!" Then she looked sheepish for her exuberance, but shared a smile with Molly and Steele.

An hour after rolling south through Blanding Utah, they reached Mexican Hat near noon.

"I'll be damned. It's still there," muttered Steele in awe.

"What is," asked Molly who had circled the place on her map where Steele and her mother had ridden the motorcycle six months before her birth? "That's it?"

"Yep. It's the Swinging Steak or something like that." They throw steaks on a grill that swings back and forth over an open fire. They say it seals in the juices."

Allie, always eager said: "That sounds really cool. Steak for lunch sounds good too! Think they have wine?"

But Molly was saddened. She had imagined there might be something about the place that might help her to understand the mother she yearned to know. She fantasized about finding traces of her imprinted in the sand—some characteristic of the place that would tell her *yes, I would have stopped here too!* Instead, all that was there was an open-air steakhouse close by a river bend surrounded by desert. She was not interested.

"Is there another place for lunch," she asked?

"Know what? That's exactly what your mother said. "Word for word she asked; 'is there another place?' Turned out there was. It was just up the road in Monument Valley. That's where we had lunch. We split a hamburger with a side of Navajo Frybread and a glass of white wine. Sat in a booth by a window and looked out over the monuments. Navajos don't allow alcohol in the valley, so it was a non-alcoholic white." *Amazed I could remember that.*

Molly perked up at the news, quite pleased that she had rejected the Swinging Steak place just like her mother had done years before. She had a file in her head where she kept precious facts about Marija that linked her to her. Her file was small. She wished it were bigger.

"She sure liked that side of Navajo Frybread," offered Steele.

"Think Emily could make it," Asked Molly?

"I think Emily can bake anything. But frybread—it's easy. Even I could make it."

"All right then. We'll make some when we get back with Emily."

"Did she like the white wine," inquired a now curious Molly?

"Hell no. Marija said it tasted like bad grape juice. Spit it out on the floor."

When they got to the Monument Valley restaurant, Steele split a hamburger with Molly and ordered her a glass of white wine in remembrance of his motorcycle jaunt with Marija. Allie also ordered the burger and frybread but ate it all by herself. Steele showed off by ordering milk. Molly noticed, but when she tasted the wine her face wrinkled up as if she had sipped lemon juice and spit it into her water glass. An older woman at a booth with her husband saw her spit and wrinkled her brow in disapproval. *Seen Molly's look before*, thought Steele as he remembered the face of Marija after she tasted Steele's Carlo Rossi white table wine on their first day together—All b*oxed and shipped from Modesto*, he told his bride to be.

Soon they were back on the road rolling toward Flagstaff to stay the night. From there, they would head on down the hills to Phoenix the next day. As the landscape flew by their windows, each mused quietly on the oddities that loomed over their lunch. Molly secured the image of her mother drinking bad wine and eating Navajo Frybread. Steele relived a forgotten memory of Marija and her taste in wine and was surprised to see a small piece of that in Molly. Allie leaned on her mother's shoulder and slept with a burger and frybread taking up too much space in her belly.

CALVARY HOSPICE

Calvary Hospice was in a bad part of town a few miles south of the high rises of downtown Phoenix. It was on the other side of the Southern Pacific tracks. Murders and robberies were commonplace there. *Just the kind of place Leon would end up in,* mused Steele as he patted the pistol in his pocket and looked up and down the cracked sun-bleached street before opening the door for Allie and Molly. Steele had never locked Mc Tavish before and fumbled with the keys to turn the locks as the girls went ahead. After finally getting Mc Tavish secured, he looked up to see Molly and Allie entering the building thirty feet down the street.

The hospice was a hulking old house with peeling white paint blistered by the Arizona sun surrounded by dilapidated homes, warehouses, and treeless lots full of blowing trash and sand. A hand painted sign above the door announced that the building housed the Calvary Hospice. Swamp coolers hummed above flat topped roofs while Jets landing at Sky Harbor Airport roared overhead and shook the ground. *No birds, no dogs, no grass* noted Steele as he hurried to catch up with the girls who had already passed through the door into the hospice—*feels dead.* Though it was already November, the sun had not yet yielded to fall. The morning sun penetrated the skin on the back of his neck. Dry air sucked the moisture from his throat and lungs as he walked briskly toward the entrance of the Calvary Hospice. He knocked on the door as he stood in the bright sunlight and cast a shadow. A man, smaller and older than Steele, opened the door and looked up at him just as a large jet roared a few hundred feet above them.

"You coming for Father Posey too," he yelled?

"What?"

"You want to see Father Posey?"

Father Posey Hell. That father of lies you mean? The man let Steele into the small lobby. At the dusty concierge desk was a box with a slot for mail. It was labeled "Signed Social Security Checks Due by Last Friday of the Month." The old man wore crumpled clothing that he had obviously slept in and wore slippers without socks. "Yeah. I need to find my daughters. Where'd they go he yelled over the noise?

"Well, one went to Father Posey's room, and the other may have gone to the Chapel at the end of the hall."

"Where's Leon's room?"

"Are you related sir?"
"Unfortunately, yes."

"Well then. He's in 104. Turn left over there. He'll be on the right. He's dying you know."

"We all are friend. We all are," he said as the din of the jet finally faded as it neared the runway.

Steele hurried down the dark hallway and turned left. Half the lights in the corridor were out, and he was still adjusting to the dim light after the bright sun outside. He nearly walked into Molly as she exited 104.

"Sorry, didn't see you coming. Is Allie in there?"

"No. And Posey isn't either. Allie ran down the hall as soon as the old man let us in. It's so dark I lost track of her."

"Shit," cursed Steele as he reached into his pocket. "The old man said something about a chapel. Maybe she went there."

"Maybe."

As they hurried down the hall, they ran into the old man again.

"Chapel is straight ahead? Asked Molly."

"Uh huh. But it's busy now. Father Leon is in there with a guest."

"Guest? You mean the young girl who just came in?" asked Molly in a pique.

"Yes. His daughter," offered the old man with an air of certainty as he turned to walk away into the darkened hallway.

Steele exchanged a look with Molly and then he burst into a run down the hallway with Molly pumping her arms and legs close behind. The door to the chapel was locked. *Father my ass*. Steele pounded on the door. "You in there Allie?"

"Yeah, she's in here," said a snarly man's voice. "She's busy."

Steele looked again at Molly whose eyes were open wide, and then he took on a determined look before stepping back to rush the door and break in with his shoulder. But before he reached the door, he heard the lock click open from the other side and then open slowly with squeaks from the dry hinge. The opened door revealed a dark but candlelit room. Allie poked her frightened face out the door as Steele looked over her head to search for Leon. When the door opened wide enough, Allie stepped out quickly and sidled up to Molly who pulled her in tight. Steele pushed the door open further with his left hand but had his right hand on the pistol grip of the gun in his pocket. Then, in front of a small altar, he saw Leon.

"Been a long time Steele," said Leon in a hoarse voice that sounded more like a whisper.

Leon was slumped sideways in a wheelchair. He had no legs from the knees down and used his atrophied arms and thin bony hands to roll himself deliberately toward Steele. Even by candlelight, the paleness of his skin was almost bright, and the eyes that once were fierce had retreated deep into their sockets. Sunken as they were, they still hinted at menace. Steele detected a hostile scowl beneath a veil of feebleness that Posey had donned over his pallid expression. He breathed heavily from the exertion of propelling his chair. A faint stale smell of urine permeated the entire room while his breath reeked of rotten teeth. Molly was revulsed. He looked as if he had leprosy or worse, though she felt an awkward sliver of pity for how far her rapist had fallen.

"You know you really didn't need to shoot my balls off Steele."

"No, I didn't. And you didn't have to rape Molly or Kill Morgan either.

"You're right." He quickly snapped as if he had been interrupted. "And it took me a long time to think that way. Losing my legs, my balls, my pecker… must have gotten my attention. I've changed Steele."

"That'll be the day."

"I'm a priest. They call me father now."

Steele hovered over the bent over the broken man in the chair. "Don't piss on my leg with that bullshit. You're nothing but a father of evil calling himself a priest and asking to be believed."

"No, it's true. Well, not like I'm an ordained priest or anything. Still, I'm a priest. Became one soon after I got here—after they took my legs—see what you did Steele?" he asked as he rolled closer to a candle for Steele to see.

Molly stood in the doorway behind the protection of Steele and listened to Leon's rendition of his redemption through god.

"Back then, Calvary Hospice took in invalids. It was a sort of poorhouse for cripples. It was only later they took in dying men. They got a license. Got approval to bill Medicare and Medicaid, and get inspected every year. On inspection day, we put a little envelope filled with hundred dollar bills marked "inspector" on the Concierge desk. We manage to pass every year despite the look of the place—heh, heh.

The priest that started it got himself kicked out of the Church for something bad he did with some little boys. Thought he better do something good in this life to make up for it in the eyes of god. So, he started this place on his own to atone for his sins. Took me in off the street, and treated me like I was his long lost son. Said I was still a good lookin' man despite the wheelchair. Took good care of me. Even said he loved me. Maybe just because I was so broken up. Felt sorry for me, no legs and all. He died years ago and left me this place full of dying men. In his will he wrote that I could have the house if I kept it open and replaced him as administrator and priest of the place. I've worn this crucifix ever since. Funny huh? How life turns out I mean?"

"What happened to your Ute woman. I suppose she took you here after I left you at the shack in the Disappointment?"

"Yeah. Chipeta took me to a hospital in Phoenix. After you shot me all up, she loaded me in her truck at the line cabin and we left the state for good just like you said to. She helped me for a time until the hospital got me a wheelchair and dumped me on the street. Wound up in this place. Said she couldn't stay. Besides, she said I wasn't no good any more to be a father. Went back to Colorado and lived on the reservation near the Uncompahgre. Heard she took up with a Navajo goatherder and had two kids—babies I mean," he snickered. "Get it? Never blamed her for leaving though. Say, I always wondered. Why didn't you just shoot me in the top of my head when you had the chance."

Steele hesitated, then quipped: that's for me to know and for you to find out."

"That's no answer Steele," he glowered with the same sinister look he used to carry around the Badwater Bar.

"It's the only one you'll get. And by the way, I'm not buying your 'redeemed by god' crap. You're not capable, and you know it. Besides, you need a soul to get redeemed and you don't have one. You got your miserable body dumped here in Phoenix, rose from the hellish ashes of your own making, and claim your soul found the wings to god. Bullshit."

Leon looked past the man who shot him to pieces. He called out over Steele's shoulder to Molly who was standing behind him with Allie. Then he donned a whimpering tone instead of the raspy pathetic timbre he had greeted them with at the door. "Molly honey, I know you're there. Sorry for you having to hear all this. And I'm sorry for what I did even though you hit me first—chipped my tooth, you did—beat me at pool too in front of my friends. Now that wasn't nice was it. Anyway, not much more I can say. Yeah, it was a mean thing to do, and I was a mean man then. I've changed as you can see for yourself."

Molly hunched behind Steele, clenched her fists, tightened her body, and stayed silent wishing she could get her hands on another cue ball. *Damn good thing my .45 in the roll up desk isn't close by you asshole.*

"So, Allie honey. You have some questions for me?"

Molly couldn't stay for this part. She put Allie in Steele's charge and then strode back down the hall to the lobby at the entrance. Her footsteps echoed through the corridor until she found a wooden bench, sat down, stared at the dirty floor. Then, she shook her head in wonderment of the evil she had just witnessed. Steele stayed with Allie but sat at the opposite end the single pew in the chapel. The hospice had salvaged it from a burned out church. Allie pulled out her list and started to ask Leon her questions. After going through the ones related to his cancer, she went on.

"You got any Indian blood in you Leon?"

"Kind of a weird question don't you think?"

"Maybe. Got any?"

"Not that I know about. My dad came from a family that came to Colorado from Germany. My ma's family was from Poland. They left and came to the Uncompahgre. Both

Grandpa's were mining engineers in the old country."

"Ever take a DNA test?"

"Now that's really weird. Hell no. Why do you even ask?"

"Paternity."

"Don't know what you're getting at. But I ain't paying no back child support if that's what this is about. Besides, the statute of limitations already run on that. Rape too," he snarled. "So no, I ain't and won't be takin' no DNA test."

"Ok. Ever own a fast car or motorcycle?"

Pleased to have an easier question than the last, he sighed at the query. "Nope. Never had more than my old truck. Can't say it was fast. Why's that important to you?"

Allie ignored the question. "You still smoke Leon?"

"Yes, I do. Never been able to give it up."

"Nasty habit. You the only one?"

"The only one what?"

"The only one in here who smokes."

"Sad to say, yes. I'm the only one. I set a bad example for my flock," he said as if he cared about his flock. "Shortens your life you know."

"You have some water around here?" asked Allie as she folded her list of questions and put them back in her pocket.

"Right around the corner. There's a cooler and some

dixie cups.

“You want some?”

“Sure. That’d be nice. Hard for me to get over there me being crippled and all.”

Allie gave him a perfunctory smile, found the cooler, and returned with the water, and made some small talk. After a sense of ending settled over them, she asked if she could take his cup. “I’ll trash it for you.”

“Naw. Thanks, but I’m still working on it. We done, honey?”

“Almost. I just wanted to say this to you. Mr. Posey that you are a complete asshole for raping my mom on a pool table in a cheap bar in front of your disgusting friends. You being a fake priest with no legs and calling me honey won’t change that. You’re nothing but a evil beast. You understand—right?”

For a moment, Leon’s eyes flashed with dark anger before remembering that her avenging angel was still in the room. Steele sat in a shaft of light which lit up his face, but he was too far away in the dark for Leon to see that he was smiling at what Allie had just said. Then, realizing he may have shown too much of who he still was, he morphed his eyes into a harmless look to avoid Steele’s wrath. But his lips went their own way and twisted into a smirk tinged by a hint of snarl—despite Steele’s threatening gaze.

With that, Allie got up. Steele rose with her but stumbled and had to grab the pew to catch himself. *Getting worse,* he grumbled to himself. Then they walked out and left Leon alone. The lasting image Allie would keep of Posey was of him lighting up a Marlborough cigarette. Smoke surrounded his head and the smell of tobacco mingled with the sour humid smell of wet urine. *He's the Lord of Hell,* she thought. On her way out, Allie used a clean tissue to pick up two Marlborough butts out of an ashtray full of sand and dropped them into a plastic bag. Silently, she vowed to quit smoking.

As for Steele, he sighed with relief. Posey's revelation of his German/Polish heritage asserted a near certain truth. Posey was not the source of the indigenous blood. Short of an interloping indigenous milkman secretly consorting with Posey's mother while Sherriff Posey was out, Leon could not have been the source for the Indian blood in Allie. DNA from the cigarettes would surely confirm that. As for Molly, she was pleased that she had trusted Allie enough to allow her to take her chance to confront Leon and ask her questions. She was ecstatic when fresh sunlight lit up her face as she escaped the dank smelly halls of the Calvary Hospice and Leon Posey.

"So, what's the verdict," Molly asked Allie as Steele looked on?

"He got the cancer from his work in the uranium mines in Urovan, not from his genes. And he's a son of a bitch."

Short and to the point, thought Steele. *That's Allie.*

EXODUS

Steele fumbled with the keys to unlock the doors on Mc Tavish again. All were anxious to rid themselves of the grimy soot that had seeped over their skin while inside the Hospice. Despite their angst over the foul odor they had absorbed, they also wanted to put some miles between them and Phoenix before stopping to clean up. After driving east for more than an hour airing out with the windows open, they found a clean motel in Globe. Steele went to check in while the girls waited. Steele entered the front office with a smile.

"Hello there. Got a room for three?"

The clerk's smile quickly changed to a scowl as she caught a whiff of Steele's stench and then pulled away from the counter. "What is that smell?" she complained.

"Bad, I know. Sorry. Ran into a skunk outside of Phoenix. We've been smelling it all the way since we left. Thanks for the key."

Allie was first to get to the shower. As she left the bathroom in a cotton robe with a white towel twirled around her head, she passed Molly in the hallway who was on her way to clean up. Allie quipped: "you're gonna need a lot of soap."

In the morning they walked up the sidewalk in bright sunshine sporting fresh clothes until they found a fifty's era diner. It had seats with red leather upholstery, black and white floor tiles, and chrome trimmed furniture. They had breakfast.

"I've been thinking," said Steele interrupting Molly's fork in midair with half a grilled sausage dripping maple syrup. I don't see any reason for you two to have to tag along while I sleuth the Apache reservation." Looking at Allie, he made a point. "That online source you showed me about my Pop being buried didn't say which cemetery. All it said was that 'there was a report that a white man named Steele is buried on the reservation.' Steele is a common name. There's nothing to say that it's my pop Leon Steele. More than that, there's five cemeteries scattered around the reservation. Hell, he might not be there at all. But it's going to take some tramping around to figure it out and that's gonna' take me some time. Why don't you two stay here for the day while I take the day to look around?"

Molly had gawked at all the antique stores lining the street as they drove into Globe from Phoenix. And Allie's curiosity was set off by a sign that said: "See the Indian ruins." Between those venues and some tasty looking places for a sip of wine and some lunch, they were happy to oblige Steele in his thinking. They also looked forward to putting some mental distance between them and their sour meeting with Posey. "Sure Pop. I'm sure we'll find something to do," said Molly speaking for the two of them as they shared a happy giggle.

FORT APACHE

Steele bid goodbye to the girls after paying the breakfast bill in cash and leaving a 15% tip to the young waitress named Tiffany. *Somehow, Tiffany's name doesn't fit with hardscrabble Globe* was his afterthought. As the girls walked arm in arm up the street, he noticed that they had the look of two excited teenagers after their parents announced they'd be out for the day. They loved Steele, and Steele loved them. But they were looking forward to some girl time and some freedom to explore the historic town on their own. And Steele had been around female company long enough to want some solitude. He was relieved to be on the road again as he nudged the old truck up the hill gear by gear toward Fort Apache. Along the way, he rolled down both windows to feel the air. It felt good to have a pine ladened breeze teasing his hair and beard as he drove Mc Tavish up the twisting highway into the Mogollon Range and to the high elevations where the White Mountain Apaches lived. *Strange*, he thought as he whizzed by pinon and juniper trees. *Looks like the western slope around Nucla.*

In the weeks before the road trip, Allie tutored Steele on the use of her laptop and google. Common as google had become, Steele had never touched a keyboard in his life, and never "done the google" as some of his fellow ranchers would say. But now, he needed research skills to narrow his investigation.

The reservation, he learned, was spread over 2,600

square miles. He had already found more than five cemeteries within the tribal boundaries of the White Mountain Apache reservation where a reputed "L. E. Steele" might be interred. There were other smaller burial grounds like the one where slain Apaches were buried after the Cibecue massacre in 1881 not far from Fort Apache. Each was a candidate for where his father might be buried. But he also found that he would not be allowed to go into any of them without the permission of the White Mountain Apache tribe. Tribal headquarters was in White River, so that was his first destination.

Tribal headquarters was housed in a modern building on a flat above the north fork of the Whitewater River. Steele went directly to the "can I help you" counter.

"Hi. I'm here to get permission to go into some tribal cemeteries. I'm looking for a man named Steele."

The young man behind the counter kept a stone face as he sized up the white man standing in front of him. "Steele doesn't sound very Apache, does it?"

"No. I'm thinking that this man named Steele is related to someone from the reservation. Possibly the son of an Apache woman and a man named Steele."

The clerk did not look Indian. The only clue to his indigenous heritage in Steele's view was the silver and turquoise bolo tie and his dark black hair; but it was curly, not straight like an Apache's.

Hoping to build rapport, Steele noted: "By the way, I like your tie. Handmade?"

"Thanks. Yes. Handmade in China. The turquoise is plastic, and the silver is polished zinc," he answered in perfect English. "Which cemetery?

"Oh," said Steele fumbling from feeling foolish about his tie comment. But he quickly got back to the clerk's question. "Yes, well, that's the thing. Which cemetery? I don't know. You see, my granddaughter took a DNA test, and it came back 1/16th native American."

"And now she wants to know if she can get Indian benefits?"

"No, it's not like that. We're just trying to determine the source of the indigenous blood. It's a genealogy thing. We've narrowed it down. It came through my father or my wife or maybe one other person, but we don't know which one yet, and that person may be buried here."

"Did you ask your wife?"

"She died eighteen years ago. But she probably wouldn't have known anyway."

"Did you take a DNA test?"

"Yes, but my results aren't in yet."

"Where did your father come from?"

"Don't know. That's part of the problem."

"Well then. Where were his last whereabouts?"

"My granddaughter located him in a census living in Black Canyon Arizona in 1960."

"Sheepherder?"

"How did you know that?"

"Because everyone that lives there works the old Spanish sheep herding trails. But what makes you think your father might be in one of our cemeteries? Black Canyon is a couple of hundred miles away."

"A message board— my granddaughter found a post that said they found a marker with "L. E. Steele" on it on the reservation, but didn't say which cemetery."

"Your name is Steele?"
"Yes, sir."

"Give me a minute Mr. Steele."

Steele thought it was a good sign that the clerk had asked so many questions. Each time he asked one he seemed to be narrowing down options for his search, and he began to get his hopes up. Steele heard a commotion behind him and turned to see what it was about. A long line had formed since the only clerk at the help desk was off looking up cemetery records for Steele. He gave the impatient group behind him a guilty smile and then turned to fix his eyes on the wall clock behind the counter to watch the minutes go by. Finally, after almost twenty minutes, the clerk returned.

"Well, Mr. Steele. I have two clues for you. The first is about a soldier named Glenn Steele, and the second is about an old Apache woman named Cocheta."

Glenn Steel? Jesus. That's a coincidence. But what does that have to do with an L. E. Steele buried somewhere on the Res?

The clerk went on. "It seems that in 1910 an eighteen year old soldier named Glenn Steele from St. Joseph Missouri was assigned to Fort Apache. He only stayed a year. The record is unclear, but he was badly injured in a barfight with an Apache a few miles from here. They discharged him and sent home to St. Joseph. He was stabbed in the eye."

"And what about this Cochekta woman?"

"Cocheta," corrected the clerk. She's a tribal elder—born in 1911, near the time this Glenn Steele was at the fort. She's 103, feisty as a 70 year old, and still smart a whip."

"And where might I find her?"

"She lives alone at the top of Seven Mile Road in an old cabin at about 6,200 feet. Hard to get to and she probably wouldn't like seeing a white man coming up the dirt trail to her place. She's armed— you might get shot. But she drives her mule and wagon down the mountain to visit the cemetery above the fort every Sunday to put flowers on her family graves and pick up supplies for the week. That'd be tomorrow and she's as reliable as a clock."

"Which cemetery?"

"The Post Cemetery."

"Why is it called the Post Cemetery?"

"That's where the soldiers who died at Fort Apache were buried. But all the military graves were exhumed except for the Indian scouts and reburied in the federal cemetery in Santa Fe. Now it's just Apaches, their families, and Apache scouts buried there."

"But like you said, Steele doesn't sound very Apache, does it? So. what's your guess about a Steele being buried there? "

"Got me there Mr. Steele. But while I was researching your questions, I did get permission for you to enter reservation cemeteries for your search—here."

"Thanks for that. You seem to know a lot for a guy who clerks the help desk."

"Could be because I just happened by the desk when you were standing there looking like you needed help. The real clerk doesn't punch in for another ten minutes. I'm a resident anthropologist Mr. Steele—cultural anthropologist. I'm interning here from Northern Arizona University. Name's Smith. Will Smith."

"Glad to meet you Will. Name's Steele— Glenn Steele."

Smith's eyes grew wide as he made quickly made the connections—the Glenn Steele standing before him, a Private Glenn Steele at the Fort in 1910, and an L. E. Steele somewhere between them possibly buried on the Res.

"Let me know how this turns out Mr. Steele. By the way, Cocheta always comes to lay flowers in the morning just after sunrise."

"How do you know that?"

"Because that's where I usually meet her and take down her Apache stories. I'm writing a book about her."

"Usually?"

"Yes. Usually at the cemetery. But I was invited to meet her once at her cabin. Interesting place. Looks more like a fort than a cabin."

Steele made a mental note about the book. "A book huh?"

Then, without a segway he asked: "Is there a payphone around here?"

"Pinetop. It's about twelve miles north. Go to the Buck Springs Resort. They have one but nobody ever uses it anymore. You can use my cellphone if you like."

"Thanks, but that's ok. I was headed to Pinetop anyway," he fibbed. He had never used a cellphone before and did not want to embarrass himself by fumbling with another man's phone. He had; however, memorized the phone numbers for Molly and Allie. Then he thought to ask Smith for his number too—just in case. All he lacked now were quarters and a ten mile trip to Pinetop. Before leaving, he asked Smith his last question.

"What's her last name?"

"Cocheta? She doesn't have one. She comes from the time they only used their given name. You know, like the Apache chief *Cochise*. It means wood, or *Dasodaha* the name of another chief. It means 'He only sits there.' Neither one had a last name and neither does Cocheta."

"So, what's Cocheta mean?"

"She won't tell me. Says it's a secret she won't tell a white man."

PINETOP

"Change for a dollar, Steele asked the clerk at Buck Springs Resort? "

Molly's cellphone only rang twice before she answered. "Hi Pop. You coming back to get us soon?"

"Hi Molly. No. Something came up. I'll have to stay one or maybe two more days."

"What came up? Where are you."

"It's a long story. Right now, I'm in a place called Pinetop."

"What are you doing there?"

"Investigating."

Molly sensed he was not being candid, so she changed the subject. "Should we just catch a bus and come there?"

"Not yet. I don't know where I'm staying tonight, but I'll call you tomorrow. By the way, has Allie ever been interested in anthropology?"

"Maybe. She's at some Indian ruins just outside of Globe right now. Why?"

"Just thought I'd ask, that's all."

FORT APACHE MILITARY CEMETERY

Graves dating to the late nineteenth century were scattered helter skelter across the fort cemetery without any sense of order. It was perched on a knoll 500 feet above what was left of the old fort on the flats below which had been turned into a museum. Steele hurried because he wanted to reconnoiter the burial grounds while there was still some light left. He also wanted to be alone among the dead and think.

A graveyard is a good place for that. Better than most. Maybe stumble across that L. E. Steele marker Allie found on the message boards, he thought. He drove Mc Tavish up a dirt road past a few houses to the top of the knoll. Steele imagined being watched from each abode as the old blue truck bounced over rough road and billowed up dust that turned powdery gold in the failing afternoon sun. The entrance to the cemetery was marked by a recently painted sign that had been carelessly lashed to a tree with scrap pieces of rusty barbed wire. It was already sagging toward the ground. Steele parked at the entrance and walked in with the low afternoon sunlight on his face that revealed deep cracks in his visage.

Other than the dozen or so graves laid out in orderly patterns with store bought gravestones or homemade markers, the rest were placed randomly as if each grave bore no duty to bear a relation to the one next to it. There were broken down crosses, graves whose boundaries were marked with irregular stones, weathered wooden markers that once had paint, markers pushed over by tree roots, and concrete markers with illegible inscriptions scratched into them with a nail or a stick just before they hardened. Some of the crosses were adorned with bead necklaces and a few had feathers tethered to them which flitted in circles in the wind. Still others had nothing more than a stake in the ground or a sunken area to indicate that the spot had been taken. Many had faded plastic flowers laid long ago at their base and then faded by the sun and forgotten. A few had wilted flowers that were fresh a week ago. But Steele ignored them all. He was looking for a metal post with a stamped inscription that said more than "unknown" of which there were many. He wanted one that said: "L. E. Steele."

The cemetery was dispersed over a wide area with graves hidden under bushes that had seeded long after the deceased was buried. Many were outside the fenced confines of the grounds and extended down the brush covered hillside where corpses were buried on a tilt. It was as if bodies were buried in the most accessible location near the road.

Thus, there were too many random places for Steele to find in one afternoon. When the sun set, Steele pulled a flashlight out of the glove box, ignored the fifth of whiskey lying next to it, and searched in the dark. Near midnight, he gave up, crawled into the bed of Mc Tavish, and got into the survival sleeping bag he always kept behind the seat of the cab. Soon he was asleep among the dead. He trusted his internal clock to wake him before sunrise.

That night as he slept in the bed of the truck, he dreamed of his father in the pasture on the ranch again. Firelight flickered from his campfire next to the old cabin where Ganiz mostly stayed. Steel saw him from a distance as he gesticulated from one side to the other as if telling a tall tale to an audience of rough men paying rapt attention to him in the Disappointment Country. But he had no voice as he spoke. Then his father noticed something in the direction of Steele and paused. His father saw something out in the dark, he thought, beyond the campfire that was blinding his eyes. Then suddenly, his face lit up. He smiled as if recognizing a friend and beckoned Steele to sit next to him on a white rock by the fire. Steele could hear his words for the first time. "Come on son. Here Glenn, sit here," as he patted the glittering white rock. Steele heard his own footsteps as they ground across loose gravel toward the fire.

That was when he heard them. "What you doin' here mister? This is no place to sleep it off." Three flashlights blinded him as he awoke to hostile voices in the dark. "I said, what you doin' here in our cemetery mister?" It was three AM.

Still half asleep, Steele searched for words to allay the angry questions coming from the men with the blinding lights. "I'm uh, I'm meeting an old woman here in the morning."

"There are many old women here old man. Which one?"

Steel tried to recall the unfamiliar name. "Cosh..., no, Cocheta." Sensing they needed more, he reached into his pocket and pulled out his permit. "Here, I have a permit."

The leader shined his flashlight on the paper. "This don't give no permission to sleep on sacred ground."

"Look, I'm told she arrives every Sunday to lay flowers on the graves of her relatives."

"Who told you that?"

"Will Smith at tribal headquarters."

"That white college boy? You working with him?"

"Maybe a little. He told me she might be able to answer a question."

"About what?"

"Personal. Personal to me and my family." The flashlights stayed glued on his face and his answer was met with menacing silence. After a pause, Steele answered. "There's a chance my father is buried here."

After some laughter, the leader spoke again. "You don't look like no Apache to me."

Steele took out his own flashlight and pointed it toward the sound of the leader's voice creating a tête-à-tête. The leader's face was unremarkable. The look leaned toward Mexican, but he could have been a white man who spent too much time in the sun. Then again, he could be Apache. "You don't look too Apache either," fired back Steele. His retort was followed by chuckles, titters, then hearty guffaws before the three of them turned and started to walk back down the road toward the houses below.

"You say good morning to old Cocheta for us mister. That kid Smith is right. The old woman will be here at dawn if she lives another night."

Steele did not relax until the voices walking down the dark road faded safely away. *Damn. I hope that didn't mess with my internal clock.* Then he went back into a fitful sleep fearful of sleeping through sunrise. He did not return to the dream of his father again. But he wanted to.

Three hours later, the dark sky to the east was turning

into a faint blue and was silhouetting trees along the horizon. Steele's eyes darted back and forth behind his lids as they sensed the dim light harkening the dawn. When he heard the snort of a mule and the sound of steel capped wagon wheels grinding rocks as they rolled slowly up the unpaved road toward him his eyes opened wide. Lying on his back on his bed in the truck, he looked up to see a white haired woman with a hand woven shawl pulled over her shoulders sitting on a buckboard with eyes that seemed to pierce through time and Steele. Then, she looked away and clicked her tongue at her mule and the wagon lurched further up the road.

Steele dusted himself off and crawled out of the truck bed to the ground. He watched as the woman halted her mule and set the wagon brake fifty feet ahead in the near darkness. Then she stepped slowly and gingerly down to the road and went to the back of the wagon. There, he saw her lift a woven basket dripping with flowers and step determinedly through the cemetery grounds wearing tennis shoes over the rough terrain. It was obvious that she knew exactly where she was going. To Steele's eyes, it seemed like a ritual playing out before him, so he remained quiet in the background until she had finished.

As she returned to her wagon with the empty basket the morning light was strong enough to make out her features. She had fiercely high cheekbones made more prominent by her age. Her black eyes were piercing, and her long white hair lifted and fell in the morning breeze. Deep lines were etched across her forehead. Crow's feet radiated from the corner of her eyes and furrows ran down her weathered cheeks. She wore a red and white calico dress, Nike tennis shoes, and a woven shawl over her shoulders. Silver trinkets around her neck and waist caught the first rays of sun filtering through the trees. She walked with deliberate steps, though age had bent her body forward, and she leaned on a walking stick to stay upright.

"You that Steele fella," she asked acknowledging Steele's presence for the first time?

"How did you know?"

"Us Indians got our ways. Been communicating for centuries," she answered sounding younger and more alert than her age but with a raspy growly voice that could have been a man's. Steele was expecting more of an accent from an Apache speaking English. But like the three men who had rousted him, there was none.

"How's that" asked Steele?

"Cell phones. Work better than mirror flashes, puffs of smoke, or reading sign. But hell, you white folks know all about that."

"Will told you?"

"Yeah, nice young man, for a white boy. So, what is it you want Mr. Steele?"

"Well, I..."

"Come on Mr. white man. You're here to find your father in our cemetery. You think Will called to tell me you would be here at the cemetery at dawn on Sunday, and he didn't tell me why?"

"Well?"

"Well, nothing. If you can't spit it out, let me tell you what you want to know. You want to know if there's a dead fella lying in this place you think is your father. Right?"

"Yes."

"Well, this is holy ground for Apache's not white men. Cavalry moved all of them white soldiers buried here from the fort to Santa Fe long ago. So, why are you looking for a white man in our cemetery. Get the hell out white man. This is Apache land, and you'd best leave now before you have some visitors!"

Steele stood his ground, put his hat in hand, and bent over in a placatory pose. "I'm sorry ma'am. But I can't leave now."

"You mean you won't?"

"Yes ma'am. I won't. You don't understand. I may be the son of a man buried here."

"Well, you got some sand mister, and you damn sure don't look Apache with that long white beard of yours. Didn't nobody tell you Apache men don't grow beards. Like I said, get out!"

With that, she boarded the wagon and snapped the reins hard against the mule's rump like a whip which made it jump forward. Steele watched as the buckboard turned around to go back down the hill and then bounced up and down the rough road. He heard rocks being crushed by steel capped wheels as it rolled away. He listened until the sound of splitting granite grew faint. When she reached the Fort on the flats below, she turned east for a mile, followed the highway, and then turned right and went south up Seven Mile Road. Her cabin rested at 6,100 feet where she lived alone among the pinyon and juniper trees on a hill above a storage pond called Tin Shack Tank.

After watching the wagon go down the hill, Steele went out among the graves to see which ones she had laid flowers on. Steele figured that if she did know Pop Steele, that she might have put flowers on his grave. That assumed she honored Leon Steele enough to do him that favor, and based on what Steele knew of his father, that was not certain. But it was worth a try.

Steel found thirteen graves with fresh flowers laid over them but was not sure he had found them all so scattered and randomly placed as they were. Those he found weren't marked in any obvious way except for the most recent burials which were store bought markers that had letters chiseled into solid marble or granite. But none of those belonged to an "L. E. Steele." In the end, Steele found nothing and needed a plan on what to do next. He also needed to call the girls who were probably worried by now.

Cocheta had ample time on her ride back to her cabin to think about the white man prowling the cemetery at sunrise. It was more than ten miles to her shack and more than a thousand feet of elevation to gain before she got there near noon. Her experience with white people had never been good and she had ample reason to dislike them. But worse than that, the man had interrupted her quiet time with her dearly departed. It was a ritual she enjoyed, and she took the job of remembering her relatives and friends to heart. *If I don't remember them, who will?* It was a duty to her.

The episode had upset her enough that she had decided not to pick up her week's supply of food at the local store and go straight home. Instead of resupplying, she checked her inventory in her head as the mule plodded along the road—half on the state highway and half on the dirt next to it. An occasional car or truck whizzed by on its way to nowhere. If a car honked in irritation at her wagon blocking the road, it was usually a white man driving. She ignored them and moved at her own pace. *Now, let's see,* she thought. *Plenty of water from the creek, a full container of Quaker Oats, some raisins and milk from her goats to go with it— also got some bread, and some corn oil, and a smidge of sugar for toast—It could last until the next Sunday. Besides,* she laughed to herself, *you don't eat as much as you used to old woman.*

The presence of the white man at the cemetery was still addling her all the way back to her cabin three hours later. *White father buried in an Apache cemetery. Bull!* After unhooking the mule from the wagon, putting him in the barn, and stowing the tack, she stepped up to her porch and entered her abode.

From the outside it was modest and crude, yet it looked like a small fortress. Closed wooden shutters hung on metal hinges and shielded the windows on all sides from view and from gunshot. Each shutter had slots cut into them large enough for a rifle to poke out and cover the ground in front of it. The walls were made of thick adobe bricks while the roof was made of corrugated steel panels. A chimney made from river rock anchored the west end of the structure. A man, or woman, could hold out in that place for a long siege if they needed to. For her own reasons, it was the only place where Cocheta felt safe.

Unlike the foreboding outside, the inside was comfortable—feminine. A large Navajo rug with abstract designs was laid over the wood planked floor and smelled of dyed wool. Above the stone hearth was a wooden mantle littered with framed photographs of her kin.

Her older sister Nachota who died in 1910 after she gave birth to her youngest child. Next to it was Cocheta's long dead husband Dahkeya and her two children Bina and Ekta. Both girls were young and faced the camera with long black hair long before they died old and gray years ago. There were also pictures of her older brother Elan as a teen just before he was hung for stabbing a soldier in the eye during a knife-fight at a bar to avenge his sister Nachota's rape.

Cocheta was born the same year, she remembered, so she never met her brother Elan nor her sister Nachota. She only knew their stories. Missing from her pictures was Nachota's baby. No one had ever bothered to take his picture. At the far end was a faded ambrotype of a handsome Apache chief named Naiche dating from the 1880's when fighting was still rife between Apaches, Whites, and Mexicans. The chief wore a cloth band around his head, breechcloth, leggings, a calico print shirt, high leather boots, and a leather vest. Cradled proudly in his arms was a Browning 1886 45-70 rifle. His face had chiseled eyes that pierced, a mouth that slashed horizontally across his visage below a well-defined nose, high cheekbones, and leather for skin. His gaze rifled through the camera lens to shoot across time and startle the modern eye of any who would look upon him. *I am still here*, said his eyes, *and I am still proud.*

Opposite the mantle with its images and memories was a rocking chair with crocheted pillows stuffed with bags of feathers for the seat and back. A .433 Mauser rifle and a twelve gage break barrel shotgun were hung at the ready on racks next to the wood-fire stove. A loaded .45 revolver pistol in a worn leather holster hung from a square nail on the wall. There was no electricity, so she only stored foods that did not need to stay cold. For milk, butter, and cheese, she used fresh from her three goats whose bells jingled gently around a wire pen built next to the cabin. For meat, there were chickens and eggs in abundance. And to protect it all was Wolf whose tail never wagged. He preferred outside to inside and slept with one eye half open except when it blinked.

Cocheta sat in her rocker and mused on the pictures as she rolled her chair forward and back while the images took her back and forth through time.

These days she lived mostly in the 19th century, but kept up with modern times. *I might be old*, she thought, *but I'm not dead!* Then she remembered. *Damn, I forgot to charge my phone!* People said her old flip phone was obsolete and it could only be used for talking. To Cocheta, that was a good thing. It used little of the battery's energy. Still, she turned it off to save what was left of the battery. *I'll get it charged next week. Besides, I can always get voice recordings from Verizon,* she remembered. *I'll check for them every once in a while, then turn the phone back off.* It wasn't that she used the phone a lot. She mainly talked with her grandniece and sometimes to that white boy Will from the university. Everyone else had already died.

Her worry about the phone having been resolved to her satisfaction, she sat back and lit her clay pipe filled with dried ditch weed plucked from the wild. One summer in the early sixties a naked band of hippies built a small commune by a rivulet near her cabin. The little stream was fed by spring water that ran year-round alongside the road to her abode. The little creeklet was also her main water source. The commune did not last beyond that summer, but in that time, they planted high quality marijuana seeds near that trickle of water until the tribal police kicked them off the land. Some of their plants lingered and went wild. The locals called it ditch weed.

Soon there were wild plants growing up and down that little creek. She had been smoking it for year. It helped her arthritis better than aspirin and she preferred it to alcohol. She had seen what liquor could do to an Apache and wanted none of it. After the marijuana had its effect, she would chant ancient Apache songs that she had learned as a child while shuffling around the floor in her white Nikes in a trance. Once, some kids from the Res were hunting for hemp by her cabin and happened to hear her singing and shuffling inside. Ever since then, she was called Cocheta, the Medicine Woman. She liked it.

PINETOP AGAIN

Steel finished at the cemetery and reached Pinetop around noon. He had some spare quarters from his last call from the pay phone the day before and dialed Molly's number.

"Hi Molly."

"Hi Pop. About time. Find anything?"

"Just enough to get my hopes up, but no, no conclusions yet. I think it's time you girls checked out of your hotel there and took the bus here. I'll be staying in a private bungalow at a place called the Buck Springs Resort in Pinetop. It's about twelve miles north of White River. Take a cab from White River after the bus drops you off."

"Ok, Pop."

Steele heard Allie clamoring for Molly's phone in the background.

"Pop. Pop, can you hear me?"
"Hi Allie."

"Good news bad news Pop. The tests came back this morning by email. The good news. Mom is 1/8th Apache."

Steele braced himself for the bad news. News that might

prove that he was not the father of Molly nor the grandfather of Allie. News that someone else contributed the Apache genes to Molly and Allie—not him. His had began to shake as he asked Allie the question that had to be asked.

"And my results?"

"Sorry Pop. It was inconclusive. We'll have to do another test."

Steele felt his body slump and tried to find a silver lining. *I can always take another test. But god damn, the universe seems to have it in for me.* What he needed now was some evidence from the cemetery that would tell him that his father was half Apache, and the only person who had the answer was an old woman who hated whites and did not want to talk to him because he was white.

Lost in thought, Steele ended the conversation. "I'll see you two tonight." Bye."

Steele hung up the phone and turned to see the clerk at the desk looking at him with concern.

"You all right mister? No offense, but you look a little pale."

"Naw. I'm all right. Just old I guess. "Have a bungalow for tonight?

THE PLAN

The girls arrived in a cab three hours after sunset. They were determined to cheer him up. Allie knocked on the bungalow door first. She carried a bag filled with Weber's bread, a quart of Vitamin D fortified Milk, four packets of sugar, and 6 pats of butter from the breakfast restaurant in Globe. She also had another bag with hours old burgers and stale fries from the Mc Donald's in White River. Molly followed Allie through the door sporting three bottles of wine—one white, one red, and a bottle of Champagne. After the hugs and hellos, Molly floated a question in a sing-song voice.

"Well, where to start. Burgers, fries, wine, or torn toast and milk?"

"Wine," Allie was quick to say.

"I'll go with wine too," Molly agreed, though the jury was still out on whether wine included champagne.

"How about you Pop, she asked hesitatingly?"

"I hear the water's really good up here. "I think I'll have water, one of those burgers, then hot sugared milk and toast for dessert." Molly and Allie smiled.

Steele took momentary pride in saying water instead of wine or whiskey. He knew there was an unopened pint of booze in the glove box of Mc Tavish, and he was starting to feel he needed a snort. *Just a snort.* But he knew where that would lead. That bottle in the truck had been there since they left Nucla. It was still there. That pint or another one just like it would always be there waiting for him, he knew. But Steele gathered himself. There was still hope. So, he barked at himself in his head. *Not tonight old man. Not tonight.*

Molly and Allie exchanged glances as Steele went to the sink and poured water into a glass from the tap. Then they gave Steele a kiss on each of his white stubbled cheeks.

"What was that for?"

"Oh nothin," Molly answered.

"Yeah, nothin' Pop," Allie repeated. And then she added; "Ok, Pop. What's the plan?"

"Don't have one yet," he responded. "That's why you're here." Then he told them what he had found out so far, what happened at the cemetery with Cocheta and how she told him to leave Fort Apache. He hoped the girls might help him find a way to locate the grave of L. E. Steele.

"So, who's this guy Smith," asked Allie?

"Will Smith? He's the young man at tribal headquarters that told me I should go see Cocheta. Said I would find her any Sunday morning at dawn at the Post Cemetery. He was right."

"Is he Apache?"

"No idea. His hair is dark enough. Might even match yours. But it's curly. And Cocheta called him a white boy. All I really know is that he's interning here with the tribe as an anthropologist. Says he's a student at Northern Arizona

University in Flagstaff. And, oh yeah, he's writing a book on Apache stories that Cocheta has been telling him.

"Sounds like an interesting guy, Allie noted with interest. "Where does he meet her to listen to her stories?"

"Says he usually meets her at the cemetery, but he met her once at her cabin."

"Well, you said you already tried meeting you at the cemetery and she told you to get out. Maybe it's time you went up to see her at the cabin."

"Maybe. But Smith said I might get shot if I do."

"Well then. Let's go see Smith first thing in the morning and ask him what to do. I mean we've come a long way not to find your father's grave don't you think?

"Yes, answered Steele. But we're a little ahead of ourselves. We don't even know if this L. E. Steele is Leon Steele, my father."

That was when Molly piped up. "What if we went with you to her cabin?"

"Nope. If she'd shoot me, she might not think twice about shooting you two."

"How about just giving her a call?"

"Never thought of that. But Cocheta did tell me she has a cell phone. Said she talks with Smith on it sometimes. Good Idea!"

"One more reason to see Smith in the morning then," concluded Molly.

Steele looked puzzled.

Molly noticed the confusion on his face. “He has her cell phone number Pop. You don’t. We have to see him to get her number.”

“Oh yeah. Good thinking,” he muttered as he wondered if his brain fade was due to age or his brain cancer.

TRIBAL HEADQUARTERS

Will Smith was nowhere to be seen so Steele asked Allie to call him on her cell.

"Hello, Mr. Smith, Allie greeted."

"Hello, but it's not Mister. It's just Smith."

"Ok, Smith." I'm Glenn Steele's granddaughter. Name's Allie. You know, Glenn Steele, the man you talked to about the cemetery?"

"Oh yeah. How did it go with Cocheta?"

"Not good. She told him to leave the cemetery. Said it was only for Apaches. She doesn't seem to like white people much. We were hoping that maybe you could help us talk with her since she knows you. We have some news that might change her mind about talking to us."

"And that news is?"

"My mom is 1/8th Apache. That makes it likely, but not conclusive that she got her Apache DNA from her father Glenn Steele. The report also says mom's DNA came from the Mogollon range. Meaning right here, just like mine does."

"What about Mr. Steele's test?"

"Inconclusive. We'll have to do another test."

Smith gave himself a moment to think about what Allie had just said. "So, you have about what 1/16th indigenous blood?"

"You got it."

"Just like me!"

"Weird. You have Indian blood too?"

"Yup. It was the only reason Cocheta ever agreed to talk with me. She still insists I'm white, but that 1/16th was important to her. Opened a door."

"What color is your hair."

"Jet black."

"Yours?"

"Jet black, long, shiny, and gorgeous."

"Wanna get married?" he laughed as he now wondered what this shiny black haired girl might looked like.

"Now that our hair color is out of the way," Allie replied, "can you help us?"

"Maybe. Where are you?"

"We're at the information desk at tribal headquarters."

"Be there in a minute."

Smith left the library room fifty feet away still carrying his phone and was in full stride when he was struck by a girl with long black hair standing next to an equally attractive but older blonde woman. Allie was talking with Steele and had her back to Smith as he sized her up. *Not too tall, but built for speed,* he thought. *She'd look good on a horse or maybe a motorcycle* was his next man thought, but he had no idea where it came from. Allie turned around just as Smith got near and fixed on his full head of long black curls. He wasn't tall, maybe her height, but his shoulders were broad, and he walked with purpose. *A medium sized big man,* she mused.

"You must be Smith?" offered Allie as she held out her hand.

"And you must be Allie? Nice to meet you," he answered as he shook her hand.

As they droned on in the fashion of young people who had just met, Steele and Molly were left out of the conversation for several moments. Finally, Allie remembered why they were there.

"So, any ideas on how you might get my Pop in to talk with Cocheta?"

"Oh yeah, well, yes I think— maybe."

"Maybe?"

"Yes. You were right when you said Cocheta does not like Whites. But since both you and your mother now have proof of your indigenous heritage, she might open up."

"But what about the inconclusive test that came back for my Pop?"

"I don't have to tell her that. The fact that you and your mom tested positive for Apache DNA is what I will tell her. I'll leave out the part about the inconclusive test for Mr. Steele."

"You OK with that? I mean it's a bit sneaky isn't it?"

"Yeah. But us Indians are known for being sneaky."

Allie looked askance at Smith trying to determine if he was serious about Indians being stealthy.

"Look Allie. The odds are high that your Pop is your biological grandpop. You just lack scientific proof. Relax. The first step will be to call her. I'll give her the news about you and your mom and see what happens. Excuse me while I ring her up with the news."

Smith dialed her number, but the call rolled over immediately to voice mail. He knew that meant her phone was off. But he left the pertinent news about Molly's and Allie's DNA and asked her to call back.

Smith let the three of them know. "Cocheta didn't pick up. We'll have to wait."

"How long do you think that might take," asked Steele.

"The last time, it took a week."

"Anything to do around here?" asked Allie.

"Plenty. There's Fort Apache, the museum there, the Kinishba ruins..."

Allie stopped him cold. She had spent the other day at the Besh Ba Gowah ruins a mile south of Globe and was fascinated by the multi-story stone structure with 200 rooms.

"How far away are the Kinishba ruins?"

"Not far. I can take you there on my motorcycle if you like. They're part of the reason I'm here. I work with a team of archaeologists from the university. They do the digging, and I do the cataloguing of the artifacts."

"That's really cool." But she had to ask. "What kind of motorcycle?"

Smith beamed. " BMW R1150R," he told her. "A horizontal twin cylinder monster painted all black. BMW called it its naked bike."

"Naked? Sounds sexy."

"Yeah. It means none that plastic fluff. Just engine and wheels."

Allie glanced over to Molly and Steele for permission, but she was determined to go with or without approval. She was almost eighteen. When both nodded reluctantly, the two young ones were off. Soon they had the wind in their hair. Will controlled the gears, brakes, throttle, and handlebars, and Allie sat behind him holding on to his waist. She donned a big grin on her face as they accelerated the beast down the road and her hair flew in the wind like Maverick's tail. Molly and Steele were left behind and watched them as they sped away on a road of their own, and both felt old in their own way. Quietly, they headed to McDonald's for a couple of cheeseburgers and fries and to wait for news about Cocheta.

WAITING FOR COCHETA

Time to get up Cocheta, she chided herself as the first rays of sun tickled the cracks between the timbers that formed the walls of her cabin. She struggled to get her bony frame upright from the cotton mattress weakly supported by a rope lattice woven beneath it. She had made the bed herself after her husband died thirty years before. It was Monday and she rose early to go through her daily routines.

First was to gather water. She had no well to draw from, and Tin Shack Tank which lay below the cabin was little more than a seasonal catch pond used for watering Cattle. It was not fit for humans to drink since cattle leave their pies everywhere including in the water where they slack their thirst. Summer to fall it was usually empty. Winter through spring it was always full from rainwater and melting snow. But from Cocheta's standpoint it was nice to look at but not to drink from. Her fresh water source was the same place as where she gathered her ditch weed on the banks of a small creek near the dirt road leading to her cabin. It would take her several trips back and forth carrying two buckets to fill the trough for her goats and then to fill her oak barrel outside the cabin with drinking water.

For breakfast she gathered two eggs from her chicken coop after chasing off the rooster in charge. Though it was close to the season that her hens would stop laying eggs for winter, she was still getting eight to twelve eggs a day—more than she could use. So, out of the surplus, she let the hens hatch a few chicks as they went into their slack season. When winter freeze settled in and they stopped laying, she slaughtered one chicken a month starting with the older hens. She used the cold outside to keep the butchered chicken fresh since she had no electricity to run a refrigerator. By spring she would only have a few mature hens left to lay eggs until the chicks that had hatched during the winter season would begin to lay their own.

As her eggs sizzled sunny side up in a skillet atop the wood burning stove, Cocheta drank her coffee and made notes on scraps of paper saved from discarded packaging of her store bought goods. The topics of her daily notes were identical. They outlined things that she wanted to remember, but kept forgetting. She thought to hold on to her most precious thoughts by jotting them down daily. On mornings when she could not remember something, she went to a drawer which was filled with scraps of collected notes from past days. She called the drawer her archive. She thought that using the repository was cheating, But ever since turning 100 years old, she forgave herself for using the archive to jog her memory.

Her last task before lunch was to check her phone for messages. But since her battery was nearly out of power, she decided to wait a few days before turning it back on. *Who's going to call an old woman anyway,* she thought. So, it wasn't until midnight on Friday that Will Smith received a crisp voicemail from Cocheta.

"I'll meet the white man at the cemetery on Sunday at dawn," it said.

SUNDAY AT DAWN

After rising at 3:00, Cocheta hitched her mule to her buckboard just before 4:00 in the morning, loaded a few things, and set off down the mountain for the Fort Apache Cemetery. The cold weather had killed off the last of the wildflowers she could pick for the graves. But she would bring flowers again in spring. Comforting her against the cold was a Navajo blanket which she pinched at her neck with one hand to keep in the warm. The fort was almost three hours away and a light snow was beginning to fall. By the time she reached the graveyard, all the flat surfaces of the buckboard were covered by two inches of soft frosty flakes.

Ahead in the dim light, she spied the back of the blue truck of Glenn Steele. When she pulled alongside, she leaned over and saw him still asleep in the bed of the truck dusted with snowfall.

"Anybody bother you this time Steele," she barked into the cold morning air?

Spluttering from being woken up so suddenly, he spoke nonsense until he settled down long enough to remember where he was and why he was there.

"No. Quiet night. Cold, but quiet."

"So, Smith tells me you want to know about a grave

where an L. E. Steele is buried?"

"Yes. Is he here," he asked as he struggled to find the zipper to his sleeping bag?

"Might be."

Steele stopped fiddling with the zipper and gave Cocheta a hard look. "What do you mean maybe?"

"It was a long time ago sonny. My sister dead, my brother dead. That white soldier with one eye."

Steele bit his tongue as she rambled. Cocheta didn't seem to understand that this was a matter that had shaped his entire life. "Excuse me ma'am. I'm here to find out if a man named L. E. Steele is buried here. It's kind of important and...."

Cocheta interrupted. "I don't know nothing about a Leon Steele. The only Steele I ever knew was one called Leonardo. Leonardo E. Steele."

Steele shuddered. He could almost feel the hot breath of his father hissing up from a hidden grave deep in the cemetery. His hand began to shake as Cocheta went on.

"Your name Glenn?"

"Yes, but..."

"That was Leonardo's father's name. Glenn Steele—a cavalry man at the fort."

Cocheta reached behind her into the wagon bed and pulled out a kerosene lantern, lit it with a stick match, then held it up to Steele's face. It cast a yellow light and made Steele squint. She cocked her head from side to side and seemed to be searching his face for some clue. Then her eyes grew wide. "I'll be damned. Didn't see it the first time. But it's clear as day now. With that scowl on your face, you look just like him."

"Just like who?"

"Just like Leonardo E. Steele. My cousin. Your father."

Steele stopped struggling with the zipper and sat dumbfounded in the bed of his truck. He was still trapped in his sleeping bag with only his face showing under the glow of the lantern. Cocheta seemed satisfied with the proof she saw in his visage. To her it was settled. The white man in the bed of the truck was kin. She snuffed out the lantern and went on talking in the dim light of dawn with her breath turning to steam above Steele's face as Steele struggled to get out of his sleeping bag.

"Well then Mr. Glenn Steele," she began as if what she had just revealed to Steele was just an unimportant piece of random of news. "There were four things about your father Eskaminzim. First, his Apache name means bigmouth. Second, he was a good liar. Always telling tall tales about something and none of it ever true. Everybody liked listening to him though. Good storyteller. Should have took up book writing—could have if he wasn't such a drunk."

"Eskaminzim," asked Steele, struggling to pronounce the strange name and struggling to imagine that it belonged to the Indian hater that raised him?"

"Yes. That was his Apache name. Leonardo was the name his white soldier father gave him along with his last name Steele.

"Now for the third thing. Eskaminzim had a vicious temper from the time he was a boy. Once saw him kick his favorite dog for no good reason then went off and cried his eyes out. Then he came back and petted the poor dog until the dog nipped his hand to make him stop.

"But worst of all, your father was a thankless kid. He hated being Apache and he hated the Res—blamed Apaches for him being Apache and not a white man—crazy? Like blaming your mother for giving you life. Leon always told everyone on the Res he was English like his father calvary father Glenn Steele. The fool even went around trying to speak like an Englishman. Got him into a lot of fights that phony accent. Later in life, Leonardo went to see his father in Missouri. It was 1918. I remember it because he left the same year when that big war ended. After he saw his father, he came to hate white men too. Never could get it right.

"Nine months before Leonardo was born, my sister Nachota went off with that cavalry man named Glenn Steele. One night, she drank too much whiskey and got herself pregnant. She said your English grandfather raped her. He said he didn't and that was that. Happened in 1910, the year I was born."

"You knew my father?"

"Grew up with him. He was my cousin. Son of my dead sister Nachota—same age as me. I never knew your white grandfather, the cavalry man at the fort. He got himself into a bloody fight with my older brother Elan after our sister Nachota got pregnant by him. My brother took his eggs.

"His eggs?"

"Yes. His ayęęzhii!"

“What’s that mean?”

“His balls. You know— his cojones.”

“Oh those,” Steele acknowledged, wincing as he remembered Leon Posey on his bloody knees and holding his groin that morning in the Desolation.

“Then, after he sliced off his balls, he stabbed that cavalry man in the eye. I don’t know why he picked his eye. Always seemed strange to pick an eye. He already had his balls. But I guess Elan thought it was the right thing to do. It all happened the same year I was born, so I never knew him either. I just heard the stories about it. After that, the army sent the soldier home to St. Joseph on account of his eye. Wasn’t no use to them no more.

"I bet he spent the rest of his life in Saint Joseph with a patch over that eye bragging to everyone he was a brave Indian fighter wounded in battle. But they hung the Apache who took his eyeball and his eggs. Like I said, he was my brother Elan whose name meant friendly. The army said it was justice to hang Friendly even though all he was doing was avenging his sister from her rapist. Never sounded like justice to me— hanging the Indian and letting the white rapist go free, I mean. Elan was just fifteen when they put the noose around his neck. But he died with his balls on. Not like that soldier man.

"o, no, I never knew your white grandfather. I only knew his son—your father Leonardo, the child of my sister Nachota’s rape. Did I tell you that Eskaminzim was a chattering fool right from the start? Sometimes I forget things I’ve already said. I’m over a hundred you know. I’m allowed. Anyway, I knew Leon for eighteen years. We were the same age. Even though he was my cousin, we grew up like a brother and sister who didn’t much like each other. My sister Nachota committed suicide after she gave birth to your father in 1910.

"My mother and father took Leonardo in and did their best to raise him in their old age. They shouldn't have bothered. He was thankless. When he was eighteen, he up and left. Said he would find his white father in St. Joseph and leave the Res forever. Denounced his Apache name and would only call himself by Leonardo—Leonardo Steele. Didn't even use an initial for his Apache name. And that was that. 'Good riddance to all you savages,' he said with his nose in the air. Burned his bridges to his own kin as you white people say.

"After Leonardo went off looking for his white father in St. Joseph in 1918, the family lost track of him. Only got one letter from him. It said his white father didn't want to see him, and told him never to come back. His fresh new bride in St. Joseph didn't know nothin' about Nachota or her half Apache son Leon who was talking with her new husband on their porch. And I expect he didn't want her to know. Probably didn't want her to know he was missing his balls either. So, he sent Leonardo away like an unwanted dog with a kick in the pants and an apple from his tree for the trip home. "And don't come back," said his father. That's all Leonardo ever got from that man. An apple and a knife.

"What kind of knife?"

"It was an old switchblade. Had some soldiers engraved on each side of the blade swinging swords at something. Probably some poor Indian fools. You know, the India Indians from India that the British liked to massacre—not Apaches though either one would have worked for them. One savage is as good as another to those Englishmen.

"Said Sheffield on the side—right?"

"Yes. How did you know?"

Steele didn't answer. So, Cocheta continued.

"Leonardo decided he would make his way from St. Joseph west across Kansas to Colorado. It wasn't until he was close to his end that he came back to the Res to eat crow and make amends. Said that's where he belonged after all. But I don't think he knew even then. Took him thirty-six years for two reasons. First, because he never could decide if he was white or Apache. Second, he didn't much like the taste of crow. He finally got back here near dead in 1964 and told us what happened.

"Said he worked here and there for after leaving St. Joseph. Drifted mainly—— hired hand, oil fields, dry farming, horse trading, sheep. Then, one day when he was drunk, he married a white woman from Kansas. Met her at a dance—Fort Hayes, he said. They won a contest or some such thing. I expect he never told her he was half Apache. Along the way they had children. I guess you're one of them. But he said he lost them all—said he did a bad thing. Something about a horse in a house. He was never very clear because he was always blubbering when he talked about it. Didn't realize how much he loved them all till it was too late. Admitted he was a fool for it.

"Finally came back a broken man who looked older than his years and had a dent in his head that he didn't have when he left. Said he deserved that too, and he was proud of the boy who gave it to him. Then he said he wanted to be Apache again before he died. So, I cleansed him with sage smoke at my house after I set him down on my Navajo rug. Said he was sorry again. Like I told you, I don't think he ever knew what he wanted out of life. But I know he never got it. He begged to be buried next to his mother Nachota, the horse thief."

"Horse Thief?"

"Uh huh. Then, after I told him I would bury him there like he asked, he walked off. Went to the cemetery, sat on a bright white rock with quartz crystals sparkling all over it. Then he shot himself in the forehead. Made a mess of that rock. You know quartz is sacred to the Apache. Our medicine men carried quartz crystal in their medicine bags."

Steele winced at the news of his father's suicide. But he wasn't surprised that his father had met a sad and violent end. It fit. "Damn—good god damn. On a white rock you say?" Then after gazing off toward the sunrise for a while, he bit his lip and turned back to Cocheta. She had been watching him as he digested the news of his father's suicide. Then he remembered something that she had just said about her sister.

"You said my grandmother Nachota was a horse thief?"

Cocheta smiled revealing two missing teeth. She was relieved that Steele did not ask for more about his father's death.

"They say she was a good one."

"So, Pop named me after his father Glenn," mumbled Steele to himself under his breath as he shook his head.

"What's that you say sonny?"

"Leonardo named me after his father Glenn."

"And you think naming you after a murdering one-eyed Apache killer was a good thing?" There's a few around here that might want to have a disputation or two about that," she said as she gave him an angry look and leaned forward while wagging a finger.

"No. Not when you say it that way. I mean he was honoring me or maybe he was honoring his father by naming me Glenn. Most thoughtful thing he ever did for me. He wasn't a kind man, especially after he got stove-up."

"Stove-up? What's it mean?"

"Long story. Short version is, he got two broke legs that were never straight again—'Stove-up.' After that, he came to be a mean drunk. Before getting his legs broke, he was just a loudmouth drunk who told good stories. I was the one who gave him the dent in his head"

"How's that?"

"He went after my brother with a knife, so I hit him in the head with something heavy."

"Fry pan?"

"Rolling pin"

She mused on Glenn's choice of a feminine weapon for a moment, then changed the subject. "He sure was good with horses. Like his mother I guess."

"His mother the rustler," he added shaking his head at the irony and giving a thought to Maverick. "So, you're my aunt?"

"For the time being— time being pretty short for me I expect."

Despite his reputation for reticence, Steele stepped toward her with his arms out. He had never known any of his extended family— not a grandmother, a grandfather, aunt, nor cousin. Without warning he surprised even himself when he pulled her in and gave her a familial hug. "Nice to meet you Aunt Cocheta."

"Hold on there sonny." Protesting mildly, she wriggled against his embrace with a smile while flashing anger from her dark eyes. Steele could not be resisted. But upon finding that she was little more than a bag of brittle bones, he held her with a light touch so as not to break anything. "Never been hugged by a white man," she complained as she dusted herself off after he put her down.

"How about if the hug came from a one quarter Apache man?"

"You know that for certain?"

"Not yet, but I will soon. I mean, who else but Leon's kin would know about that Sheffield knife or his kindness with an apple. So, we ever going see my pop's grave auntie?"

"Soon."

Cocheta then reached into her buckboard and pulled out the Navajo blanket she had worn during the long ride from her cabin. "They make better blankets than us Apaches. That's all right. We Apaches make war better than them." Then she spread the blanket on the ground and ordered Steele to sit.

After Steele was in place, Cocheta reached again into the wagon and pulled out a bag full of sage and lit it. She took the liberty of adding some ditch weed to the bundle to sweeten its effect. Then she waited until the flames died out and only smoke and embers were left. Waving the smoking bundle of brush over Steele, she closed her eyes, went into a stepping motion while incanting words she had learned as a child but no longer understood. Steele instinctively used his hands to pull the smoke up toward his head and breathed in the spicy aroma of singed sage and ditch weed. It refreshed his soul almost like a washing of his face in a cold creek.

"There now. That better sonny? You know, you keep this up you're gonna need an Apache name."

What'd you have in mind?"

"Dunno. I'll have to think about it...sonny."

Steele sat on his haunches and smiled at the notion as he traced a twig from a juniper through the snow. Then, after a pause, the tone of Cocheta spoke in a voice that had shifted in tone. It signaled a segue and she donned a somber timbre out of respect for the dead they were about to walk among. Leonardo was Steele's father after all, and Steele was part Apache to boot, just like his pop. *Respect is in order*, she conceded to herself, *even if he isn't full blooded.*

"Follow me," she said as she donned the Navajo blanket over her shoulders and led the way with her walking stick weaving circuitously around trees and grave markers. When she came to the apex of the knoll, the early morning sun lit the underside of a passing cloud turning it bright orange against a dark purple sky. Their footprints in the shallow snow marked their path through the trees and up the hill. There at the top was a three foot long stake that she had driven into the ground at the head of a grave. She and a grandson had dug it for Leon some fifty years before. The stake was made of galvanized steel and showed no rust. Attached to the top with a brass screw was a shiny aluminum coin. It was like the ones you get at a carnival where pull a handle on a machine and it stamps your name and date letter by letter and number by number as a souvenir. Hanging from a string of beads was a feather and a knife—a switchblade knife. At the base of the stake was a snow dusted pile of week-old wildflowers and a blood red apple.

"Aren't you afraid someone will steal the knife?"

"No. Apaches don't steal much from their own. The especially don't steal when everybody knows who the thing belongs to. And it belongs to me, Cocheta." She said her name as if it contained power and threat. "I was all he had left when he went out of this world. Besides, it's a sacrilege to steal from a place for the dead. Been hanging there since 1964, and nobody's touched it."

"All right then, but why the apple?" asked Steele.

"Long story."

"And?"

"Well, I told you Leonardo was an ornery boy right from the start. And he was. But there was this one little thing he would do. Whenever he got hold of an apple, he never ate it all himself. He always came over and gave me a slice without saying a word—just put it in my hand and went off. He could be an ass before and after, but in between there was this slice of an apple. I think he was saying he liked me and maybe that he wasn't quite as bad as I thought. It was the only way he could do it."

"I know."

"You know what Steele?"

"That was the only way he could show he liked you." Cocheta nodded at him and gazed out at the morning sun.

Then, after a pause, Steele asked her more about the knife.

"It was his prize possession," she answered. "Never let it out of his sight."

Steele noticed another batch of flowers laid over a grave next to his father's. The perimeter of the grave was marked with Quartz stones outlining the grave below. "Is that my Nachota's grave?"

"Sure is sonny. Right where Leonardo said he wanted to be—next to his Apache mother—your grandmother Nachota. And at her feet is Elan her son—the brother I never got to meet.

As Steele lowered himself to inspect the medallion and the knife, he asked where his father's head might be beneath the ground. Before she answered, he felt his hand twitch as he conjured the image of his father's forehead with a hole through it.

"Right under where your knee is headed. I know, I helped bury him. Never will forget that dent in his head—the bullet hole neither."

With that, Steele lowered his knee over the grave as gently as his aging body would allow and then donned his glasses to read the medallion. Cocking his head to the side and squinting in the morning light, he read: "L. E. Steele. Coyotero White Mountain Apache 1910-1964."

"Dort," muttered Steele as he stood up from the grave.

"What?"

"I lost a man named Dort that same year in Vietnam."

"A friend?"

"No, just a young man. It was my fault. I ordered him to do something dangerous, and he got shot in the head."

"You pull the trigger?"

"No, no. He was shot by the enemy," he answered, exasperated at the suggestion.

"You led men into war and thought none of your boys would get killed?"

Steele thought hard on her question which reflected her Apache view of war. It was a simple question he had never asked himself even though he was always proud to say that Dort was the only one he lost in combat. Then he blurted out a new truth. "Yes. At the time that's what I thought."

"Never was your fault. Never was, she said as she turned to walk back down the hill to her wagon.

"You mean about Dort?"

"No. I meant your father. Your Dort was just a soldier that got himself killed. That war took a lot of boys just like Dort. Some even came from this Res. You had nothin' to do with it.

The sins of your father and his father, and the fathers before were theirs, not yours. You inherited nothing from them except maybe a weakness for whiskey. But you are the one that put that dent in Leonardo's head and rightly so. You probably saved your brother's life. Time to let that part go sonny. This boy Dort had nothin' to do with it," she asserted as she stepped up into her wagon.

"How do you know that? "How do you know that?" he

yelled.

She snapped the reins on the mule and the sound of rock being crushed again by steel wheels echoed back as they rolled down the hill toward Fort Apache for supplies and to charge her phone. Without looking over her shoulder, she yelled.

"If you want the knife…take it."

When the sound of the wagon disappeared in the distance, her firm words finally pierced the veil of guilt he had carried like a shadow for a lifetime. They cleansed his soul like the sage scented smoke she had waved over his head while sitting on her Navajo blanket. Finally, he allowed the words.

Cocheta and Cohen were right. None of them were your fault Steele. Not a one.

Then he dropped back on his knees near the head of his father and dropped tears into the snow.

BACK TO THE RANCH

Molly, Allie, and Steele all agreed that they would grind out the miles back to the ranch in one day without a stop. Allie had one request. She wanted to see the campus of the Northern Arizona University in Flagstaff and pick up some brochures. After that, they burned up the desolate highway for miles until Steele suddenly put on the brakes and pulled to a stop beside the road where a barbed wire fence guarded Navajo cattle from straying into traffic. The girls watched Steele in silence as he exited the truck and strode with purposeful steps over to the passenger side. There he opened the door and pulled out a fifth of Jack Daniels from the glovebox, opened it, and took a sniff. Molly and Allie had a worried look until he replaced the cap, gave them a wry grin, and put the bottle on top of a fencepost. Then, without warning, he pulled out his pocket pistol, extended his arm, aimed, and fired one shot shattering glass and whiskey all over the shoulder of the road.

"Now that felt pretty damn good," he said as he ambled back to the truck.

"Hold on Pop," barked Allie. "Can I borrow it?"

"Borrow what?"

"The pistol."

"Sure can." Then he handed her the pistol with the slide

opened, the chamber empty, and the loaded clip separated from the weapon.

Allie pulled a hardpack of Marlboros out of her shirt pocket where she always carried them. With a wink to her mother, she placed the box on the same fencepost Steele had used to shoot the bottle. Then she backed up toward the truck as she loaded the clip with a click, released the slide with a snap to load the chamber, and aimed. With a pow from the pistol, the shot-through box flew through the air spewing tobacco and paper into the wind until it all landed among the glass and sticky whiskey.

"You know that's called littering," taunted Molly as she scowled at the mess?

Blowing smoke from the barrel of the pistol like a gunfighter, Allie answered.

"Yeah, but it was for a good cause," she quipped as she popped out the magazine, pulled back the slide, and caught the ejected cartridge in the air as it flew out of the chamber.

"Amen," said Steele as he and Allie bent down to pick up as much of the sticky trash as they could find and dropped it in the litterbag behind the seat.

Five hours later they were back at the ranch. Emily had the table set, dinner was hot and waiting, and Potiča still baking in the oven for dessert. Fergus greeted them by jumping on everyone as they exited Mc Tavish. Arrate wagged his long tail, but arthritis kept him lying down by Ganiz's rocker. But he offered a whiny groan which was dog talk for *glad to see you*. Maverick and the old roan joined in with whinnies of their own. During the road trip, Emily had tended the ranch and had moved her things into the master bedroom so she could stay with Molly. She also put clean sheets on the bed in the cabin for Steele, and got Allie's room ready for her as well. The weary road warriors could not stay up long after supper despite their late evening coffee and Potiča. Soon Allie was in bed asleep. Emily retired next leaving Molly and Steele together.

"Pop?"

"Yes, Molly."

"I've been thinking about calling myself Amelia."

"Well, it's what's on your birth certificate—sort of rhymes with Emily too."

"No, I mean what would you think of me if I did that? I'm your Molly, after all."

"Amelia's your name and you have a right to it. I think maybe I should have left well enough alone and not started calling you Molly back when you were still a baby. You know your mother made me promise to name you Amelia, and I did—legally anyway. But I fudged and started calling you Molly soon after you were born. Don't quite remember why. I thought it fit your birthdate better—Fourth of July and all. But I never felt quite right about that. It wasn't mine to change. You come from a long line of Amelias, and I shouldn't have taken that link from you."

Molly looked at Steele with a wrinkle in her brow. "You never told me that. The long version I mean."

"Sorry."

She paused on Steele's words and then abruptly announced: "I'm going to visit my mother's grave this

Christmas. Then I'm going on to Leadville."

"Leadville?"

"Yes. Because that's where my great grandmother Amelia is buried with great grandfather Franz. I want to put some Potiča on each of their graves. You know— like the promise Marija made to her grandmother Amelia to put food on her grave. Did she ever keep it?"

"Keep what?"

"Her promise to place Potiča on her grandmother's grave on Christmas?"

"No. Marija was different," answered Steele.

"Different how?"

"Just different," explained an exasperated Steele who was still trying to understand his long dead wife.

"Do you want me to come with you to Leadville?"

"No Pop. I need to do this one by myself. I mean, just me and Emily."

"Do me a favor?"

"Sure Pop."

"When my time comes, bury me beside Marija, and bring Potiča to our graves at Christmas."

"Ok, Pop. What about some torn toast and milk?"

"That and maybe a little Carlo Rossi white for the road too."

With that, Molly went to be with Emily in the bedroom where Steele and her mother Marija Amelia Brankovič once slept together forty years before.

"Good night, Amelia"

"Good night Pops."

After two gulps of milk, Steele walked out the door over to his cabin in the pasture feeling an afterglow of revelations revealed and a tryptophan calm from the milk. Then he got into bed, fell asleep, and began to dream. His dream was not of guns firing, det cord exploding, empty magazines ejecting from rifles, nor the rat-tat-tat of a Thompson machine gun. It was the sound of crackling wood from a fire and a gentle voice from afar in the night.

POP IN THE PASTURE

"Hey Glenn. Glenn Steele. You in there?"

Steele's eyes opened wide as he lay on his pillow. "Pop. That you," he asked into the dark?"

"No. It's just you thinking it's me in your dream son."

"I'd rather it was you Pop. We need to talk."

"All right then. I'm here by the campfire. See me? Over here."

Steele opened a window, put both hands on the sill, and leaned out. To his left he saw a campfire burning bright in the pasture fifty feet away near a water trough nestled under a stand of Junipers. Warming his hands by the fire was Pop Steele who sat on a brilliantly white rock. Embers from the flames flitted like gnats afire and flew in panicked directions under a flickering canopy of Rocky Mountain stars. Steele stepped barefoot out the door into the dark, across the porch, down the three stairs, and over to the campfire.

"Good to see you son. You know you're not wearing any clothes?"

"I do that sometimes," answered Steele as he sat on a cold rock beside his Pop and began to warm his hands like his father while his shoeless feet chilled against the icy ground. "New blood pressure medication."

"Say what?"

"Nothing. Its personal."

"So, what is it we have to talk about son?"

"You still have that dent I gave you."

"Yep. Right where you put it."

"Good. You deserved it."

"I did. That it?"

"No. There's more. You know I felt guilty most of my life for having bashed you in the head with mom's rolling pin. I was only twelve for Christ's sake. It got you banished forever. Just like that, you were gone. You left me with your whole family. Did I mention I was twelve?"

"Yeah, I know. I'm sorry kid. I never wanted that for you."

"Did you even think about it?

"Not until I took stock when I was about to die. Took me a long time to sort it all out. You see, I had some problems with my own dad. More than a boy should have had."

"Sins of the father eh Pop?" Steele went on without waiting for an answer. "Then mom died. Then Dort."

"Dort? Who's Dort?"

"Nobody Pop. Just a kid who died young."

"Oh, well about your mom. I felt bad for her. Ginny never deserved the life I gave her. Maybe if I hadn't been stove-up it would have been different. Maybe we could have just gone on dancing. Or maybe I was just born ornery and being stove-up was just an excuse to be mean. Who knows? Too late for what ifs. What if is a waste of time you know? The accounting's been done, and the book's been closed; I was evil."

"That's bullshit Pop."

Pop turned toward Steele and took on a look of astonishment as Steele continued.

"Evil is different than pathetic Pop. You were just a self-centered, self-pitying, and an all-around weak confused jerk most of the time—especially after you got stove-up and drank yourself to death. Trust me Pop, I just left evil in Phoenix. You were a paltry excuse for a husband and father, but you weren't evil. Besides, there was that apple."

"Apple?"

Soon after he said *apple,* a bright red one dropped from one of the Juniper trees near the fire.

"Apples grow on Juniper trees," asked Steele?

"Must be," answered Pop. "Got a knife son?"

"In your pocket Pop."

Pop Steele reached into his pocket and pulled out a switchblade knife and inspected it by firelight. He pressed the button on the side and the shiny blade swung open with an ominous whack that jerked his hand. "Almost killed Jesse with this thing," he lamented.

"In a drunken rage Pop," consoled Steele. "Did you really have a mind to kill Jesse?"

"Hell no. Hell no! I didn't mean to kill anyone. It was just being my natural self, I guess. Somebody left me outside in a wagon in the cold. Besides, it wasn't Jesse I was afraid of. It was you. You were the strong one. I was just slashing about like always, and Jesse happened to be the first one in my way. I was drunk and hot-tempered; you know? I mean, who rides a horse into their own house waving a knife at his own kids?"

"You were afraid of me?"

"Who took over the family after I left son?"

"Well, me. Somebody had to. But it's not what I ever really wanted. And yes, we all knew about your temper Pop. That's why I left you passed out in the wagon in the first place that cold night on the way back from the Desolation.

"That was you? Figures."

"Yeah, it was me. I wanted to get away before you woke up and took your orneriness out on me." As they talked, Pop cored and quartered the apple and offered Steele two slices.

"You never gave anyone more than one slice Pop. And you always went off with your share to eat alone."

"Yeah. Times are different now," he said as he chomped on his share of the apple and Steele chomped on his. Now we're just two old drunks who ran out of time sitting side by side on rocks in front of a campfire watching embers flitting up to the sky and sharing an apple. The only difference is that I'm wearing clothes—and you're not. Wanna hear a good story son?"

"Sure Pop.

"Want a drink first," asked Pop as he held out the bottle to Steele?

"Naw," answered Steele while raising his hand up in refusal. "I quit. And make your story short Pop. I'm dying you know."

BOOKS BY THIS AUTHOR

Laguna Diary

A COMING OF AGE STORY SET IN MID-CENTURY LAGUNA BEACH, CALIFORNIA

The House Of Ilya

A LOVE STORY SET IN THE WILDS OF RUSSIAN SIBERIA AND ALASKA

Made in the USA
Middletown, DE
22 September 2022

10841592R00156